SELF-ASSURED

Nicholas Rhea titles available from
Severn House Large Print

Rest Assured
Some Assured

SELF-ASSURED

Nicholas Rhea

Severn House Large Print
London & New York

This first large print edition published in Great Britain 2006 by
SEVERN HOUSE LARGE PRINT BOOKS LTD of
9-15 High Street, Sutton, Surrey, SM1 1DF.
First world regular print edition published 2005 by
Severn House Publishers, London and New York.
This first large print edition published in the USA 2007 by
SEVERN HOUSE PUBLISHERS INC., of
595 Madison Avenue, New York, NY 10022.

British Library Cataloguing in Publication Data

Rhea, Nicholas, 1936-
    Self-assured. - Large print ed.
    1. Insurance agents - England - Yorkshire - Fiction
    2. Yorkshire (England) - Social life and customs - Fiction
    3. Large type books
    I. Title
    823.9'14[F]

    ISBN-13: 9780727875686
    ISBN-10: 072787568X

Printed and bound in Great Britain by
MPG Books Ltd, Bodmin, Cornwall.

One

'A gale smashed the vestry windows and sent lots of rubbish, including the vicar's sermon, swirling among the tombstones.'
                                    From a claim form

We bought the house. We couldn't afford it, but we bought it and afterwards spent weeks and even months wondering whether we had done the right thing. It seemed such a huge place by comparison with the tiny one we had vacated and I wondered about the cost, not only of buying it but maintaining it, and paying my household bills. Somehow, I would have to earn, and keep earning, enough to pay the mortgage, the rates, the electricity and the heating bills in addition to keeping the fabric of the house in top condition. And I would have to do all that while supporting my family with essentials like food and clothing.

£1,350 was a massive amount of money for me to pay for a house, even if I had thirty years to pay off the loan. Thirty years! I'd be an old man by the time I'd finished and dared not calculate the total amount due to the interest on the mortgage. The interest would add substantially to the cost of the loan even though I had obtained very favourable terms from the Premier Assurance Association. They had loaned me the money because I was an employee – the Premier's staff mortgage was formulated with advantageous rates and it was one of the perks of my profession. Another bonus was that it contained a built-in mortgage-protection policy.

That was invaluable if I died or became incapable of work; it meant the mortgage would be paid and that Evelyn would be very secure. Such considerations rarely affected rented properties. Widows or people without work could not afford to remain in their former homes and many had been thrown out due to their inability to meet payments. I was determined that sort of thing would not happen to my family – Evelyn's security, and that of little Paul, meant a lot to me.

The former owner of the house, our then neighbour Mr Browning, had become too old to look after his spacious and rather splendid home and had decided to go and live with his daughter. Knowing we would dearly love to buy a property, he had given us first refusal on his house, allowing us time to consider his offer before placing it on the open market. That was an example of his kindness and thoughtfulness. Since moving next door to him, we had become quite well acquainted. A quiet, fit but rather reserved gentleman of about seventy-five years of age, he had constantly shown unexpected kindnesses towards us, the most recent being permission to use his garage to house our little Austin 10 car, Betsy. It was also large enough to contain my Coventry Eagle motorcycle, now used only sparingly.

Mr Browning had no car of his own, consequently his garage was empty apart from one or two household items he stored there. As he had no further use for it, he'd said he was delighted to offer it to us for as long as we needed it. He had admired Betsy's shining chrome and gleaming paintwork and thought our pride and joy would be much better living in a garage than standing overnight in the uncertain and sometimes ferocious weather of the moors.

He refused to take any money from us even though I had offered to pay a fair rent and I think it was after our purchase of Betsy, and during subsequent chats with Evelyn, that he had learned of our property-owning desires. In return for the use of his garage, though, Evelyn would give him samples of her baking and cooking, sometimes even inviting him in for Sunday lunch, when he would entertain us with tales of his family and his earlier life in the highways department of the local rural district council. In some ways, I thought he regarded us as a substitute family because his wife had died some years earlier and his only daughter lived about seventy miles away. For much of the time he was on his own, and I know he enjoyed our companionship.

In spite of his kindness and his offer to show us around the property with early indications of its probable price range, the decision to buy Daleside was not easy. For one thing, it was far larger than the cottage we rented, and Evelyn wondered if it was too big and too ostentatious for us, but in my opinion its overall size, particularly its interior accommodation, was a huge bonus. As I worked from home, I needed space for an office, in addition to which the nature of my work meant that customers and potential customers came to the house to discuss their business and personal requirements. Confidentiality was therefore important. In a small house with a young child running around, coping with our domestic routine as clients awaited my attention was far from straightforward and not at all desirable. It was frequently unavoidable because many arrived either during the evenings or at weekends, often without an appointment.

Furthermore, I was growing busier, which meant dedicated office space was becoming increasingly necessary.

Thanks to my tours of Daleside with Mr Browning, I knew the house had enough rooms to provide a downstairs office quite separate from the rest of the domestic accommodation. The room in question was big enough and secure enough to permit me to discuss confidential and personal business with my clients. There was also access from outside, through the garden and via the veranda door, without tramping through the kitchen or living room. For me, it represented a kind of workaday heaven, even if I was going to commit myself to a huge financial responsibility over the coming years.

Daleside was a spacious end-terrace house built of local stone with a blue-tiled roof. It was actually No. 1 Miners' Cottages, Micklesfield, one of six houses in that terrace, located at the east end. An earlier owner had given it the name. Our first house with its two bedrooms and two downstairs rooms was next door, i.e. No. 2, and it seemed to be tightly squeezed between Nos. 1 and 3. Certainly it was very tiny by comparison with both Daleside and No. 3. Upstairs, Daleside had a spacious loft with flooring, three large bedrooms, a bathroom containing a toilet (which had been converted from a previous bedroom) and a spacious landing. Downstairs there were four large reception rooms like quarters of a square, with a glass-fronted veranda running the entire length of the south-facing frontage. There were two further rooms at the rear, both very small and attached to the main building, almost as an afterthought. One was called the pantry and the other the scullery.

There was a backyard with a very useful coalhouse, an outdoor toilet and wooden wash-house. That had water laid on and a copper which we could use for washing the clothes. The wash-house was large enough to contain a washing line so that clothes could hang in there to dry when it was raining or snowing, while to the rear of that outbuilding was a sort of lean-to, a corrugated-iron roof on posts. This contained things like garden tools, the wheelbarrow and piles of logs for the fire.

To the east of the house was the huge garden, an acre and a half according to Mr Browning, and it contained a lawn at the front of the property, a rockery, lots of space for growing vegetables and soft fruit, a second larger lawn which had once been a croquet green, a single garage, two pigsties and five stone-built sheds which would be

10

wonderful for accommodating all my clutter, especially those oddments I collected from hard-up customers in lieu of their premiums. Not only that, there was an orchard with a hen-run and sixty apple trees to the north of the property; that lay across the back lane which served the row of houses, and there was a wooded drive leading to the southern entrance. That small wood, called the Drive, was about a third of an acre and full of deciduous trees. It belonged to Daleside although the road which passed through it served all the houses in our row. Furthermore, there were long reaching views from Daleside's south-facing rooms and garden; the terrace was built along a lofty hillside and so the orchard on the north side was higher than the house with the front garden sloping south and catching all the sunshine. In fact, the veranda with its rows of windows was just like a hothouse, ideal for summer days and lazy evenings. It would be perfect for indoor plants.

Anyone with a lot of money could transform Daleside into a wonderful home ... but I did not have that kind of cash to spare. I would have to occupy it as it stood – and it did need some attention and modernization. With a bit of luck and lots of hard work, that could come later. In the meantime, a few licks of paint and some fresh wallpaper

11

would work wonders. I could do that myself but could I earn sufficient both to buy and maintain a place of this size? As a young couple with a child, could we enjoy Daleside without it becoming a financial burden?

In considering all the factors, I could see a potential income from those expansive grounds – I could market the apples, for example (there would be far too many for our modest household), or I could fell the existing trees in the Drive, sell the timber as firewood, and replant it with Christmas trees. They grew quickly and always sold well. I could produce all my own fruit and vegetables, I could keep pigs and hens and even repair motorbikes in the garage. But, of course, all those schemes would have to be accommodated in addition to my work for the Premier. That must always remain my main job and primary source of income.

The more I thought about it, the more appealing it became. I had long been advised by friends, family and some of my customers that ownership of land and property was the key to wealth and security, and that large houses could earn their own keep if one was wise, innovative and hard-working. Certainly, Evelyn's father thought I would be silly to ignore this wonderful opportunity but I must admit that the two weeks of considering whether or not to go ahead were full of self-doubt.

I kept thinking it would be an easier decision if Daleside had been smaller but it was Evelyn's father, Big Deck (Derek) Mead, owner of the Unicorn Inn in Micklesfield, who finally convinced us of the wisdom of buying it. He helped us raise the cash for the 10% deposit – my savings could never have produced the necessary £135, nearly five months' wages – and so it was Deck's highly practical support which convinced us that purchase of Daleside was the right thing to do. If the very experienced and successful Big Deck thought it was a good idea, who was I to disagree? I recall him saying, 'Matthew, you're in business and that means you have to show confidence in yourself. By buying Daleside, you'll be doing that, everyone round here will think you're doing very well and that will give them confidence in you. Confidence in yourself will produce confidence in others; they'll respect you, they'll want you to deal with their personal concerns, like money and security. I remember my days at school, we did Milton. You know, the poet. He wrote something along the lines that *nothing profits more than self-esteem, grounded on just and right.* That's not vanity, it's confidence. I've always remembered that. So there you are, that's my bit of advice to you and Evelyn. And good luck.'

And so we bought Daleside.

On the Thursday following our grateful but tearful farewell to Mr Browning, we were due to move in. The task would not be difficult because we lived next door and possessed very little in the way of furniture and household goods – but quite a lot of oddments I'd amassed through my bartering and business dealings.

We did not go to the trouble of hiring a removal van but, thanks to Big Deck's recruitment of some strong lads from the pub's darts team, we decided to manhandle everything from one house to the other. Quite literally, it was simply a question of lifting our meagre belongings over the garden wall. That wasn't as simple as it sounds because it meant coping with two flights of steps, one at each house, not to mention the rather narrow front passages leading to each front door.

As we began our task, I must admit our new home looked very large and empty. I began to feel the entire experience was rather like someone from a one-bedroom prefab moving into a mansion. There didn't seem to be enough furniture to make the place look lived in! And I must say that in spite of Big Deck's reassuring advice, I began to experience renewed worries about the wisdom of what we were doing. I tried to convince myself that everything would be all right once we were settled in and I tried to take Big Deck's advice to heart by telling myself this *was* our house, and that it was a very wise move, from both a business and a personal point of view. After all, it was ours, it was not rented. We could live here secure in the knowledge that we would not be asked to leave. And I would have an office.

On the day of the move, Baby Paul was being looked after by his Aunt Maureen while Evelyn was doing sterling work by keeping the kettle boiling for countless cups of tea and guiding our willing helpers as to where to place our belongings. Tea, we discovered, with the occasional bottle of beer, provided a miracle fuel for the men because it certainly enabled them to work without any real rest periods.

In the midst of all this activity, I found myself helping to carry heavy stuff like the wardrobes and boxes full of crockery and wondered how professional removal men coped with this kind of heavy physical activity every day of their working lives. Things were going very well until one very tricky moment with me at one end of the settee and a youth called Jim Kitson at the other. We were struggling to lift it up some steps and over the garden wall which separated the two houses, the difficulty being the confined space in which we had to operate. As I got my end lifted higher than his with my face almost buried in the upholstery, a voice said, 'Are you t'insurance man?'

I had no idea where the voice was coming from because I couldn't move my head to take a look, but managed to utter a very muffled, 'Yes, that's me. Matthew Taylor.'

'Aye, well, I need a bit of advice.'

'Can't it wait? I'm rather busy right now.'

'No, it can't wait, that's why I'm here. If you just put that thing down for a minute or two, I'll explain. That's all it'll take, a minute or two.'

'I can't put it down ... we're in no-man's-land ... it's got to be moved one way or the other, we can't leave it on top of this wall and there's nowhere else to put it.'

'I can see you've never shifted a settee before, come here, let me do it.'

'No, it's quite all right, once we get those castors over this wall and above that top step, and let that arm into the dip at this side of the wall, we've got it. It's all a question of getting it at exactly the right angle for the next move.'

'By gum, lad, you're making hard work o' that.'

'It'll be easy once we get that manoeuvre done. Then I can talk ... would you like a cup of tea? If you can find your way to the kitchen, my wife will put the kettle on.'

'No time for tea, I can't hang about all day talking. Now look, you leave off and give that end to me. I'll have it shifted in a jiffy ... I'm not a warehouseman at Blenkins for nothing, you know.'

And the fellow, whoever he was, almost shouldered me away from my end of this operation, seized the settee in powerful arms and began to shout instructions to the lad at the other end. And it worked. In no time, the clumsy lump of furniture was over the wall and up the steps, managing to navigate a tight corner before being ushered on one end through the veranda door into the front of the house. With some relief, the two men placed it on the floor and I could then see the newcomer.

'You should have asked me to help you shift this stuff,' he said. 'There's a knack in shifting big stuff, you know. If it got into the house it'll come out, that's what we say. Anyroad, Mr Taylor, can you spare me a minute now that's all over?'

'My pleasure,' I said. 'Thanks for your help out there.'

'Say nowt about it. One good turns deserves another. Sorry to come at a time like this, I'd no idea you were flitting today but if you'd asked me, I'd have got you settled in in half t'time. Thursdays aren't bad days for

17

moving house but you aren't supposed to get married on a Thursday, it brings losses, so they say. I hope you spread salt in every room before you moved in, brings luck, it does. Anyroad, it's up to you, Mr Taylor, it's your house.'

'I'm sorry I can't offer you a seat in my new office.' I chose to ignore his old superstitions about house moving. 'But at least we can talk while the work goes on. So what's so urgent?'

He was a stoutly built man with a round, rather gloomy face topped by a flat cap under which I could see thick grey hair. He wore a brown tweed jacket, a dark green shirt and heavy brown boots and I guessed he was in his mid-fifties. I did not know his name and felt I had never previously encountered him.

'Like I said, I need advice. Well, more than advice. T'vicar told me to come and see you. It's about our Sylvia's wedding, it's this coming Saturday, the day after tomorrow.'

'Right, well I'm sure I can help, fire away. And you are?'

'Jack Watson from Gaitingsby. Curlew Cottage, on t'road out to Baysthorpe, just over t'railway bridge.'

'Right,' I said. 'I know the house.'

'We've not met because I work in Guisborough, but I've taken time off this week to

18

get this wedding sorted out.'

'So Sylvia is your daughter?'

'Right. She's getting wed in Gaitingsby church, All Saints. You'll know it. She's marrying a fellow called Ferguson, Jim. From Lexingthorpe. Nice chap, good family, plenty of brass.'

'I know the family, yes, and that church is the one with the extremely tiny tower, it's halfway up the hill.'

'Right, well, the Reverend Redhead's doing t'honours, a decent bloke as clergymen go. Half two on Saturday afternoon. Reception in t'village hall afterwards. Honeymoon in foreign parts, t'Channel Isles wherever they are.'

At this late stage, I had no idea why Mr Watson should suddenly decide he wanted to discuss insurance connected with his daughter's wedding and he seemed to be taking a long time getting around to the point of his visit. As pieces of our furniture and chests full of our belongings were being carried past, Evelyn directed the bearers to specific parts of the house as she coped with endless cups of tea. In spite of our somewhat meagre possessions, there was much work to be done so I tried to steer him towards the purpose of this chat.

'So how can I help?'

'T'vicar says we'll need t'bridesmaids

insured.'

'The bridesmaids?'

I had never come across this before and I couldn't imagine the Reverend Redhead suddenly deciding to be awkward about anything that was routine for most weddings. Even during my short time as an insurance agent, there had been several weddings in that church and the vicar had never previously issued this type of request. Why on earth would he want these bridesmaids insured? And what sort of insurance did he have in mind?

'The bridesmaids? Why? Are they likely to be doing something dangerous?'

I wondered if there was going to be an archway of ploughshares or swords or blazing torches or something equally risky. They weren't going to fire a cannon, were they? Or swing on a trapeze? Or use roller skates down the aisle?

'Not that I know of, they'll just be there, taking part.'

'Supporting the bride?'

'Aye, as bridesmaids do, walking behind her, dressed for t'occasion, looking good, that sort of thing. In t'procession.'

'Did the vicar give any reason for wanting this?' I asked.

'Aye, it's in case summat gets damaged.'

'Damaged?'

'That's what he said.'

'So why does he think your bridesmaids are likely to damage something?'

'Well, there'll be t'wedding cars outside, pews inside, yon church floor, folks in smart clothes ... and mebbe summat else I can't think of.'

'I'm still puzzled by this, Mr Watson. So who are the bridesmaids?'

'Dolly and Daisy,' he said. 'I thought you would have known that, it was in t*'Gazette* last Friday.'

'I didn't get chance to read it, I was too busy preparing for this move. Are they sisters?'

'Aye, twins. We use 'em for all our important family do's, funerals, weddings, anniversaries, christenings and such like.'

'Use them?'

'Aye, that's what I said. They're very good, very patient and calm, never get flustered, and there's nowt better looking when they're all done up in their finery, manes and tails decorated with coloured ribbons...'

'So we're not talking about two girls as bridesmaids?' The penny was now beginning to drop but I was still puzzled. 'So just who are Dolly and Daisy?'

'Hosses,' he said. 'Shires. I thought you would have know that, Mr Taylor? Everybody round here knows we breed Shires, and then there was that bit in the *Gazette* with a photo. Fair capped they were, that reporter and photographer, they reckon they'd never seen bridesmaids like 'em.'

'You mean your daughter's bridesmaids are a pair of Shire horses?'

'Aye. Mares. That's what she wanted. It's her wedding.'

'She'll have plenty of lucky horseshoes, then?' I joked.

'Oh, aye, she'll be carrying two, one from Dolly and one from Daisy, all polished up. None of your cardboard shoes for our Sylvia. She'll have t'real thing. I reckon that'll make sure everything goes well on the day, but yon vicar's a bit governed by rules and regulations, and by his parish council. It was them who said he had to get insurance, for t'hosses to go into church.'

'I think he has a point, it's not every day someone wants to take a pair of carthorses into church!'

'Our Sylvia says there's nowt unusual about it. She's grown up with them hosses, like sisters they are. She can ride 'em both bareback an' all. And she reckons if Dolly and Daisy can carry her awd granny off to her funeral, they can come to t'wedding and play an active part in that. So they'll all be dressed up in wedding colours with brasses for good luck and they'll accompany t'bride to church and then down t'aisle and off to t'reception later. We might even let 'em have a drink o' champagne and some cake.'

'And the vicar says it's all right, does he?'

'Oh aye, once he got used to t'idea. After a bit o' deep thinking, he reckons animals are part of God's kingdom and he does 'ave that annual sheep-blessing service, and one for pets, so if sheep can come to church and dogs and cats and guinea pigs, he sees no reason why hosses can't come. And there's nowt in t'rules to say hosses can't be brides-maids. Mind you, once they get into church, we'll have a chap standing by with a brush and shovel.'

'So what precisely is the vicar's concern?'

'Well, he wondered if summat might startle Dolly or Daisy, and they might lash out and kick somebody, or accidentally smash a car headlight or stand on somebody's foot and knock things over in church and mess all over t'carpets ... that sort o' thing. He doesn't want t'church to be liable if owt goes wrong. Flashing cameras might scare 'em or champagne corks popping ... I told him nowt'll scare 'em, those hosses are as calm as any, nowt fazes 'em. You could drop a bomb near 'em and they'd never flinch an inch. But vicars are vicars and I can understand him wanting to do things right. So there we are, Mr Taylor. How much will it cost to insure my hosses against causing damage on t'wedding day?'

'I've no idea,' I admitted. 'I've never had this kind of request before. I'll have to ring my District Office. How urgent is it?'

'Well, t'wedding's on Saturday, day after tomorrow, so we'll have to get summat sorted before then.'

'And the vicar is adamant, is he?'

'Aye, he's not gone so far as to say he *won't* allow Dolly and Daisy into church without insurance but I think his parochial church council's putting pressure on. They once had a cow got into church when t'door was left open and it nearly wrecked t'spot, they've never forgotten that. So I want to do what I can to make things easier for him.'

'Fair enough, I think you're doing the right thing. I'll ring my bosses now,' I said. 'But this telephone isn't connected up, not until tomorrow, so I'll use my old one next door. Come along, you'd better be on hand to answer any questions.'

When I spoke to my District Manager, Leonard Evans, he said, so far as he knew, there had never been a precedent whereby horses had been used as bridesmaids inside a church, but on the other hand there were plenty of examples where animals were taken into a variety of buildings, sometimes on special occasions. There were pet shows,

24

for example, and pet shops, artists' and film studios, veterinary surgeons' premises, zoos, agricultural shows and more, plus of course, private houses with animals both as residents and occasional visitors. Many people did not worry about insuring their premises against damage by animals and Mr Evans did tell me he knew of no specific insurance policy which catered for horses in church.

However, he did know that the Premier had several clients who were undertakers, and their black horses were insured because of their unique role. The insurance covered their use throughout the whole of any funeral, including their passage through public and private places with or without motor traffic, and the policy also covered them whilst they were on church premises. In the case of undertakers who still made use of horses, their policies were renewed annually.

The Watson wedding was different, being a one-off occasion. In short, there was no ready-made policy to cater for it. Having listened to this, and bearing in mind the wedding was the day after tomorrow, I said, 'Can we adopt one of those funeral policies for the wedding? There's not a lot of difference between a horse attending a funeral or a wedding. Both involve churches. Cross out the word *funeral* wherever it occurs and substitute *wedding*. If we've got a policy which covers the horses when they're on church premises, surely that will suffice? There's no need to specify why they're actually going to the church. Surely, church premises are church premises, inside or out, and there's no real difference between a funeral and a wedding, so far as the presence of horses is concerned.'

'I couldn't agree more. You might have solved your own problem, Mr Taylor. Hang on, I'll read through our undertakers' policy so far as horses are concerned ... it'll only take a moment, we have copies available.'

I hung on to the line as he ferreted among some papers and I could hear the rustling followed by a long silence.

Then he said, 'Right, we can do it. It's very easy to adapt a funeral director's horse-use policy for your wedding. So, yes, Mr Taylor, tell your client we are prepared cover him and if it's only for the one day, we're talking of a very low premium. Say 12s 6d. If your client gives you that money now, I'll talk to him on the phone right away, and I can complete the proposal form from what he tells me and send it out for him to sign. But we'll cover him as from now which means he can go ahead with his arrangements.'

And so the deal was done and I found myself not at all angry or upset at the interruption. I was pleased the wedding could proceed just as the bride had wished. Having dealt with that small matter, the remainder of my removal day went smoothly without interruptions from clients. When everyone had gone home, Evelyn and I celebrated with a bottle of champagne I'd managed to buy from Big Deck at the Unicorn. He wanted to give it to me, but I insisted on paying, telling him I had saved up for it by selling some of the oddments I'd accepted in lieu of premiums over the past few weeks. And I bought a second bottle which I gave him as a thank-you for his help in securing Daleside.

Later, Sylvia's wedding photographs with her magnificent wedding-clad horses at her side showed that the day had been bright and sunny, and it had been a huge success. Not surprisingly, her picture appeared in several newspapers and the official wedding photographs highlighted the unusual nature of the celebration. In fact, I was given one as a present.

From what I heard later, Dolly and Daisy had behaved impeccably both in church and outside but, of course, they did not accompany the happy couple on their honeymoon to the Channel Isles.

On that occasion, the bride was attended only by the groom.

Horses have long been associated with important moments of our personal lives as well as English history and public ceremonies. Until the advent of the motor vehicle and railway train, we depended heavily upon them for haulage and transport, either for riding at leisure or making an important or lengthy journey, and even fighting battles. Following the invention of trains and cars, horses have continued to be used for ceremonial events such as state funerals, coronations and royal weddings. People have long felt that well-trained horses in all their finery, controlled by drivers equally well turned out, are far superior to mere motor vehicles. One need only watch film and television recordings of major British events to fully appreciate this; the horse has a dignity and presence which no motor vehicle can match and that makes it ideal for all sorts of important occasions.

Not surprisingly, therefore, even in modern times horses have continued to be used for weddings and funerals, especially in rural areas, although they seldom appear as bridesmaids as they did at the Watson wedding. Instead, they are utilized to haul impressive vehicles whether they be coaches specially adorned as wedding transport, or black four-wheeled structures used as horse-drawn hearses.

For a long time in the moors, horse-drawn hearses were something of a rarity among working people and the poorer classes, most of their corpses being carried by hand in coffins or even hammocks as they were transported across the wilds to the nearest church. These routes, several miles long, became known as corpse ways and some continue to exist as parts of long-distance footpaths; there was an ancient belief that when a corpse was carried over land in this way it became a public right of way, and there is little doubt this was widely accepted. These routes were sometimes known as the church road, a name which appears in some villages today. Once a corpse way had been established through common use, then no other route was used for carrying the dead by hand. Bearers would stubbornly carry coffins along those corpse ways in spite of deep snow and dangerous floods, refusing to make use of other less dangerous or easier routes. In some areas of Yorkshire there are reports of bodies being washed away from their bearers while crossing flooded rivers, never to be seen again.

The wealthier people, or those who owned horses such as farmers and tradespeople, made good use of these biddable animals to haul funeral vehicles. Initially, these were little more than a cart which was adorned for the occasion, but it didn't take the manufacturers long to realize there was a good market for specially designed and beautifully constructed horse-drawn hearses. There was, however, a type of horse-drawn vehicle known as a coffin cart, but this was not a hearse – it was nothing more than a tiny one-seater vehicle which looked little bigger than a coffin, hence its name.

Horse-drawn hearses were much more ornate. There were extremely elegant, usually with four wheels containing slender spokes. The rear portion, over the back wheels, was a box-like container large enough to accommodate a coffin and almost invariably it had glass sides. Glossily painted in black, the hearse was often heavily ornamented with silver fittings while at the front was the driver's seat, suitably attired in funereal purple. And, of course, it was drawn by a team of black horses suitably attired, sometimes sporting black plumes on their heads.

When professional undertakers appeared on the scene it was logical they would make good use of specially designed horse-drawn hearses and it must be said these did vary considerably in design. Some undertakers would also keep a team of their own splendid black horses especially for funerals, while wedding organizers kept similar teams of white horses.

So far as undertakers were concerned in Delverdale, I knew of none who were full-time operators. Usually they had other interests; most were joiners although some were general builders or even small garage owners, their funeral activities being a sideline which, with the passage of time, became rather more formal. In later years they became known as funeral directors, many of which expanded to deal with those matters on a full-time basis, sometimes with a monumental stonemason as part of the team. Even today, however, many rural builders and joiners continue to operate as funeral directors, probably because their woodworking skills mean they can construct handsome coffins, often to very personal specifications. Those experienced in stonework may also create wonderful tombs or merely plain tombstones.

When motor vehicles became more commonplace, it was inevitable that specially constructed motor hearses made their appearance but even so many rural funeral directors kept their old horse-drawn showpieces. Sadly, some were allowed to quietly rot and deteriorate until they were beyond use, although some were maintained in splendid working order, with others finding their way into museums. Quite often, one of those retained hearses would make an appearance by special request when someone expressed a wish to be carried to the grave by a team of black horses, and so it was that I received a visit from Jacqueline Pollard, the clerk of Micklesfield Parish Council. Mrs Pollard was secretary of almost every organization in the village, in addition to sitting on countless committees. Her visit reminded me of that Premier policy which catered for horses being used on church premises.

'I like your new house,' she said as I settled her into my office. She had admired the view from the veranda and nodded her approval. 'It's a nice place, I'm pleased for you and your family. You need somewhere like this, a nice office.'

'So how can I help?'

'It's about the parish hearse,' she began.

'*Parish* hearse? I didn't know Micklesfield parish had a hearse!'

'Oh, it's been here for years. No one really knows how old it is.'

'I've never seen it used,' I had to admit.

'I'm not surprised, it goes back a long time and hasn't been used for years,' she smiled. 'There used to be a parish coffin as well but I think that's fallen to pieces. We've no idea where it went, people prefer to use their own these days.'

'A parish coffin? You mean it was reused?'

'Yes, by families who couldn't afford a coffin of their own. Bodies were carried to the graveside in the parish coffin, and then buried in a shroud. The coffin was kept for another time. There's still one in the church at Easingwold near York although I must say it's no longer used.'

'It seems I'm learning something about Micklesfield history. So if we still have the hearse that belongs to the parish, where is it kept?'

'In the hearse house,' and she smiled. 'Or t'eearse 'oose, as the locals call it.'

She pronounced eearse rather like ears, albeit with a shorter, harder letter s; it was the local dialect pronunciation.

'So where's that?' was my next question.

'You know the chapel of rest? The one used by Jedd Stoker?'

'Yes, it's up the dale, near the Dalehead Methodist Chapel.' Jedd Stoker was our local undertaker, his funeral business being run in conjunction with his joinery.

'Right, well, the hearse house adjoins it, it's a small stone shed behind the chapel of rest – it looks more like a small extension. The hearse has always been kept there because it's so handy, it's immediately available. Pop the corpse into the chapel of rest, and pop the hearse into its stable next door to await the next customer. A simple system.'

I knew the extension in question but had never considered it anything more than a tiny outbuilding, the sort that might house an earth toilet or cleaning materials for the chapel. I voiced my thoughts. 'That little shed doesn't look big enough to contain a horse-drawn hearse.'

'Oh, it's not horse-drawn,' was her next surprise. 'It's propelled by hand, by bearers in fact. It's got four wheels, like a pram, and stands about waist high. The coffin is placed on the board which forms the top and it is then wheeled to the church; the hearse is narrow enough to be guided down the aisle to the altar of churches hereabouts and it can also cope with small chapels. It was used to transport heavy coffins along narrow footpaths and through woods, places where horse-drawn vehicles couldn't reach. There were a lot of those around here in the past.'

'It must be very manoeuvrable if it can cope with footpaths. I wouldn't fancy trying to push a pram through a wood or along some of our moorland paths!'

'It is very light and it's got big wheels, rather like a pram, as I said. And, don't forget, there wasn't just one man pushing it. There was a team of four or even six bearers, they could manhandle it through very difficult areas with a coffin on board.'

'I'd imagine if the going became very rough, they'd lift the body off and carry trolley and body separately for as far as necessary?'

'My grandfather said they used to do that, to get it over bogs and rock-strewn paths, over ditches and so forth. Some of those corpses had a very rough final journey, not the sort of smooth trip enjoyed by bodies in modern motor hearses.'

'So this contraption isn't really a hearse?' was my immediate thought. 'It's more of a trolley. It just happens to be for corpses, not luggage or heavy commercial stuff. Even though it carries people, I can hardly call it a pram!'

'Oh, I agree. You couldn't say that old Mrs Whatsit was ferried to her grave in a pram, Matthew! In our parish records, it's a hearse; it would be very undignified to call it the parish corpse trolley! We must always refer to it as a hearse.'

'I must go and have a look at it, and that brings me back to you, Jacqueline. Obviously, you've come about the hearse and I'm guessing it's something to do with insurance?'

'Yes, the parish council has asked me to explore the possibility. In short, Matthew, it's not insured and it is vulnerable out there,

there's no lock on the door and one of our councillors thought it might be valuable. As an antique. We wouldn't want it stolen or destroyed, but if something did happen, we felt any insurance money might enable us to have it reconstructed or repaired. We could even build a similar one to replace it.'

'If I send a proposal form to the Premier, the first thing they'll demand is a lock on the door, and if the hearse turns out to be very valuable, they might want it removed and stored in some place where it's safe. Like a museum.'

'The door's never been locked, Matthew. It's always been open to families. Bearers could always help themselves whenever they wanted, that's part of our tradition. Remember there were no undertakers in its early days, families arranged their own burials. There's a notebook inside to record who's got it, just in case two families wanted it at the same time. It might have been eight or ten miles up on the moors, getting loaded up for a trip down to church, when the second lot wanted it ... you can't insist on a door lock, Matthew, or moving it to a museum. It has to be there if it's needed.'

'Surely no one will want it today? Not with motor hearses and the occasional horse-drawn one still available?'

'Who can say what anyone might want in

the future? In short, Matthew, the parish wants to maintain the tradition by having its own hearse always ready and available even if it's highly unlikely to be used. Because it is so unusual, we felt it should be insured. It's not just against theft, of course, there's always a fire risk or damage if the building collapses in a storm or leaks water on to the hearse, or even damage if it's taken out for use during a funeral. It could damage a wheel or get hit by a car ... .'

'I understand, Jacqueline. All I can do is ask you to fill in a proposal form – which will ask for a valuation – and I will submit it to my District Office. It will need signing either by you or the chairman of the parish council.'

I found a proposal form and suggested she describe the vehicle as simply the parish hearse, without saying whether it was hand-propelled or a motor vehicle.

I also suggested she give it a reasonable value, say £15, and I felt she could say that, when it was not in use, it was stored at the Chapel of Rest, Micklesfield, making no reference as to whether or not it was locked up. She completed the form, signed it and left. Next day, I posted it to my District Office at Ryethorpe and drove up the dale to have a close look at the hearse.

Certainly, it was a splendid vehicle. It was

eight feet long by three feet wide, its top being a flat surface with slightly raised edges to prevent the coffin sliding off. That surface was three feet from the ground, with leather straps attached to the sides so that they could be fastened over the coffin to secure it. Beneath was a framework of oak, looking like several letters X leading down to the axles. It had six spoked wheels, rather like those of a pram, all with solid rubber tyres. Along each side were six brass handles, with other single ones at the front and rear. It was in pristine condition, thanks to the care lavished upon it by parish councillors, and looked secure and safe in its shelter beneath the chapel of rest. Having seen it, I now felt confident enough to answer any questions from District Office, for surely there would be a query or two.

The phone rang a few days later; it was my District Ordinary Branch Sales Manager, Mr Montgomery Wilkins. After a few pleasantries, he said, 'Mr Taylor, the proposal for the parish hearse. It seems it has been undervalued.'

'Undervalued?'

'Yes, £15 seems rather low for a hearse, whether it is a motor vehicle or especially if it's one of those splendid horse-drawn examples which have survived.'

'Oh, it's neither,' I told him. 'It's hand-propelled.'

'A hand-propelled hearse? I must admit, Mr Taylor, that in all my long years in this profession, I have never encountered a hand-propelled hearse. Are you sure that's what it is?'

'Absolutely,' and I gave him a short account of what it looked like and how it was used.

'Well, I am sure we can cover it for all risks but I do need to categorize it. As I am sure you know, vehicles are placed in categories for road-traffic regulations, that is, carts and wagons; pedal cycles; hackney carriages and stage coaches; public-service vehicles and mechanically propelled vehicles which can include steam rollers and traction engines. When we insure a vehicle, it is one of the conditions of our policy that it operates within the existing laws, Mr Taylor, so how would you categorize this one?'

'Well, it's not mechanically propelled, and I'd say it wasn't a public-service vehicle even if it does carry the public for hire or reward, although only when they are dead, and I don't think it is a hackney carriage or a stage coach and certainly not a pedal cycle. That only leaves carts and wagons.'

'If we decide it is a wagon, it will need the owner's name and address on a conspicuous part and, of course, it will have to meet the law on things like lights and brakes.'

'It can't be a wagon or cart,' I decided. 'It's not drawn by horses. It's a pedestrian-controlled vehicle.'

'Ah! Like a perambulator or a wheelbarrow. Well done. But there are rules about lights which pedestrian-controlled vehicles must carry during the hours of darkness, it all depends on their dimensions...'

'I don't think the hearse will be used at night,' I told him. 'And I don't think we need worry about overhanging loads or the antidazzle regulations. And those regulations only apply if it is used on public roads. This one is mainly used on footpaths and church premises.'

'Hand cart!' he said. 'It fits the category of a hand cart, and although it would need lights if it exceeded certain dimensions, I think that will satisfy our Head Office. I shall describe it as a hand cart, specifying that it is used only during funeral processions and that it carries the coffin and corpse.'

'But it is the parish hearse, Mr Wilkins. I think the parish will not want it degrading into something as mundane as a hand cart.'

'Apt descriptions are so very important, especially if there is a claim of any kind. From what you have told me, Mr Taylor, this is nothing more than a hand cart which happens to be used for transporting deceased human persons. That is a very accurate description of your parish vehicle.'

Then I had a flash of inspiration. 'How about a bier?' I put to him. 'A bier with wheels.'

He remained silent for a moment, then said, 'A wonderful compromise, Mr Taylor. It is, after all, a bier because a bier is a stand upon which a coffin or corpse is placed. The fact that this one happens to have wheels to facilitate its transportation from site to site is immaterial, and if it is not going to be used on public roads during the hours of darkness, then we need not concern ourselves with lights, nor with matters like names on the sides, number plates, brakes, audible warning instruments and efficient windscreen wipers.'

And so, for a very modest annual premium, I was able to insure the Micklesfield hearse for all risks, with no questions being asked about whether its house was locked or not. I think the fact it was kept at the hearse house adjoining the Chapel of Rest satisfied my scrutineers, the belief being that theft from such a place was highly unlikely, and the parish council had no qualms about it being described in the policy as a wheeled bier. I suggested to the council, however, that they continued to use the term hearse house, or the dialect t'eearse 'oose, as the name for its accommodation.

Bier house sounded too much like the local name for a pub.

Two

'I had to swerve all over the road several times before I hit the man.'

From a claim form

Following the move to our new house, it didn't take long to settle into a familiar routine and I was surprised how quickly my clients, both existing and potential, discovered I had a different address, although I retained my earlier telephone number. The pensioners who moved into our previous house at No. 2 Miners' Row did not want to retain such a new-fangled contraption as a telephone and felt they had no use for it, so the GPO said it was a simple matter to transfer it and its number – Micklesfield 27 – to my new house. I arranged for some business cards to be printed bearing my telephone number and new address, and decided I would distribute these as I toured Delverdale. I could leave some in post offices and shops, and I'd also leave some in my

Bottle and Jug space at the Unicorn.

With Evelyn through her driving test and rapidly gaining confidence in driving alone, she could accept offers of supply teaching with greater ease, while her sister Maureen was very happy to look after baby Paul when Evelyn and I were both at work. Paul was a cheerful playmate for her three-year- old, Bernard, and that made things easier for Maureen. She did not have to worry about keeping her lively lad occupied. When Evelyn wanted to use Betsy, our shining black Austin 10, I tried to restrict my work either to my office or to Micklesfield village where I could walk to make my regular collections or do a spot of canvassing.

The alternative was to use the train to reach the villages within my agency or else to return to my former transport, the Coventry Eagle motorbike, which I had not yet sold. Certainly our lives had changed for the better. Our income was increasing, partly due to my efforts and the extra commission I was earning, but also through Evelyn's work as a supply teacher, even if it was far from regular. She might do two days in one month, none in the next and ten in the third; the work was very spasmodic so we did not rely on her earnings. They were a bonus, and I felt she should use the money to buy new clothes or provide herself with a treat of some kind. There is no doubt that a useful percentage of my commission came from new business with car owners – more and more people were buying cars, but similarly, many were also buying new electrical apparatus for their homes. Electric ovens had become commonplace instead of those which were part of the fireside range, electric carpet sweepers, kettles and clothes irons were proving popular, with their proud owners taking out insurance in case those things overheated and caught fire. In some rural areas, there was still concern about using electricity for things like heating and cooking and it was a fact that badly wired installations did cause fires. In all, therefore, it was a good time to be in insurance. The truth was that home insurance was quite a new concept for many people living in the countryside, although some would not entertain it because they thought it was akin to gambling. Some were even superstitious enough to think that insurance against fire was a sure way of causing a blaze, or insurance against injury was a guarantee they'd suffer from a broken leg, a crack on the head or some unspecified accident. This followed the similar logic that if one made a will, it was a sure way of attracting an early death.

Generally, I found people were willing to listen to my sales patter and financial advice and it was pleasing that many did come to appreciate the value of wise insurance. I was not too interested in earning high commission – I was far more concerned that my clients would receive the very best of cover through their investment with the Premier and so I never sold insurance to those who could not afford it or might have difficulty paying the premiums. Among the more popular of my policies were the various life-insurance schemes, either endowment policies with profits or without profits, or a straightforward policy based on the whole life of the assured person. The earlier in one's life these were effected, the better were the returns they promised. These were steadily replacing the old funeral clubs where people in a community or place of work, say an entire village or perhaps a factory, put a small amount of money aside each week so that a useful fund accumulated during their lifetime. The money was paid to the club treasurer and so it became a form of enforced saving, except that such savings did not generate any kind of interest on the deposits. The idea was that this would pay their burial costs when the time came – they'd have a 'bit put by' to avoid the disgrace of a pauper's burial – and for this reason, lots of funeral club members saved in this way for most of their lives, literally from the cradle to the grave. But various forms of insurance, with far superior financial returns, were quickly rendering such clubs obsolete.

In addition to this regular routine, I continued to pay my Wednesday visit to Micklesfield market on its site outside the Unicorn Inn, owned and run by Evelyn's parents. The cobbled frontage was an ancient marketplace dating back centuries with the market continuing as it had always done. It was a modest market by town or city standards but it sold fruit and vegetables, eggs, milk and cheese, household goods and some small livestock like chickens, ducks and sometimes puppies and kittens. From time to time, the occasional stall would appear bearing other items, such as parts for cars, bikes and motorbikes, or cakes and jams, fish, woollen garments and even boots and shoes. The market was well patronized, with the local bus bringing customers and scheduling its Wednesday runs so they could spend time browsing or having something to eat and drink at the Unicorn. Evelyn's mother, Virginia, always made sure she had an ample stock of sandwiches, soup, tea and coffee for those who might not want to drink beer or spirits, and she had a special room set aside from the bar in which ladies could rest and enjoy a chat over a modest meal.

Ladies seen alone in the bars of public houses were thought to be wanting in morals, but a special ladies' room provided a retreat for them; in this case, it was called the tea room.

The reason for my weekly visit was that Big Deck, Evelyn's father, had allowed me to use the Bottle and Jug as a form of outdoor office. In the days before I had an office in my house, I had nowhere private to which I could invite potential customers for a leisurely discussion and so Deck had said I could rent space at the Bottle and Jug.

That was the theory – in fact, he allowed me to use it free of charge, doubtless because my presence did attract customers who spent money in his bar. That part of the pub known as the Bottle and Jug was no longer used by patrons of the Unicorn. In the past, they would arrive at the exterior of the inn to buy ale to take home in their jugs or by the bottle, and their business would be conducted from outside the premises. Children were often sent to collect beer in large jugs and this business was conducted literally through a large hole in the wall which opened on to the end of the bar counter. On the inner edge was a large sliding window bearing the legend *Bottle and Jug*; that was still in position at the Unicorn but the outer part comprised the thickness of the solid wall, at least the length of a man's arm. About chest high to the average man, and with a flat base about two feet six inches long by eighteen inches wide, it was dry and shielded from the weather. It was ideal for my purpose, for I was allowed to spread out my leaflets and sales literature – and my newly printed business cards. People, if they wished, could help themselves without having to speak to me. However, it meant I could, if necessary, stand near my stock of literature to deal with enquiries, but whether or not I was there, my papers would be safe from the weather and readily available. I found that most people liked to browse without my intrusion – and they would approach me if they wanted further information or advice. Now that people knew I was available here at a particular time, lots made a point of visiting me during the Wednesday market, and I do know that some called merely to pick up an informatory leaflet or proposal form.

I marked these proposal forms so that when I received one through the post or by hand, I knew where it had originated. In that way, I could gauge the volume of new business which came from this source. Clearly, my system was beneficial and so it was that my Wednesday afternoons were committed to the Bottle and Jug. Because I had my weekly accounts to prepare before one o'clock on Wednesdays, in order to catch the post office and pay in my monies before it shut for the afternoon, I did not spend those mornings at the market. Early on Wednesday mornings, however, I made a point of going to the Unicorn to stock the hole in the wall with my literature, always ensuring it was up to date, and then returned home to complete my week's accounts.

Because the system appeared to be working very satisfactorily, and in spite of having a nice new office in my new house, I decided to continue with my Wednesday 'office' or 'surgery' at the market. As a direct result, I was approached one Wednesday afternoon by Sally Webster, a widow who lived at Peat Hill Farm Cottage in the dale head at Freyerthorpe. Her son, Henry, now farmed at Peat Hill having succeeded to the business upon the death of his father, who was also called Henry. Sally lived in a cottage on the farm land. She was a jolly woman with an infectious sense of humour and when she burst into laughter, her entire body joined in the fun and wobbled about almost as if it was out of her control. Round-faced with red cheeks, she was rather heavily built and somewhat squat in appearance, with some people saying she was as broad as she was high, or that she was as wide as a carthorse and as tall as a staddle stone.

A staddle stone was in fact very short; it looked rather like a large mushroom with an umbrella-like top and a thick stem. Standing about two feet high with the base of its stem about eight inches square, its purpose was to support a stack of straw or hay. Several staddle stones were arranged in the shape of the stack's base and planks were laid across them to form a platform; the stack was then built upon that base so that it was some distance off the ground. This in turn meant that rats and mice could not climb into the stack to make their homes there because they could not negotiate the undersides of the overhanging lips of the staddles. Why Sally should be likened to a staddle stone was uncertain, except that someone let it slip that she'd once worn a massive hat at someone's wedding, this making her look rather like one of those stones.

'Glad I caught you, Mr Taylor,' she beamed, with her red cheeks creasing in a huge smile. 'I knew you'd be here. I picked up some o' your leaflets last week. I wish we'd had this kind of insurance when I was a lass, my Henry didn't have any life cover or owt like that. Mind you, we couldn't afford it when we were young. It was all work and no 'olidays with very little by t'way o' wages.'

'That's what I'm finding as I go about this dale,' I agreed with her. 'In many ways, I'm

breaking new ground, I just hope the younger folks will see the sense of sound investments and good insurance cover.'

'Young folks don't often see sense in anything.' She grinned widely. 'Which is why I
want to talk to you.'

'Well, I'm happy to listen,' and I looked
around for somewhere more private,
although none of the market customers or
traders seemed to be taking any interest in
our conversation. 'We can chat over there.' I
had spotted a deserted space near the end of
the Unicorn's front wall.

'So what can I do for you, Sally?'

'My grandchildren. I'd like to insure 'em,
give 'em summat for t'future, summat me or
my kids never had. I'm not badly off now, I
don't have t'expense of running t'farm and
feeding t'workers, but I still get a share of
t'profits so I can afford to give summat back
to t'family. I'm thinking of taking out a life
insurance for each of 'em.'

'Well, I'm sure the Premier can do something although in the past, some insurance
companies wouldn't insure youngsters
under twenty-one. It was all to do with the
high infant mortality rates. Then some companies brought in what they called deferred
assurance. Under that system, you could
take out a policy for a child until he or she
was twenty-one, and if they died before that

age the premiums were returned to the family, with no interest on the money. If they survived beyond that age, though, the policy could be converted into a normal whole-life or endowment policy. So you can see that insuring children wasn't easy, rather like insuring the elderly, although you might have got a very small insurance under some industrial policies, many hardly worth the paper they were written on. But now, Sally, the Premier will happily accept proposals for the insurance of children. It's done by adults on their behalf because minors – people under twenty-one – can't legally enter into contracts, and an insurance policy is a contract. So what do you want?'

'I want to make sure all my grandchildren get good life insurances, all of 'em, all eight. I reckon I want a long-running endowment policy apiece, all with profits, that should do the trick. I've looked at your leaflets and can afford summat for every one of 'em, I'll pay t' premiums until they're twenty-one and then it's up to them.'

'I could arrange policies which mature when they reach twenty-one,' I suggested.

'Nay, lad, if we do that, they'll spend all their cash on summat stupid and unnecessary. I reckon we need to be thinking of 'em continuing until they're mebbe forty-five or even fifty and sixty, summat like that. Long term, Mr Taylor, summat to see 'em into their old age. There's no pensions in farming, you know. They'll need summat to see 'em into old age or to help their families if the Good Lord takes 'em early.'

'Have you seen anything in my literature which appeals?'

'Aye, like I said, those endowment policies with profits. They sound a good idea to me. You get more out than you put in, and it builds up as you go along. That makes sense to me. A good and painless way of saving.'

'If you've decided on that, I'll need to complete a proposal form for each grandchild, and you'll have to sign each one. It'll take quite a long time.'

'What if I come to see you at your house? With details of all t'children?'

'Great idea. I'll need their full names, addresses, dates of birth, any medical history, that sort of thing. I think we'd better make an appointment for this one, it's quite a project.'

'Tomorrow morning? Strike while t'iron's hot and all that?'

'Ten o'clock?' I suggested.

Next morning, Sally arrived at Daleside on time and she was clutching a large brown envelope full of family facts and figures. I took her into my office where she plonked the envelope on my desk and settled on a chair before me. Evelyn was at home and organized a pot of tea with milk and sugar, along with some slices of fruit cake as we settled down to our business.

'Right,' I said when the pleasantries had concluded. 'Who shall we start with?'

'Henry IV and George III,' she said in all seriousness. 'And Margaret of Anjou. Our Henry's children.'

'Henry's your son. The eldest?'

'Aye, Henry II,' she told me.

'You husband being Henry I?' I commented.

'No, he was Henry VIII,' she said. 'His dad was Henry V and his dad before him Henry VII.'

I was lost now. If Henry II was her son, logically Henry III would be her grandson. But he wasn't; it was Henry IV. So where was Henry III? I knew that lots of moorland families named their sons after the father, and so a name like Henry would have been the name of each first-born male child in each family for many generations. It was confusing when checking family histories – in this case, there seemed to be a lot of Henry Websters but they did not appear to be named in numerical sequence.

I knew some families who might have referred to such men as Henry the Elder, Henry the Son and Henry the Younger to cover three generations, Henry the Son becoming Henry the Elder upon the death of his father with Younger moving up to become Son. Or they might be Henry the Grandad, Henry the Dad and Henry the Lad.

But this family was doing things differently and I needed to get it straightened out in my mind. I needed to know what lay behind this odd practice because, sure as eggs were eggs, District Office would query the proposals if I added those numerals after the names.

'I'm baffled,' I admitted to Sally.

'It's easy,' she chuckled. 'Us Websters just call our children and grandchildren after kings and queens. When I married into t'family, I was expected to continue wi' that tradition. So my Henry was Henry II, there was a vacancy for that name, you see.'

'I can understand that,' I told her. 'What baffles me is why your son was Henry II when his father was Henry VIII.'

'It's so we don't get confused with all these Henrys,' she said. 'If we just called 'em Henry, then few folks would know which Henry we were talking about. So we add a bit to their name. Like t'kings did. We don't have second names – I mean, we might have had Henry John or Henry Simon or Henry William, but we think it's easier to use king's names.'

'So the king's number is used instead of a second Christian name?'

'Yes, simple, isn't it?'

'Are you telling me you've got other names like this, apart from the Henrys?'

'Oh, aye, there's a few Georges – our Henry's second lad is George III and our Catherine's second lad is George II. We've ever so many Williams, James and Charles, not to mention Elizabeth I, Margaret of Scotland, Mary Queen of Scots and Anne. They're all good names, Mr Taylor. Well, they would be, wouldn't they?'

'I agree, the royal family never goes in for silly names. So what you are saying, is that names of this kind are the full names of your grandchildren? Their legal names?'

'Oh aye, they were christened with 'em, and registered. Not just the grandchildren, of course, My own children. I've an Elizabeth I, Catherine the Great and Charlotte. Just Charlotte. That's nice and simple. Like Victoria will be when we use that. But we allus use their full names on official documents.'

'In that case, I must include them on the proposal forms,' I capitulated. 'So, let's make a start. You'll see on my desk I have spread out some tables of premiums which vary according to the age of the children in question, and there are notes of the operative period of the policies, based on years. They can be tailor-made to fit the requirements of each child.'

And so I settled down to complete the first proposal form, which was for Henry V or Henry The Fifth Webster to give him his full name. It was followed by George III, or George The Third Webster, and then by Margaret of Anjou Webster, followed by James IV, James the Fourth Brown, and Mary II, Mary the Second Brown; then Richard III and George II Smithers, and finally Charles II Williams, these latter three families being from Sally's daughters which meant they did not have the Webster surname. From my literature, I calculated the premiums for each child and Sally said she would pay once a month by cheque, her payments ending with the twenty-first birthday of each child. It would then be the decision of each child whether or not to surrender the policy or keep it active.

But Sally had done her bit and when she left, I collated the various forms and put them in the post for my District Office. I was not in the least surprised to receive, a few days later, a telephone call from Montgomery Wilkins, my District Ordinary Branch Sales Manager at Ryethorpe.

'Mr Taylor,' the high pitch of his voice sounded exaggerated over the telephone, 'the names of those children on the Webster proposals, am I right in thinking we can dispense with all those numerals? Can we just call them Henry or George, or whatever? Head Office is bound to query them.'

'No,' I said, and explained the reason. 'Those are the full legal names of those children.'

'Well, blow me,' he said. 'I've known boys be named after football teams or actors, and people be given all the names of Old Testament prophets, and there was even one of my clients who was working through the alphabet, giving his first child a name beginning with A, the second with B and so forth. He was hoping to get to Z eventually, although his wife wasn't too keen. By the time I left Birmingham, he'd got to J. John, I think. Or was it Jennifer? And there was another fellow who used Latin names for numerals ... I recall he had a Sixtus, a Septimus and an Octavia but I can't remember the rest. But I've never come across anyone using the actual regal title of a sovereign. Their forenames, yes, but full regal name? Blow me, Mr Taylor, you learn something every day. All right, I'll submit these. There should be no problems.'

And so it was that people like Charles II, George II, Richard III, Henry V and Margaret of Anjou had their lives insured by me and the Premier. It was a few weeks later when I got a call from Head Office to say I might be very interested to know that they also currently had, as policyholders, an Oliver Cromwell, a Guy Fawkes, a Robin Hood, several William Shakespeares, a Nell Gwynne, a Florence Nightingale and a Grace Darling.

It follows from this incident that names can be both amusing and important, and the correct recording of them in official documents is essential. Even in my locality, the spelling of names, both forenames and surnames, could vary and so I often asked my clients to spell their names, just to be sure I had them correctly recorded. For example, there are lots of ways of spelling Derek – Deric, Deryk, Derrek, Derrick, Derik, Derick and probably others, while simple names like Brown might end with an 'e', or Smith might be Smyth or Smythe, Murray might be Moray, Readman might be Redman, Reid might be Reed or Read, Derby could be Darby and Barclay might be Berkeley.

There were others like De Ath, Beaver spelt Belvoir, Powell spelt Poel and Cockburn pronounced Coburn, but in general, I managed to complete my forms without any problems. That was until I had to complete an accident report involving a motor car driven by a man called Amariah Browne – with an 'e'. Mr Browne, a Welshman, was on holiday in Delverdale and staying a week with relations at Goldrigg. He was the owner of a smart grey Sunbeam Rapier car and when he had been driving across the moors between Goldrigg and Lexingthorpe, a sheep had wandered onto the carriageway and he had collided with it. He had been unable to avoid the animal because another car had been approaching from the opposite direction which meant he could not take the necessary evasive action. The sheep had been killed and there was considerable damage to the front nearside wing of Mr Browne's car. The headlight, sidelight and bodywork had all suffered, although the vehicle remained driveable and there were no personal injuries. Mr Browne had done the right thing by contacting PC Fletcher, the village constable at Lexingthorpe, and he had taken the necessary details for compilation of the official accident report. The police would provide the sheep's owner with details of Mr Browne and in turn, PC Fletcher, upon seeing that Mr Browne's motor car insurance was with the Premier, advised him to contact me. And so it was that he rang me that same evening. He called from his cousin's house and so I said I would drive out there the following day to leave a claim form for him to complete before he returned to Wales. And so I did, but when I arrived at his cousin's cottage, Mr Browne had left to visit an elderly uncle before returning to Wales.

It seems the old man had been taken ill very suddenly and wanted to talk to him. I left the form, told his cousin how to complete it and said Mr Browne, or someone else, could either post it to me, call with it at my home or drop it through my letter box. Filling in such a form was comparatively easy, and once that was done, I would send it to our Claims Department, who would contact the county police to ask for an abstract of their official accident report. Following that, there would be a decision as to whether or not the Premier would accept liability and meet the costs of Mr Browne's accident which would include death of the sheep and repairs to his car. In the circumstances, I did not foresee any difficulties in the Premier covering all Mr Browne's costs.

When the form arrived at my house, having been pushed through the letter box whilst I was out, I read it carefully to check that all the salient details were included and correct. It was then that I realized there had been another person in the car at the time – Rupert Browne, aged eleven. He had not

62

been injured, however, but Mr Browne had included his name as the only witness. From a legal point of view, a passenger could not be regarded as an independent witness and I felt Rupert would not have been interviewed as such by the police. If he had been interviewed to help ascertain the cause of the accident, it would be recorded in the police accident report and the Premier would ask for an abstract of that. There was no requirement for me to interview Rupert and so I endorsed the claim form and posted it to our District Office in Ryethorpe. A week later, the District Commercial Manager, Mr Clemminson, rang me before I set out on my rounds.

'Mr Taylor,' he began. 'Forgive me for ringing but it's about the claim form for the Browne accident. You'll remember it, he hit a sheep on the moor, but there were no personal injuries. However, our Claims Department has raised a query.'

'Really? What sort of query?'

'They have received the abstract of the police report and it contains no mention of Rupert being in the car at the time of the accident. Did you speak to Mr Browne about this accident?'

'Only on the phone,' I admitted. 'I left the claim form at his holiday address, he was out when I called. And he, or someone else, pushed it through my letter box. I had no call to speak to him, he's not one of my clients. I must admit he didn't mention Rupert on the phone.'

'Obviously there's a slight discrepancy and Claims want us to clarify the matter even though there are no personal injuries. It's probably them being over-cautious in case we get a later claim for other injuries arising from this accident. People do that, you know, make substantial false claims later. We've got to be on our guard against that sort of thing. So can you check?'

'I'll have words with the local constable, he interviewed Mr Browne and compiled the accident report. Mr Browne will have gone home to Wales by now.'

'Good, you'll let me know in due course?'

'I'm going to Lexingthorpe today, collecting. I'll call on PC Fletcher.'

By the time I arrived at Lexingthorpe, PC Fletcher had left his police house, which explained why no one had answered my earlier phone call, but by asking at the garage, post office and shop, I tracked him down to a farm just off the road to Baysthorpe. It was Crag Farm, owned by the Hughes family, coincidentally clients of mine. PC Fletcher's pedal cycle was standing against the kitchen wall and I guessed he'd be inside enjoying a cup of tea and a slice of cake. Or two. When Mavis Hughes answered my knock, she invited me into the kitchen to join the party – her husband Geoffrey, the policeman, the stockman and she were all enjoying their feast, and before I could say whether I would stay or not, a large mug and plate appeared and a chair was hauled to the table.

'Well, well, this is quite a gathering!' grinned Geoffrey. 'So what brings you out this way, Matthew? It's not your calling day, is it?'

'Not for you, no. I'm chasing PC Fletcher, I need to have a word with him. I've tracked him here!'

'Me? It sounds you've been doing a spot of detective work, young Matthew,' smiled the heavily built policeman. 'So how can I help?'

I wasn't sure whether my quest was highly confidential or not, but I thought I'd let the policeman be the judge of that. 'It's about that accident the other week,' I reminded him. 'The Welshman who hit the sheep on the moors above Lexingthorpe.'

'I remember it. So what's the problem?'

'I've got a query from our Claims Department and thought you might help me sort it out. I don't know whether it's confidential or not...'

'You're among friends here, Matthew. So

what's the query?'

'When Mr Browne filled his claim form in, he named a passenger, a Rupert Browne aged eleven. He's not mentioned on the abstract of the accident report which our Claims Department has received from your Headquarters.'

'No, he wouldn't be. He's a dog.'

'A dog?'

'Yes, Rupert is a dog. He wasn't injured and on my Form 96, it only asks for human passengers who have injuries and those who don't. Rupert wasn't injured so there was no need to include him in my report.'

'It seems Mr Browne has listed him as a passenger and a witness.'

'Then I think your claim form need amending, Matthew. I suppose, if he was a pedigree and got hurt, it could be a costly job but that's the situation. Rupert is a golden retriever, by the way. And if your lot are worried about any future claim, the dog wasn't injured. I have that fact noted in my pocket book even if it's not on the accident abstract.'

'I'll tell my boss,' I said.

When I rang Mr Clemminson he sounded very relieved but said he would send a special addendum form to PC Fletcher for him to complete, just in case Mr Browne attempted to win some later claims from the

Premier.

I learned a lot from that minor accident – for example, names are not always what they seem and one must also be wary of the wiles of others. So far as I know, no further claims were submitted as a result of that accident but if Mr Browne had tried, he would have been unsuccessful.

Rupert the dog did not have his day.

Names are very much a part of the insurance world and it is quite odd how a person's forename will suit his or her character or personality. I have often wondered if people grow into their names – for example, would you expect to find a heavyweight wrestler or boxer called Clarence or Crispin? Or a female ballet dancer called Winifred or Brenda? Lots of firemen and policemen are called Dave, not David, while Fred, not Frederick, seems to suit a high proportion of farmers. I couldn't imagine a male ballet dancer called Sid, for example, or a butcher called Peregrine. Or a top soprano called Maud or Agnes. But I could be wrong.

As for people suiting their names, one fine example was Major Roderick Tattersall, one of several retired military men who lived in Micklesfield. He was a regular sight, always impeccably dressed in his cavalry twill trousers, tweed hacking jacket, range of smart waistcoats, expensive shirts and ties, brown brogue shoes and a brown trilby hat with a jay's blue feather in its band. A well-spoken, rather small man with a neat moustache and an erect carriage, he strode briskly around with his shoulders back while sometimes twirling his walking stick like a propeller.

He always made sure that he raised his hat to every lady he encountered and bade good morning, good afternoon or merely good day to everyone he met.

Like so many soldiers, he did not talk a great deal about his wartime exploits although it was known he had served in the cavalry under Field Marshal Viscount Allenby against the Turks in Palestine during the First World War, and afterwards, in civilian life, had established a highly success-ful racehorse-breeding establishment on the outskirts of Micklesfield. Now in his early sixties, he had sold his business and lived peacefully with his wife, Maisie, in a splen-did home called Kirklands House. He had made enough money to live comfortably upon his investments and there would also be a modest military pension; he also earned a few extra pounds in retirement by acting as a judge on local racecourses and writing for Yorkshire newspapers and magazines about horses and the role of the cavalry in the First World War. On that topic, he was said to be an authority and I believe he had written one or two books on the subject.

He did not take a great part in community matters, preferring not to get drawn into things like the parish council, parochial church council, village hall committee, cricket club and so forth. He used his considerable charm to tell those who invited him to serve on some committee or other that he was now in his sixties and looking forward to a long and happy retirement with no additional responsibilities.

I had very little contact with the Major, as he was affectionately known around Micklesfield, because he was not one of my clients, although I was on nodding acquaintance with him.

If I encountered him during one of his stick-twirling walks around the village he would stop and politely pass the time of day with me, but he never entered any kind of deep conversation. I think if I had shown an interest in horses and cavalry history, or perhaps horse-racing, we might have become more friendly, but the sad thing was that the cavalry, as a highly effective arm of our earlier war efforts, had been replaced by tanks, motor vehicles, high-powered guns, aircraft and bombs. What had once been the Major's entire life was now consigned to history and was little more than a memory for most. World War II differed vastly from the Major's experiences, and he had not fought in the Second World War; perhaps that is why he rarely discussed his war-time experiences and I had heard that he preferred to be known as plain Mr Tattersall rather than Major. Then I received an unexpected telephone call from him. He rang shortly after nine o'clock one Tuesday morning.

'Roderick Tattersall here, Mr Taylor. Hope I'm not ringing at an inconvenient moment?'

'Not at all, sir, I'm just about to set off on my rounds.' I called him 'sir' almost without thinking, a throwback to my own army service as one of the more lowly ranks even though he had not introduced himself by rank, as some retired military gentleman were prone to do.

'Good show. Then can I ask you to pop in? For a chat? Perhaps a modest amount of business for you.'

'Yes, of course. What time?'

'To suit you, old boy, I'm free all day. I live at Kirklands House.'

'Thank you. I'll be leaving home in about twenty minutes on my rounds. Say nine thirty?'

'Absolutely splendid. See you then,' and the phone went dead.

Prompt at nine thirty, I drove on to his spacious forecourt where I saw the green front door was standing open. As I eased Betsy to a halt, the Major appeared in the doorway and waited until I had gathered my briefcase. He led me deep into the house where we turned into his study, a book-lined room facing south with a massive walnut desk in the centre.

'My den,' he said with evident pride. 'I come in here to lose myself, there's always something to do, something awaiting my attention. But I wouldn't want it otherwise, Mr Taylor, I can't bear the thought of growing old and having nothing to get out of bed for. Anyway, take a seat and I'll let Maisie know you're here, you'll join us for coffee?'

'Thank you, yes.'

'I appreciate your quick response, Mr Taylor, very impressive,' and he went to the door and shouted to his wife that I had arrived and would love a coffee.

'I like to deal with things straight away,' I told him when he returned to sit opposite me. 'I can't bear unfinished matters littering my desk – or my brain!'

'A man after my own heart. You'd have made a good soldier. Now, while the coffee's on its way, tell me a bit about yourself, then we'll get down to business.'

I told him how I had been an apprentice butcher at the village shop and how I had been persuaded to make a change to insurance, referring to my brief spell in the army where I had been trained as a mechanic, specializing in motorcycles. I told him Evelyn and I had recently bought a house, which he thought very wise, and we both agreed that my little son Paul now provided a strong focus in life and a motive for hard work and enterprise. When the coffee came, Mrs Tattersall said, 'Shall I pour, Roderick, or will you do the honours?'

'You can join us if you wish, Maisie. This is Mr Taylor from the Premier. Mr Taylor, my wife, Maisie.'

'I'd love to join you but I've some cakes in the oven and have a lot to do.'

With the major saying he would act as host, she left us alone with the coffee.

'Well, Mr Taylor,' he said at last. 'You'll be wondering what this is all about, me not being one of your clients.'

'I must admit I did wonder.'

'It's quite simple. I need some insurance and thought you were the fellow to approach.'

'But surely you are already insured? The house, car, a life policy perhaps? Personal belongings and so forth?' I did not like to deliberately poach customers from my competitors, although if they volunteered to join the Premier, then, of course, I was very happy and would do all I could to make the transfer possible.

'I am, Mr Taylor, and quite adequately too, I might add. When I was in business, I was granted very favourable terms for my stables and horses, and Equine Equitable extended my policies to include my domestic belongings, house, car and so on. I cannot back out of it, nor would I wish to. The company is utterly reliable and my terms remain highly favourable.'

'And I would not even try to persuade you, I don't believe in stealing my customers from other companies.'

'I've heard that, which why I have approached you. I believe, where possible, in giving local people my custom. I also choose local practitioners for work about the place, carpenters, builders and so forth.'

'Thank you, I appreciate that. So how can I help?'

'Over the years, Mr Taylor, I have amassed a huge collection of memorabilia associated with the cavalry – everything from uniforms, medals and badges to documents, old records, saddlery, equipment of every kind ... you name it, I've got it stored here. Most of it was discarded by the army when cavalry units became operationally obsolete, but I managed to salvage a lot of it. Much would have been lost otherwise. Before I die, I want to give it all to a military museum, probably that one at Richmond, but in the meantime I have been asked if I will arrange a display in the Territorial Army Hall at Guisborough. It will take place over a week in August. You can guess my next comment – I need to have the entire collection insured, Mr Taylor, both during its time in the Hall, that's night and day of course because it will remain there throughout the period, and during transit. Is that something you can arrange?'

I explained that this kind of insurance, covering private and personal objects and artefacts on show in public places, was regularly effected by the Premier. To accompany the proposal form, I would need a general list of items, an idea of the total value and some indication of those pieces with either a rarity value or high commercial value, along with a detailed description of each such object. I told him I wouldn't need every badge listing, for example; all he need record was, say, 150 cap badges, ten corporals' uniforms, twenty sets of spurs ... and so on. He would also have to convince the Premier that the display was secure while the Hall was unoccupied, especially at night, and one way to achieve this was to notify the local police of its presence. Their routine night-duty patrols would check the Hall during the hours it was closed.

I gave the major a proposal form and said

he could complete it at his leisure and return it to me at his convenience; in the meantime, I would get in touch with my District Office to get some idea of the cost of the premiums he would have to pay. And so I left, thinking this was a small but very nice policy to secure.

Major Tattersall rang me a few days later to ask if it would be convenient to call with his completed proposal form, along with a typed resumé of the artefacts to be placed on show together with a note of their value or rarity, and I agreed to see him at ten the following morning. When he arrived, I took him into my new office, settled him down with a cup of coffee and a biscuit, and prepared to read through his proposal just in case there were any queries I could deal with before posting it to District Office.

The first error I spotted was at the very beginning. The form had spaces for one's title or rank, Christian names and surname. In the space for title or rank, the Major had written 'Mr' and where it asked for Christian names, he had written 'Major Roderick'. I thought the form should be as accurate as possible – either I could amend it or he could complete a new one. The form itself was quite simple to replace because the objects to be insured were presented on a typed list.

'Er, Major,' I said. 'Would you mind if I corrected this form? You've entered Mr where Major should be, and you've put Major in the Christian names section.'

'No,' he smiled. 'No, Mr Taylor. Everyone makes that mistake. Everyone calls me Major, which is really a Christian name. I am not a major by rank, in fact I was only a corporal. My parents christened me Major for reasons I shall never know.'

'But everyone in Micklesfield thinks you are a retired major from the First World War.'

'Not through anything I have said, I assure you, Mr Taylor. I keep trying to tell people that I am not a retired major, I try to get them to call me Mr but I cannot seem to get the message over. I am Mister M. R. Tattersall, nothing more.'

'I noticed your wife called you Roderick when I called, and you introduced yourself to me as Roderick.'

'I did. She always refers to me as Roderick because she hates calling me Major. If she uses that name, it sounds as if she's being pompous and unable to cast off our military background. All through my life, Mr Taylor, I've had to tolerate this misunderstanding. Heaven only knows why my parents called me Major. I think they must have had delusions of grandeur – I think my father was rather disappointed when I rose to nothing higher than a corporal during the war – but of course, I was Corporal Major Tattersall! I never even got to be Sergeant Major Tattersall! But it all got a laugh or two from my mates.'

'I think I must put a short explanatory note in with your proposal form when I submit it,' I told him. 'I know our office staff will query it, as I did. So I must stop calling you Major – now you've explained things, it all sounds rather too familiar.'

'Don't let it bother you, Mr Taylor, I am very accustomed to it by now. I answer to most things! I suppose I should be grateful I wasn't christened Earl, Duke or Prince.'

Somehow, his revelation helped to reduce the formality of the occasion for, being an ex-soldier, I had always felt I should be respectful to his rank and call him sir. Now he was plain Mr it would make a big difference to our relationship even if I found it difficult to accept immediately. I still thought of him as a military officer whom I should call sir – most certainly he had that air of authority. In spite of that, his application was approved within a few days and his exhibition went ahead.

But a note in the local paper announced it as 'Army Officer's fine collection on show. Major Roderick Tattersall of Micklesfield has kindly allowed his collection of cavalry memorabilia to be on display in the Territorial Army Hall next week...'

I knew he would be on show too, and I knew his instinctive behaviour and deportment would convince everyone he was a retired major. He acted the part even if he did not want to be known in that way.

Like so many other people, he had grown into his name.

Perhaps that is what his parents had wanted? If they were alive, I felt sure they would be proud of him. There would be no doubt in their minds that Major Roderick Tattersall had become a very important person.

Three

'The accident scene was visited by an Irish seaman.' (This was later amended to read: an RAC man)

From claim details by telephone

A substantial amount of insurance is arranged because of risks arising from the actions of others, whether intentional or not. It is perhaps unfortunate that we cannot always anticipate what those actions might be – if we are a car owner, of course, we might assume that some clown will run into our vehicle but we don't know where or when that might happen, or if we are a house owner, we might think the neighbours could accidentally set fire to our garden fence and shed when their bonfire, which is always far too big and smokes too much, gets out of control.

We are at risk from others in all sorts of ways, but we are also at risk from ourselves – through our own carelessness, we might lose something valuable during a journey or mislay our house keys so the door has to be smashed down to effect an entry, or we might fall and break a leg through not looking where we are going or even while playing some supervised sport like football. The scope for accidents and mayhem is endless.

And that is precisely how I regarded the activities of Crocky Morris. He had an uncanny ability to cause others to have accidents and many of the claims which came through my hands were the result of his presence in some unwelcome or unexpected way. There is no doubt he was a liability, particularly in my field of work, but I could never persuade him to get himself insured.

I thought he should take out some kind of personal insurance, just in case he was ever sued for damages by those who unsuccessfully crossed his path. And they were many!

Crocky was a pedlar who lived at Crossrigg. He travelled throughout Delverdale, visiting every village by train on some kind of rota system in the hope he could sell a few items of crockery from his basket. The moment he arrived at the village of his choice, his first action was to visit the pub and have a few pints of beer. Then he would hoist his heavy basket of pots on to his head, make sure it was balanced and embark upon his rounds. Even when he had enjoyed rather too many pints and when his feet tried to go in a direction different from the one he intended, he never dropped his basket. Not only that, others would challenge Crocky's basket-bearing skills either by getting him to race against the clock or compete against others with similar skills, or to carry other heavy objects upon his head – and he always won and never dropped one of his burdens. And for a man well into his seventies, that was an astonishing achievement.

When I attended my weekly 'surgery' outside the Unicorn Inn at Micklesfield, Crocky was invariably inside the premises. He made the occasional appearance outside, wandering among the market stalls with his basket aloft in the hope of selling a few plates, cups and saucers. He knew that the shoppers changed every half-hour or so as customers left and others arrived and he could usually time his appearances to coincide with the appearance of the local bus. I think he wanted the passengers to first spend money with him, and then go about their normal business.

The money from those casual sales would invariably be spent at the pub's bar within minutes of him receiving it, although he always seemed to have a pocket full of ready cash, in both notes and coins. Clearly, he managed to keep some money for future events.

And then, one Wednesday afternoon, he appeared among the market stalls without his basket and there is little doubt this caused something of a stir. Seeing Crocky without the basket on his head was rather like seeing something unreal, a vision or even a ghost, or someone completely naked. But that vision was real enough. There were shouted comments such as 'Lost your pots, Crocky?' or 'Sold out, have you?' or 'Fallen off at last, has it?' or 'Had a few too many?' but he just smiled one of his semi-toothless grins and waved a fistful of paper in reply.

'T'basket's in t'pub. Got summat else for you all,' he said to everyone. 'Twopence a sheet.'

'What is it?' I asked when he approached me.

'A recipe,' he said. 'For elderflower fizz ... if you've never 'ad elderflower fizz, young Matthew, now's your chance. Get that missus o' yours to make it and you'll love it ... it's got bags o' bubbles, as good as or better than champagne.'

'So where did you get the recipe?' was my next question.

'Never you mind that, young feller-me-lad. I'm a businessman and guard my special suppliers as much as them guards look after Buckingham Palace. But make no mistake, this is good. And I'm t'sole supplier in this dale. You'll not get this recipe anywhere else. Not at only twopence a sheet...'

'You've quite a handful of copies!'

'Aye, I've a friend who got 'em printed for me. Going like hot cakes they are ... if you want one, young feller-me-lad, you'd better take it now before I sell out.'

And so I bought a copy of his recipe.

It read: *This is a recipe for a lovely summer drink which is simple and quick to produce. Ingredients: One gallon of cold water, one and a quarter pounds of sugar, seven heads of elderflowers, two lemons and two tablespoonsful of white-wine vinegar. You will need a large bowl to contain these. The flowers should not be washed or rinsed with water as this reduces their flavour, but insects should be removed by hand. Boil the water and pour it over the sugar, stirring to melt it. When this is cold, add the seven florets of elderflowers with the sliced lemons and white-wine vinegar. Cover the mixture with a cloth to keep off the flies, and leave for twenty-four hours. Siphon it off and bottle it, making sure it is firmly corked because it is a very fizzy drink. It can be drunk almost immediately but if it is left for, say, four years, it resembles the best hock wine. Elderflowers, which are heavily scented, can also be eaten raw direct from the bush and make a very cooling snack on a hot day. The flowers can also be made into a face cream, skin ointment and eye lotion.*

I was happy to hand over twopence for this and bore it home in triumph. When Evelyn saw it, she nodded and recalled her grandmother talking about the wonderful elderberry wine which is supposedly health-giving.

But she also knew about the famous summer-day drink which so many likened to champagne. Evelyn decided to follow Crocky's recipe so that we had a stock of nice summer drinks. We had a few elderberry bushes in our garden; some people did not like them but in the past, householders deliberately encouraged them to grow near their homes to protect them against witches and the evil eye.

Later, when our elderflowers were blooming, Evelyn set about making some of the special drink. We picked a handful of florets and managed to get some corks and used wine bottles from Evelyn's parents at the Unicorn. Soon, and with surprising ease, we had a few bottles of the clear liquid. Believing that it improved with keeping, albeit recalling that it could be drunk almost immediately, we popped our collection into the pantry and waited for a hot summer day.

I have no idea how many people bought the recipe from Crocky, nor do I know how many made the drink and then decided to drink it almost as soon as they had made it. However, it did become apparent that a considerable number had decided to brew substantial quantities and allow their creation to mature in bottles, even if that period of maturity was only a few weeks rather than four years. I became aware of this when I received a phone call asking me to pop in and see Maurice and Dorothy Blackburn of Elm House, Walstone. I did not know the reason for the request because Evelyn had taken the message while I was out and the Blackburns had not given a reason. Evelyn had said I was due to visit Walstone the following day because I would be collecting in the village and she would pass the message to me, promising I would call.

The Blackburns were already clients of mine with their car, house and life insurance. They were a nice, quiet and rather shy couple without any direct family, i.e. no children and no brothers and sisters. They were totally alone with only themselves to consider, both having recently retired after working in the York offices of the recently nationalized British Railways. Upon their move into the moors, administration of their insurances had been transferred to my agency. They had moved to Walstone because they liked the countryside in and around Delverdale, having often visited the region at weekends to pursue their hobby of bird-watching. They had found Elm House, a small cottage with a big-sounding name, close to a small copse near the banks of the River Delver. It was their dream cottage with plenty of walks and bird life around them, and so they had happily settled to a life of complete contentment in rural Walstone.

When I arrived I was shown into the small sitting room where Mrs Blackburn, a neat grey-haired lady wearing a tartan skirt, offered me a cup of tea and a home-made rock bun. Her husband joined us a few moments later, having been into the village to obtain some groceries, and after the pleasantries, he explained his problem.

'I'm not sure whether I am covered for this sort of thing, Mr Taylor.' He was a quietly-spoken man with a rather serious approach to life. 'We have had an explosion, you see...'

'Explosion?' This puzzled me as I knew the village was not connected to the gas network, and I'd received no suggestion that unexploded bombs in gardens or other war-time souvenirs like hand-grenades had been causing recent problems.

That kind of thing did happen from time to time, with unexploded bombs being found on the moors and indeed in several villages, and sometimes accidents occurred through former soldiers keeping unsafe, and

probably illegal, explosives like hand-grenades in their garden sheds, but Mr Blackburn smiled and shook his head.

'No, nothing quite like that. It's our wine,
you see. Dorothy made a few bottles and
some have exploded, they've made quite a
mess, I must say, blown a window out and
ruined the carpet and wallpaper...'

'Really? Where did this happen?'

'In our back bedroom,' said Dorothy. 'We
left it as it was in case you wanted to see the
damage.'

'Yes, if it's a big claim, our assessors might
want to examine it so I think I'd better have
a look first.'

It emerged that Dorothy Blackburn had
made eight bottles of home-made elderflower fizz by using Crocky's recipe and had
decided to store them in the back bedroom
until they decided to open them, one at a
time as required. They had drunk one of the
bottles, leaving the other seven to mature,
with Mr Blackburn adding that it really was
a superb drink. When I arrived at the bedroom, there was a scene of utter devastation.
I did not go inside but stood in the doorway
to absorb the scene. It was just as if the room
had been blitzed by a bombardment of
exploding bombshells – two panes of the
window had been blown out, the wallpaper
was stained with fluid, two pictures had been

blown off the walls and their glass smashed and there were pieces of broken bottle all over the carpet and bed, both of which were soaked.

There was other minor damage too, such as some china ornaments which had been blown off the dressing table and smashed, and a smartly dressed doll who was sitting in a corner with a look of utter surprise on her face which now had one eye missing.

'Are you sure the elderflower fizz caused this?' I had to ask the question.

'Absolutely,' said Maurice. 'Five of them have exploded, almost all at once.'

'So where are the others?' was my immediate concern.

'We've drunk one as I said, it was lovely, but the other two are at the bottom of the garden. I daren't keep them in the house, not after this.'

'And they've not exploded?'

'I'm not sure, but I fear it could happen at any time. I daren't go near them, I put them in a dustbin and held the lid on top when I moved them, they're still there, still in the bin. I daren't go near the thing!'

'You managed to move them without any mishap?'

'More by good luck than good management, I suspect. But we wondered if our insurance covers us for this damage, Mr

Taylor. I mean, we're only pensioners with not a lot of money to spare and although we can wash the bedding and clean the carpet, there's the window to repair and all that wallpaper to replace...'

As we chatted with the devastation before us, I could see Dorothy was becoming upset at the prospect which faced her. Their house, which was so neat and tidy, had been sullied, but upon first appearances I didn't think there was a great deal of damage; it was more mess than destruction.

Much of it was superficial – replacing the broken window panes, for example, would not be very expensive although I did not know whether Maurice Blackburn was personally capable of redecorating the room. There would be some expense, however, such as having the small bedroom carpet cleaned, and some ornaments had been damaged beyond repair.

'You will be covered by your house insurance,' I told them. 'You are covered for loss or damage caused by fire, explosion, lightning, thunderbolts, earthquakes, falling trees or parts of trees, larceny, attempted larceny, burglary, attempted burglary, housebreaking, attempted housebreaking, arson, malicious damage, collisions by motor vehicles, carriages, aircraft, other airborne devices like balloons, trains, riot, civil commotion, political disturbances and escape of water. And most other things including subsidence and avalanches. Clothing, linen and personal belongings are covered in addition to the buildings. I think your experience can be attributed to an explosion but my District Office will need to know the cost of the damage and any replacements. Clearly, they will also need to know how or why the explosion occurred, and whether it could have been avoided. I will leave a claim form with you, so perhaps you could make an estimate of the costs involved – I might add that our claims assessor might want to see the damage, so can you leave things as they are for a day or two, just in case?'

We returned to the sitting room where I provided them with a form and helped them to complete it, but when we reached the point where I had to specify the cause of the explosion, I was not quite sure how to phrase the relevant sentence.

'What made the bottles explode?' I asked.

'I've no idea.' Maurice shook his head. 'We did everything according to that recipe, and the other two bottles don't seem to have blown up, those outside in the dustbin. If some have exploded and some haven't, there must be a reason for that.'

'So what sort of bottles did you use?'

'Old lemonade bottles and wine bottles.

Some I'd kept in my shed.'

'Lemonade bottles?' I queried. 'Those with screw tops?'

'Yes, the recipe said we should make sure the bottles were firmly corked because it was a very fizzy drink, so I thought lemonade bottles would be ideal.'

'I used the same recipe,' I told them. 'I used old wine bottles I got from the Unicorn, and some corks which I fixed with one of those things for pushing corks into narrow bottle necks. But not screw tops.'

'The ones which haven't exploded are the wine bottles,' he said. 'We corked them like you said. I make home-made wine so I have the corking device...'

'It seems to me,' I said with all the wisdom of a very young lad, 'that the stuff you made was like champagne – very fizzy indeed. That's why they secure champagne corks with wire caps. But I'm amazed your others haven't shot out their corks...'

'We had two brewings ... they might not have been the same strength...'

And with that, there was a loud clattering of metal in the garden and when we peeped out we were in time to see the dustbin lid rolling across the lawn and a fountain of something shooting from the inside of the bin, rather in the manner of a newly discovered oil well or a burst water pipe.

'There goes the rest of it!' and I was pleased to see Dorothy was now laughing.

'Oh dear,' she shook her head. 'That must have been the best wine we ever made and now it's all gone.'

There was no damage to the dustbin and neither bottle had exploded. All they had done was to shoot their corks high into the air with the power of a shotgun, with one bottle probably activating the other and I guessed the reason for the explosion in the bedroom was that the lemonade-bottle corks could not be ejected in that manner. Being screw-type corks, they were very firm indeed, so much so that the bottles themselves had exploded.

I rushed home to remove my bottles into the outside shed, but they did not explode. I think the Blackburns had probably amended the recipe to suit their own taste but the Premier accepted the claim and paid for the Blackburns' repairs and damage. As I toured my agency in the days which followed, I heard of other exploding elderflower bottles, one of which had sent a cork through the plaster of a ceiling, another which had smashed several bulbs in a chandelier and a third which had wounded a passing crow. All had acquired their recipes from Crocky but when they complained, his only reaction was to grin widely and say they shouldn't have used so much sugar.

But no one else made a claim from the Premier. I think such people did not want anyone else to know they had actually bought the recipe from Crocky, neither did they want me, or my colleagues at the Premier, to know they had been drinking such powerful stuff within the secrecy or confines of their home.

It was fortunate that the incident at the Blackburns' home did not affect or harm anyone else. If the couple had not used the correct corkage for their home brew, then it could be argued they were entirely responsible for what later occurred even if, in insurance terms, it was a fairly low-key accident. While some might have suggested Crocky was somehow blameworthy, others might have said that common sense should have warned the Blackburns about using screw tops for very powerful fizzy concoctions, particularly as they admitted to brewing home-made wine.

But common sense, in spite of its name, is not at all common. It is a quality not possessed by everyone and it could be said it was not present in the character of a man called Frank Wishart. Frank and his wife, Jenny, lived at Crossrigg. Their home was called High Rigg House, and it was a smallholding near the summit of the hills behind the village. In the North Riding of Yorkshire, the word *rigg* means the ridge of a hill, so his home was aptly named because it was on top of that ridge. His smallholding, covering several acres, was untidily spread across a large expanse of that hillside, much of it rough heather-clad moorland useless for cultivation, with scores of large boulders and half-buried rocks. On the summit was the dwelling house, surrounded by an array of weather-worn sheds and buildings which housed hens, ducks, geese, turkeys, pigs, sheep and goats. Scattered around the spread were the remains of hundreds of re-dundant machines, such as ploughs, binders, motorbikes and cars, mangles and lathes, carts and traps, along with rusting metal and decaying timber of all descriptions, includ-ing zinc bathtubs, milk pails, wardrobes, tables, armchairs and much else.

The place looked like a massive dumping ground for unwanted items and certainly it was an eyesore when viewed from any angle. It could be seen from a great distance and even though the parish council tried to force Frank into tidying his smallholding, he steadfastly ignored all the pleas as more rubbish continued to be deposited on that once-beautiful hillside.

Frank had lived there since his marriage to

Jenny. The smallholding had belonged to her parents and upon their death, she had inherited it, moving in with husband Frank. But Frank was no farmer, something which he readily admitted, and he earned his living as a dustman, leaving the agricultural work to his hard-working wife. It was she who cared for their menagerie of livestock in addition to running the household. Frank was in his mid-fifties and Jenny perhaps five years younger, and there were no children at home; they had one son, who worked overseas in some obscure profession. It was Jenny's aim to sell up one day in the not-too-far-distant future and move into Whitby to a small house with no land and no animals. That was her dream – all she wanted was time to relax and wander around the shops.

But Frank needed all that space for his hobby and so he was reluctant to move into something smaller. High Rigg House, with its lofty open aspect and range of outbuildings, was perfect for him and his hobby. His hobby was collecting and restoring old things, and he came across most of his raw material during his bin-collecting rounds. If, for example, someone placed an old mangle outside for collection, he would ask whether he could take it away for his personal use. The owner invariably agreed – all they wanted was to be rid of the thing.

Frank would not take it away in the dustcart, but would return later with his private van. In this way, he took home all manner of trophies large and small – and that is how his premises came to be littered with such an array of useless and decaying objects. He took them for a reason, however. In his heart of hearts, he had an unfulfilled dream – he had a great urge to restore such things to their former glory and saw himself as the eventual curator of a rural museum of some kind, filled with wonderful restored and working examples of bygone machinery and artefacts. As a dustman, he knew that thousands of historic and valuable artefacts were thrown away every day, so he did his bit for posterity by saving them.

One day, he told himself, he would fix that old mangle, make that old plough fully operational or restore that old oak wardrobe without any feet, top or back. He would put everything back to its original condition, and when he got his museum fully operational he would show an adoring public just how wonderful such things could be. But he never had time. Something always cropped up to frustrate his latest effort, but this did not prevent him bringing home more and more potential projects, large and small. The snag was that his shortage of time was due to his work, but he needed his work to find more projects, more things which others had discarded. And being a dustman with the rural district council was the perfect job for that kind of thing. What other job enabled you – and paid you – to collect the cast-off items of others? Frank Wishart found himself in a perpetual circle of wishing he had more time to complete more projects for his long-term dream of having fields and buildings full of gleaming reminders of former times.

Not surprisingly, the villagers nicknamed him Wish Hard Wishart.

And then he found something which created even more of a spark of determination in his mind. I first came across this yarn during my rounds and later as a result of a subsequent claim but I will relate it in sequence.

Along with other members of his team, Frank was collecting rubbish during his bin round at Baysthorpe. It was mid-afternoon by the time the cart arrived on the outskirts of the village; it had attended to the centre and was now heading into the neighbouring countryside to service farms and outlying houses. One of those was the ruined Baysthorpe Castle with Castle Farm attached, and the smaller Castle Cottage nearby. The cottage, owned by Baysthorpe Estate, was occupied by Miss Hester Clarke, a retired maid who used to work in Lord Baysthorpe's house about half a mile from the castle.

Whenever the binmen called at Miss Clarke's there was a cup of tea and a biscuit for them, because she felt rather lonely after working in such a busy place at Baysthorpe Hall. She was accustomed to having people around her and so she enjoyed the weekly session of tea, chatter and banter with the dustmen. They told some wonderful stories of their work and she responded with tales of life in the big house, each of them relating yarns about the people with whom they had had to deal. And so it was that Frank Wishart and his team arrived one day just as the kettle had boiled. They settled down in the kitchen as she fussed over their tea and cakes.

'I've something in the garden which I want you to take away,' she said eventually. 'No one wants it, I don't want it taking up valuable space in my vegetable plot and it will only clutter up the castle and go rusty if we put it there, with no roofs or shelter, so I've had a word with the estate and they told me to get rid of it.'

'Sounds like summat for you, Frank!' laughed one of his mates.

'What is it?' asked Frank with only a modest degree of interest.

'I think it's an old cannon,' she said. 'Either that or an ancient water pipe, or even the remains of a drain. It's very old and encrusted with dirt. No good to anybody.'

'I'll have a look before we leave,' he promised her, now very full of interest. Being the owner and restorer of an ancient cannon sounded highly intriguing for Frank. After their break, Miss Clarke led them into her garden where a corner had been partially excavated.

In the hole was a long tubular earth-encrusted lump of what looked like dark-coloured cast iron with remnants of timber at one end, a touchhole in the top at the same end and what appeared to be a bore running down the centre. Its apertures were blocked with soil although there had been a half-hearted attempt to remove some of it with a stick. The object was probably five feet long by more than a foot in diameter and stacked nearby were half a dozen round stones, all of the size that could be accommodated by the hollow tube, which was about five inches in diameter.

'I reckon it is a cannon,' said Frank. 'And those are cannonballs. Stone ones, that's what they did, years ago, fired lumps of stone.'

'The estate were digging there,' she explained. 'I wanted a new washing line at the end of my plot and they started to dig to put concrete foundations there, that's when they found it. They told the boss and Lord Baysthorpe about the find, but they don't want it. They said if I could find somebody to take it away, all well and good, and if I couldn't they would come back with a cart or truck to put it in and take it to the council tip. I said you were due today so I'd ask you.'

'Right, I'll take it,' said Frank without waiting for any other suggestion. 'I can clean all that muck off to see if it really is a cannon, and then it can go in my display of renovated objects, when I get it all ready. It'll look good standing at the entrance to my museum, all cleaned up and in good working order. I'll come back later for it with my van.'

'It's too big for you to shift on your own,' pointed out one of his pals. 'You'd strain yourself trying to lift it.'

'Can we get it on board the dustcart?' asked Frank.

'We might,' smiled his pal. 'With a bit of persuasion.'

'All right, two bob apiece says we can get it aboard, but that's if we drop it at my house on the way back to the depot.'

And so the deal was done. Four hefty men, all accustomed to lifting full dustbins onto their shoulders, hoisted the cannon from its resting place and bore it towards the dustcart where they placed it alongside other bulky items.

It was quite normal for the cart to carry items which were too large to go into the enclosed area with small rubbish. The cannon was strapped in position on a platform at the side and off they went to complete their rounds. Later that day, it was delivered to Frank's place at Crossrigg, and carried to a pair of flat raised stones upon which it was placed. The five stone balls were put beside it. Because it was resting on the stones, Frank could work on it from all angles, including the underside, and so, now a very happy man, he and his pals continued to the depot. Frank was now the owner of a very ancient cannon and some cannonballs in remarkably good condition. It wouldn't take much to restore the weapon, if he had the time.

I learned more of this story when Jenny asked me to call because she wanted to amend their car insurance to take into consideration their current car, a replacement for an earlier one which had literally dropped to pieces. The replacement wasn't a great deal better, but at least it was a runner with a body in reasonable condition, and I had to record the change. As we chatted, she took me outside to look at Frank's latest acquisition, wondering whether such a thing should be specially mentioned on their house insurance.

I felt not – it was not of any great material value and could be considered part of his general collection of rubbish, all of which was accounted for in general terms on his policy, just in case he stumbled upon something valuable. And, in its present state, it could not be considered dangerous, while its sheer size and weight rendered it unlikely to be stolen.

Then Frank surprised those who knew him.

He tackled the renovation of the old cannon with uncharacteristic gusto and determination, even going to the trouble of finding books in the library which provided information about these ancient weapons. He discovered most were so large and heavy they could only be transported upon their own specially built wheeled platforms, although another use for the wheels was to absorb the violent recoil when the cannon was fired. He was particularly fascinating by the history of Mons Meg, the huge cannon at Edinburgh Castle. At thirteen feet four inches long, with a twenty-inch bore, it is a monster weapon as it sits on its four-wheeled wagon. Its massive barrel had burst in 1680 and it was years later, when Sir Walter Scott renewed interest in the gun, that it was eventually restored and taken to Edinburgh Castle in 1829 for permanent display. A highly visible permanent display outside his premises was just what Frank desired for his cannon and it was perhaps this famous weapon, supposedly named after the noisy wife of its maker, which provided him with such inspiration.

Frank's cannon was less than half the size of Mons Meg but it presented a formidable challenge as he first set about constructing a strong four-wheeled chariot for it to sit upon, making good use of ingredients among his collected rubbish. With its base complete, he began the task of cleaning the cannon both inside and out, carefully removing centuries of dirt as he worked down to the bare metal to find it in a remarkably good state of preservation. Its barrel was as smooth as the proverbial baby's bottom.

The touchhole in the top was easily cleaned too – this gave access to the gunpowder which was rammed into place before the cannonball was pushed home down the tube. And when all was ready, the gunner ignited his fuse, pressed it down the touchhole where it caused the gunpowder to explode and so propel the cannonball to its target.

Sadly, some of the earlier cannons exploded at this point, killing those who were nearby, although some larger ones, such as the seventeen-foot-long bronze cannon owned by the Sultan of Turkey in 1464, could fire a half-ton ball for almost a mile. Certainly, the power of such huge weapons was awesome but, in practical terms, such huge guns were not very satisfactory – moving them from site to site was a very laborious business and once there they could only launch one ball at a time. There were instances when battles were over before such guns could be reloaded and, of course, they destroyed property, not armies. They were very effective in smashing holes through walls and doors, but little else.

But that kind of historic background did not greatly concern Frank. Fired with enthusiasm, he worked late at night and at weekends on lovingly restoring his magnificent gun as the focus for his dream museum of rural equipment. Finally, it appeared to be finished. It had been a lengthy task of devotion and endurance; Frank had actually achieved something of merit, a rare event, and his cannon was ready to be towed into its important and imposing place at the entrance to High Rigg House. Before then, however, only one test remained.

He wanted to know whether his restoration efforts had put the cannon back into full working order. It looked splendid, but could it actually fire one of those stone cannon-balls? He did not want to risk losing the balls, so reckoned an iron ball of similar size would suffice – and he happened to have one among his rubbish. He showed it to me during one of my visits, wondering what on earth it might have been. In my view, it looked like a massive ball-bearing, but I couldn't think of anything it might have been used for. I wondered if someone in a foundry had made it out of spare raw materials, perhaps as some kind of souvenir or keepsake. And so it was that Frank Wishart, aided by a willing tractor, towed his cannon into position so that he could test it by firing a cannonball upon his land.

His cannon was tiny in comparison with some of the giants he had read about during his research, and his expanse of rough land, isolated from the rest of the village, was spacious enough for any shot from his weapon to be totally harmless. He would direct it away from those parts occupied by outbuildings, hens and other livestock and his test would reassure him that his cannon was in perfect condition. No one else but he would know about this test; it would be conducted in great secrecy.

Or so he thought.

He knew that some of those ancient cannons had had severe flaws which had caused them to explode while being fired, but this one appeared to have been very solidly constructed. He did not think it would blow up in his face, or worse.

He also knew, through his dedicated research, that the gunpowder used in these cannons varied in strength, often according to the gunner's recipe, or the way that recipe was mixed. Even so, the basic ingredients were simple – sulphur, charcoal and saltpetre, preferably with the charcoal being made from the wood of the hazel. The charcoal was pulverized and mixed with the powdered sulphur, with the saltpetre being added later, and it was recommended that these ingredients be carried separately and mixed shortly before being used. The most important of the ingredients was saltpetre because it contained oxygen and this allowed the other two substances to burn extremely rapidly even when cut off from a supply of air. When a flame was applied, ignition was instantaneous and dramatic, sufficient to produce a massive noisy explosion which would forcibly propel a missile over a long distance. Bearing in mind the size and bore of the cannon, and its anticipated range, the critical point was to get the quantity of saltpetre exactly right for the task in hand. And for that, Frank had to make an inspired guess.

One Saturday afternoon when his wife was away on a shopping trip at Guisborough with friends, Frank relished the solitude as he mixed his gunpowder in one of his out-buildings. Then he towed the cannon to the site he had determined for its test and placed some chocks behind the wheels to prevent it recoiling too far backwards upon ignition. Next he squatted on his haunches to aim the barrel so that its projectile would fly across the open expanse of his land towards the distant boundary, to drop harmlessly on to the sloping moorland beyond.

Happy that his plans were adequate and safe, he thrust the gunpowder down the barrel, slamming it in with his home-made ram. Then he popped the iron ball into the mouth and watched it roll down the slight incline to rest against the impacted gun-powder. Now it was time to light his taper and insert the flame into the touchhole – 'light the blue touchpaper and stand well back' as the advice was printed on Bonfire Night explosives.

Somewhat gingerly, he lit his taper, waiting until it was burning brightly and then, heart in mouth, popped it into the touchhole. Almost instantly, there was an almighty ear-splitting explosion as the gun hurtled back-wards over its chocks and turned onto its side, but its cast-iron projectile was already on its way somewhere. Frank had no idea where it was heading because he was lying on the ground, not injured but somewhat startled by this unexpected turn of events. He rose to his feet rather shakily, seeing a lot of smoke, as he realized his hearing had been affected by the explosion, hopefully temporarily, but of the cast-iron ball, there was no sign. It had not landed upon his property. Where it had landed, he knew not. Indeed, he did not know if it *had* landed.

Later, I discovered the true course of events. The cannon had indeed ejected its ball in a spectacular and highly efficient manner and it had sailed across an open patch of Frank's smallholding. As it was passing over the moorland beyond, it had begun its descent, albeit still travelling at a very fast rate rather like a meteorite dropping from the heavens, but that descent was gradual.

It was rapidly heading for earth at an angle of about forty-five degrees but before landing it struck a large boulder half-buried in the heather. The boulder itself had a sloping surface and so, when the flying cannonball hit it, it served as something akin to a secondary launching pad and the ball ricocheted off to continue its journey in a completely different direction. Frank, happy that his cannon had not suffered any damage, had no idea where to start looking and, not surprisingly, was rather hesitant about knocking on doors to ask for his ball back.

It so transpired that, at the moment in history, retired Colonel Dudley Smithers and his wife were sitting in their conservatory having afternoon tea. They were rather taken aback by something which smashed through an upper window, hurtled across the room and, by a miracle of marksmanship, disappeared through a second small window which led into the lounge. There, with its velocity much reduced, it fell towards the ground and landed in the goldfish tank, to expire in a hiss of water with much flying glass and gasping fish.

'Hello, is that the insurance man?' It was the accent of a man of importance. 'Colonel Smithers here.'

'Yes, Matthew Taylor speaking,' I responded.

'Tell me, Mr Taylor, am I insured against meteorites or shooting stars which come to earth through my conservatory?'

'Your household policy covers things like thunderbolts and aerial devices and articles dropped from aircraft,' I said. 'I am sure it will cover a meteorite.'

And so he told me the story over the telephone.

Later, after checking the situation with District Office, I called on the Colonel with the claim form and he showed me the meteorite, as he honestly thought it was. As I weighed it in my hands, I knew I'd seen it before and it didn't take long for me to realize it was Frank's cast-iron cannonball.

'Rest assured you're covered for the damage,' I told the Colonel. 'But this is not a meteorite, it's a cannonball. Well, it might be something else in reality but it's been used as a cannonball.'

I told him all about Frank's labours to get his gun in full working order and he took it all in good part, expressing a sneaking admiration for a man who could revive something as ancient as the old weapon, and actually persuade it to fire a shot. I advised him on completing the form, saying the Premier would claim the cost from Frank's insurance, but as Frank was also insured by the Premier, the matter would be dealt with internally. There were no problems so far as the Colonel was concerned.

'So what happens to this ball?' asked the Colonel before I left.

'I'll speak to Frank about it,' I promised. 'He might not want it back, clearly it was expendable.'

When I explained all this to Frank, he was most apologetic and said he would visit the Colonel in person to apologize, saying he could keep the ball as a souvenir if he really wanted it. Frank had no further use for it –

he had no intention of submitting his cannon to another test. Besides, he still had the five stone balls and he was still determined to re-establish his cannon at the gate of his yet-to-be-built rural museum.

Some months later I discovered the villagers were in the firm belief that a meteorite had crashed through the Colonel's conservatory; such is the power of a good story. The fact he had kept the object in question and had put it on display in his conservatory as a talking point was further proof of the tale, and there is no doubt he loved telling everyone about his brush with death.

But then a thought occurred to me. If no one knew where that ball had come from, or why it was made, could it be a genuine meteorite? One which might have landed years ago without anyone realizing? And was it really made of iron, or some other mysterious metal? On occasions such things did fall to earth from the heavens. A fairly local example was the missile which crashed to earth at Wold Newton on the Yorkshire Wolds in 1795, and which is now in the Natural History Museum.

I made a mental note to speak to District Office and clarify the situation so far as falling meteorites were concerned.

Four

'I saw the surprised expression on the old gentle-man's face as he bounced off the bonnet.'
From a claim form

'Know your clients' was the advice often given by Mr Montgomery Wilkins, my District Office Ordinary Branch Sales Manager – Life. In relating his experiences in Birmingham prior to transferring to the very rural North Riding of Yorkshire, he would tell me about some of his adventures as a means of advising me to become closely acquainted with the background and family details of all my clients. 'Know them and know who you can trust,' he would often say. 'Don't take everyone at face value, dig a little deeper into their backgrounds, talk to neighbours and the local business people. Shopkeepers, garages and such. See if there are financial problems. You can learn a lot from friends and contacts, and from a person's way of life.'

When in this kind of mood, he would

remind me quite frequently that dishonesty could affect the insurance world just like any other. False claims were surprisingly common; indeed, he told me, they were all too numerous, especially in his former agency, where hard-up people tried all kinds of tricks to reclaim cash from their policies, such as pretending their car or bike had been stolen, their house had been broken into and money taken, or that they had a long illness which meant they could not earn a living, hoping their ill-health insurance would pay the bills. I tried to counter this by saying that my clients were all very honest country folk who were more accustomed to hard work and honest living than trying to defraud the Premier.

In response, he would nod his head in what he regarded as a sage manner, reminding me to be eternally vigilant.

Although he would often arrive to give me a pep talk, urging me to produce lots more business in the form of new policies, I had come to realize that he enjoyed his visits to my agency. Quite often, he would arrive when I was holding my 'surgery' outside the Bottle and Jug at the Unicorn Inn, and would then spend time chatting to the young women who attended the market or having some kind of banter with the stallholders. In some ways, he was an odd figure among all those country people – small in stature, with his distinctive black beret, brightly polished shoes with pointed toes and high-pitched voice, he was immediately recognizable as someone who was not a dalesman or even a countryman. It did not take long, however, for the stallholders and regular attenders to realize who he was, and they were more than happy to chat to him, often relating stories of their own very rural worlds whenever he referred to life in Birmingham. I was not sure whether they were jollying him along or even making quiet fun of him, but I realized that he was chatting to them so that he could absorb a great deal of information about them; that was part of his technique for getting to know the local people and then he would come to me and suggest I talked to Mrs So-and-So about a life policy or per-haps some other form of investment or cover. With his surprising charm, he had often broken the proverbial ice and it was then up to me to consolidate the deal. In watching him at work like this, I had to admire him for his ability to get on with people whom he did not know.

Certainly, he could put people at their ease and even charm them into revealing their hopes and desires before he persuaded them to take out a policy with the Premier. There was no doubt he was a very good insurance salesman, that he believed in what he was doing, and that he was willing to teach me some of his skills.

It was during one of those visits that he wanted me to undertake rather more canvassing than I wished among those attending Micklesfield market. He drew my attention to a middle-aged man who was wandering around the stalls. Montgomery touched my arm and, with an inclination of his head, indicated that he wanted me to move away from our present location. He led me to my display of literature at the Bottle and Jug and we stood with our backs to the pub wall, watching the passing show. There we could chat without being overheard, and we also had a wide view of the entire market. The man was moving quietly among the stalls, occasionally picking up something to examine and then returning it, but ignoring the food, fruit and vegetables. He was more interested in things like home-made crafts, second-hand goods and furniture, second-hand books, paintings, tools and clothes.

'Watch that man,' Montgomery whispered from the side of his mouth like someone from a spy film. 'The man with the brown trilby.'

The fellow was about fifty years old in my estimation, quite stockily built and of average height with grey hair showing beneath his hat. He wore a tan gaberdine raincoat, a blue and red tie with a white shirt, brown trousers and brown shoes, nicely polished. On his back, he carried a large ex-military haversack which currently looked empty.

Having heard Montgomery tell me to watch him, I did so even if I had no idea why he wanted me to. Neither of us spoke for a few minutes as I saw our target moving steadily among the stalls, sometimes picking up an object to ask the stallholder about it, sometimes holding a piece of glassware up to the light to get a better view but all the time moving slowly and methodically about his mission. Nonetheless, it was difficult to know whether he was looking for something in particular or merely browsing through everything in the hope he might drop across something valuable. I did know, of course, that antiques were now becoming very fashionable, with people beginning to realize that old paintings, china, furniture, silverware and such could bring huge rewards. Quite literally, many people had no idea of the value of some of their household contents, such a vital aspect of the insurance business. This man appeared to be browsing among that kind of merchandise and then he would buy something, hand over the cash and pop it into his haversack. Having done that, he would produce from an inside pocket a small red-backed notebook and write in it, presumably recording details of his purchase.

'A dealer, is he?' I ventured to ask, in what might be described a stage whisper.

'He calls himself an antique dealer,' Montgomery told me with more than a hint of confidentiality. 'His name is Dawson, George Dawson, from a village near Scarborough. Remember that. If he realizes who you are, he might attempt to take out fire insurance with you. If he does, refer the case to me at District Office.'

I sensed an air of mystery about all this, but with people milling around it was clear that Montgomery was not going to explain. I could see that he was very closely focused on Dawson's activities and then, after about half an hour, the fellow bade his farewell and left the marketplace. Minutes later, I saw him drive away in a dark blue Morris 10.

'So what was all that about?' I asked.

'Let's walk along the lane,' said Montgomery. 'Away from flapping ears.'

When we were about a hundred yards from the Unicorn, he said, 'That man is a long-term suspected arsonist. A clever man, Mr Taylor, a devious rogue to be more accurate, one who has never been caught. Suspected, as I said, but never prosecuted, although I must say we are 99.9 per cent sure about his activities.'

'You know him?'

'Yes, although we have never spoken to each other. I know him by reputation, not on a personal basis. You might appreciate, Mr Taylor, that in some instances, the insurance companies of this country pool their knowledge when it concerns matters of mutual interest. That man is the subject of such a pooling of knowledge, which is why you must refer to me any attempt by him to secure fire insurance through you. Having seen him at your little market, I felt I should alert you to this.'

'George Dawson.' I repeated the name to make sure I had got it right. 'I can't think I've come across him yet, and to my recollection, it's the first time he's attended this market. So why has he raised this kind of suspicion in you? And other companies?'

'Just after the war he established an antique shop in Scarborough, selling artefacts he had collected around the district, just as he was doing today. Nice stuff – local arts and crafts, antique furniture, paintings, silverware, jewellery, pottery, books, toys ... you name it, he had it for sale in his shop. All quite legitimate.'

'Not stolen property?' I asked.

'Oh, no, he's much too clever to risk selling stolen goods, Mr Taylor. All the contents of his shop were bona fide antiques and second-hand goods, all bought and sold at fair prices and all in good condition. Everything looked absolutely right, he didn't sell rubbish and he was known to be a reliable dealer. His stock was comprehensively insured by Kingston, the specialist antique insurers – he was covered for everything, floods, fire, malicious damage, theft, burglary ... the lot.'

'But, if you pardon my interruption, the stuff he was buying here didn't look like valuable antiques. It was more like second-hand stuff you can pick up at any market.'

'You're ahead of me, Mr Taylor!' smiled Mr Wilkins. 'What I said was that he sold good-quality antiques and fine second-hand goods in his shop. And then he had a fire. Not at his shop, Mr Taylor, but in his warehouse, which was some distance away. It was gutted and the entire contents destroyed. From what they found, the fire brigade and Kingston's assessors could only decide it had been due to an electrical fault, and so they had to pay out on the policy – for a warehouse full of valuable antiques, all destroyed by fire. The ashes showed a lot of stuff had burned.'

'But there was a problem?'

'There was a full investigation into the cause of the blaze, with fire brigade, police and insurance experts examining the charred remains. And there was little more than ashes, everything had been totally destroyed. But there was a firm belief, Mr Taylor, that the warehouse had contained rubbish, cheap furniture, old chairs and such. It was the considered opinion of the experts, but they had no means of proving that. Certainly there were grounds for suspicion but positive proof was lacking. After all, how can one say whether the scant charred remains of a chair leg were a Chippendale or just an old dining chair of similar design and matching wood?'

'So the fire had destroyed a load of rubbish but Dawson was paid for a warehouse full of high-value goods?'

'Yes, he made a substantial claim for the loss and we think it was a clever fraud. By we, I mean a pooling of expertise from the insurance business, particularly those in the fire and accident departments. He had a record of all the contents, you see, a very comprehensive list. Due to that list, no one could dispute his claims about the losses. He was making a list today, Mr Taylor, he is very good at making lists, keeping records. False ones, we are sure. It meant, of course, that no one could prove he was lying. He provided the assessors with a very comprehensive list of everything in the warehouse, and its value. So he claimed.'

'A clever fraud! So was it arson?'

'Almost certainly. We think he engineered an electrical fault, not a difficult task if you know what you are doing. It's comparatively easy to get apparatus to overheat or for a short circuit to be created.'

'I have known some electrical plugs and wires grow very hot, and if something combustible was touching them...'

'Exactly, Mr Taylor. But in his case, he got away with it and made a handsome profit from Kingston. That enabled him to expand his business.'

'So the fire wasn't the end?'

'By no means. With the payout, he could afford to buy, and continue to buy, very good antiques and make a lot of money. He kept the shop going, extended it and rented another warehouse, a larger one.'

'So am I right in thinking he repeated the fraud?'

'Several times to our knowledge. But eventually Kingston refused to accept his proposal to renew his insurance with them. They didn't tell him that, they simply raised the premium so high that he couldn't afford it, so he went to another company, a smaller one. It was one of those new cut-price companies which are springing up even as we speak. He took them for a ride as well, it cost them thousands. Again, there was no proof it was arson, it was another electrical fault which destroyed his warehouse full of antiques. He's done it several times, Mr Taylor, always without being prosecuted, but he's been lying low for a long time. I know he was questioned by the police, who left him in no doubt about their suspicions, and the fact any future fire would be rigorously investigated. That might have persuaded him to stop. Certainly, he's been quiet of late. He still has his shop in Scarborough and has opened another in Bridlington, all bona-fide antiques. But his last fire must have been four or five years ago.'

'Perhaps he's reformed now? Or perhaps they really were all accidents?'

'Then why is he here, buying rubbish? Men selling fine antiques don't go around village markets buying rubbish – oh, I know they like to hunt for valuable things others might have overlooked, but he was buying rubbish, Mr Taylor. He would know it was rubbish. That's why I was watching him.'

'You mean he's planning another fire?' I was beginning to see Montgomery Wilkins in a new light. So what precisely had he been doing during the war?

'That's exactly what I think. It's almost certain, in those earlier fires, that he bought a load of junk which he intended to be burnt beyond recognition. He scrounged a lot of

122

old furniture too, things no one wanted, so in fact his warehouses were little more than a heap of bonfire fuel. Stuff he could afford to burn, a sort of investment, I suppose. He keeps the best stuff in his shops. So if he's buying up rubbish again, I must alert my colleagues. We do operate an early-warning system for things of this kind, and I shall also warn the local police, Mr Taylor, and the fire brigade.'

'Has he tried to obtain insurance from the Premier?' I felt I had to ask.

'If he has, he was unsuccessful. His name is not among our list of clients, past or present. But there is always a first time, Mr Taylor. If he has tried, it was before my arrival.'

'So who is he insured with now? Do we know that?'

'I have no idea, Mr Taylor, but my guess is that it will be one of those small new companies, those who offer cut-price deals, or, of course, he might not be insured at all. If the premiums he has been quoted have all been very high in view of his past record of fires, which is possible, he might have risked running his business without any kind of insurance cover. After all, there is no legal obligation to take out insurance as there is when using a motor vehicle on a road.'

By this stage, we were walking back towards the market which, at this time of the afternoon, was dwindling in numbers of customers and stalls. Its regulars, mainly housewives or pensioners doing their shopping, had all gone home to prepare tea and so the stallholders were packing up and preparing to leave.

'Will there be a something to drink at the Unicorn?' Montgomery asked somewhat unexpectedly.

'Yes, it's open all day on market day,' I told him. 'The market-day licence, it's called.'

'Oh, I don't mean alcohol,' he smiled. 'I don't drink alcohol when I am at work, although I might indulge in a small sherry when the day is over, nor do I drink stimulants like tea or coffee. But I could do with a nice glass of cool liquid, lemonade perhaps, or even a squash of some kind.'

'I'd welcome a cup of tea and a rock bun,' I told him.

As we sat with our drinks at a table in the restaurant portion of the inn, the one where women came for their refreshments and a gossip on market day, he told me he always enjoyed his visits to my Delverdale agency.

He added that today had been rather special due to his sighting of George Dawson. I gained the impression he was highly excited about observing Dawson in action in Micklesfield and that he would set in motion some kind of observation or monitoring system in the coming weeks. He told me he was pleased with my efforts; he liked my 'surgery' here at the Unicorn, and was delighted by the way the market traders helped each other, and me, to conduct our businesses. And then he left as I decided to return home to complete the necessary entries in my books. That day, I told him later, twenty-five of my leaflets had been taken from the hole in the wall, and I felt sure some would be returned to me as proposals.

In the days which followed, I thought little more about George Dawson because he lived a long way from Micklesfield and was some distance from the boundaries of my agency, but three Wednesdays later, I was back at my hole in the wall and doing my stuff at the market. I was kept busy with en-quiries, some genuine and others doubtful, and then I saw George Dawson. As before, he was moving among the stalls, inspecting all manner of small but curious objects before buying some and placing them in his haversack. Judging by the stalls he was using, I think he was buying pieces of lace, miniature oil paintings, wood carvings and similar arty things, although he did purchase a three-legged milking stool, an old piano stool and a child's small armchair, all of which he carried to his car.

And then I was aware of him approaching me. For a moment, I wondered whether my facial expression would betray my knowledge of the suspicions which surrounded him, but I managed a smile and said, 'Good afternoon.'

'I believe you are Matthew, of Matthew's insurance?' he spoke in a refined accent, not in the least like the Yorkshire accent of these moors.

'Yes,' I smiled anew. 'That's me.'

'They've talked about you on the market, saying how obliging you are and what good insurance deals you can arrange. I thought I might be able to put a little business your way.' He smiled broadly at me.

'I'm always interested in new business.' I spoke the truth in saying that. 'But you are not a local person, are you? I can't say I recognize you.'

'George Dawson of Oyster Antiques, Scarborough.' He held out his hand for me to shake and I took it. 'I have just discovered this little market, one never knows when one is going to discover a gem of some kind. My shop is closed on Wednesday afternoons, you see, and that's when I go out seeking new items of stock in addition to those brought in to my shop. I tour the district, dropping in on markets like this, or even visiting other dealers. And I must say I have not been disappointed with these small markets, they are often full of surprises. And here you are, doing the same as the other traders, selling your wares on the open market. Quite charming, I must say.'

'I regard this as my office,' I told him. 'And I do good business from here.'

'Just what I want to hear, Mr Taylor, or may I call you Matthew? Everyone else does.'

'Yes, of course,' and already I was being seduced by his charm. 'So how can I help you, Mr Dawson?'

'The insurance on my premises is almost due for renewal,' he said. 'I have the shop in Scarborough, another in Bridlington run by a manager, and two warehouses, one in each town. The warehouses are separate from the shops, in case of fire, you understand. One can't be too careful in this business. So what I am seeking from Matthew's insurance is comprehensive cover of both shops and warehouses, plus of course their contents, which will inevitably be valuable, or even irreplaceable.'

'That's our business,' I returned. 'But with high-value contents of that kind, at four different locations, our assessors might want to examine all the premises, to assure themselves about matters like security and the fire risk, as well as anything else, flooding even.'

'Exactly as one would expect from a good insurance broker, Matthew. So if I want you to insure me, how do I go about it?'

'You start by filling in a proposal form,' I told him. 'I will send that to my District Office who will examine it before making a decision. If they need further information from you, or want their antiques experts or assessors to call on you, they will contact you direct.'

'That all seems perfectly normal, so right, Matthew. Have you a form here?'

I reached into the hole in the wall and passed one to him. It was then that he saw the heading – Premier Assurance Association, with its headquarters address in London.

'Oh, I see you're with the Premier, I thought you were operating a much smaller company or that you might be a broker. There are lots of new insurance companies these days, they said you ran Matthew's insurance.'

'I wouldn't work for one of those cut-price companies,' I told him. 'Neither would I take out a policy with any of them. If a difficult claim arose, you'd probably find you weren't covered, but the Premier is the best in the country. If you'd like to complete this form and return it to me, or even send it direct to our District Office in Ryethorpe, then we can take things further.'

'Yes, well, yes, I will think about it, Matthew,' and he pushed the leaflet into his pocket. 'Thanks.' And he left.

I never saw him again. He did not complete the proposal form, or if he did, he did not submit it to me. I told Montgomery Wilkins of that encounter and he assured me he would record it in whatever system his office operated to prevent fraud. But I never heard any more about George Dawson and never again saw him at Micklesfield market. Certainly in the months which followed there was no fire at any of his premises. I don't think he could ever get the necessary insurance cover thanks to the underground intelligence system currently operated by the insurance companies, but I was quite proud that he thought I was running my own insurance business. I had forgotten that my work in the dale was called Matthew's insurance.

But it did make me realize that the best way of preventing a fire at Oyster Antiques was *never* to insure the building and its contents. Following this development, I wondered what he had done with all that rubbish he had bought.

If he hadn't been able to burn it in one of his fires, I guessed he must have sold it at a handsome profit, perhaps coming to realize that honesty is always the best policy.

One of the most common frauds in insurance is – or perhaps was – the inflated claim about the loss of money in the form of cash, perhaps through burglary or housebreaking, or perhaps through something as simple as losing one's handbag or wallet, or having them stolen. If someone breaks into the family house and ransacks the place, the chances are they are looking for easy money. If a person has a secret hiding place such as a vase on the mantelpiece, a cash box hidden under the cushions or a pillow case stuffed with pound notes under the mattress, it is highly likely the thief will find it and make off with the loot. Whatever brilliant and original hiding place a householder will devise, it will not be as secret as he or she believes. A professional or skilled thief will find it within a moment. Precisely how much money was concealed in such places is often a secret between the householder and the thief – people hide money for all sorts of reasons. In farms and businesses, it might be a means of defying the tax man, or in the house it might be a means of a wife keeping her savings secret from her husband or children, or money might be hidden simply as a safeguard against theft.

If, therefore, a householder makes a claim from his insurance company when his house is burgled and states he had £10,000 in notes hidden in his secret place, who is to know whether or not that is a true and accurate amount?

And similarly, if a lady loses her handbag containing her make-up, driving licence, personal letters and some cash, who is to know the precise amount of cash it actually contained? The answer is no one but her and the thief.

It follows that dishonest or opportunist losers found it easy to inflate the figure that was lost or stolen in the hope the insurers would repay the amount they had falsely claimed. If a woman had her handbag stolen with £5 housekeeping money inside, how easy was it to complete the claim form and say it contained £50? And if one's house was burgled during the night-time hours with the culprit finding a hoard of hidden cash amounting to £500, how easy was it for a wealthy property owner to claim that £5,000 in notes had been stolen?

In their attempts to halt or perhaps reduce this kind of swindle, the insurance companies did two things – first, the claimant in such cases had to report the loss or theft to the police, who would decide whether the matter was a loss or a crime, and the insurers would then contact the relevant police station for confirmation of the report. The second thing done by the insurers was to impose a limit on the amount of cash that could be claimed as the result of loss, theft, burglary or housebreaking. In the case of the Premier, that amount was £10 0s 0d, and it was stated in all household insurance policies which covered matters like burglary, housebreaking, theft or loss. Many of those policies also covered the policyholder for loss or theft of other valuables when away from the home. The Premier, being one of the best of British insurers, provided total cover in such cases – but always with a limit of £10 0s 0d so far as stolen or lost cash was concerned.

If an insured man lost his wallet containing £150 0s 0d while touring the country, then he could expect only £10 0s 0d from his policy, and the same applied if a burglar stole cash from someone's house. Even if £2,000 in cash was stolen from the house, the policyholder's refund from his insurers was limited to £10 0s 0d. This was considered necessary to prevent or reduce fraudulent claims.

With this in mind, I found myself dealing with the loss or theft of Miss Florence Parkin's handbag. A retired bank clerk in her late sixties, Miss Parkin lived at No. 5 Moorland Terrace in Ingledale. It was her own property, which she had managed to buy while working for the bank, and now, in her spare time, she helped with the church flowers and cleaning, and was president of the WI and secretary of the village-hall committee. She was a grey-haired, thickset woman who dressed in heavy tweed costumes and wore spectacles with thick lenses but she was a tower of strength in her work for the people of her village. And her honesty could never be doubted.

I knew her because she had a small household-protection policy with the Premier. I called once a month to collect her premiums, but I had noticed that in recent weeks she had become rather vague and forgetful. There were days when she had to hunt for her handbag so that she could find money for me – for example, one day she was sure she'd left it on the kitchen draining board when in fact she found it on the dining-room table. A simple error and not at all serious, but perhaps an indication that she was becoming rather fragile with her advancing years. From her policy documents, I knew she was sixty-seven years old, but even if her age was taking its toll she continued with her various voluntary tasks and pursued an active social life.

Then late one Saturday afternoon, I received a telephone call from her. 'Mr Taylor –' she sounded very upset – 'I have lost my handbag, I have told the police and they suggested I contact you, they said I might be insured.'

'Lost it? Or do you mean it was stolen?' Quite often, people would say they had lost something when in fact it had been stolen, and similarly the police would sometimes record property as lost when in reality it had been stolen – that happened when there was no evidence of a crime.

'Well, I am not sure, it might have been stolen, but I have told Guisborough police. I lost it in Guisborough, you see.'

'I'm so sorry to hear this. Was there much in it?'

'All my savings,' and she started to sob into the phone. 'A hundred and twenty-five pounds, Mr Taylor. And other things, cosmetics and so forth. And my grandmother's necklace. Well, it was eventually my mother's and she gave it to me.'

'Oh dear, this doesn't sound good. Look, will you be at home if I come straight up to Ingledale to see you?'

'Yes, yes of course. It's very kind of you, I don't really want to be a nuisance especially on your weekend, but it was such a shock.'

'Give me twenty-five minutes,' I said. 'I'll bring a claim form with me.'

I knew that Miss Parkin would never falsely claim that her £125 had been lost or

134

stolen but I now had the unenviable task of telling her that even if her household policy covered loss or theft of valuables when away from her house, it would only be for a maximum of £10 0s 0d, so far as cash was concerned.

I had no idea how much the bag itself and the rest of its contents were worth, especially the necklace, but that might be determined during my chat with her. Precisely what cover she had for the loss would depend upon the provisions of her rather modest policy.

When I parked Betsy outside, Miss Parkin immediately opened the front door; clearly, she had been watching for my arrival and as I was ushered into her neat little sitting room, I saw the table bore a tea tray with cups, milk and fruit cake. There were also some papers – her insurance policy and lots of receipts for premiums.

'The kettle has boiled,' she said. 'Sit down, Mr Taylor, and I'll be back in a moment. My policy is on the table in case you want to look at it, I took it out long before you replaced Mr Villiers, so you might not be familiar with its provisions.'

When I read the relevant clauses, it was just as I had expected. Loss or theft of valuables was covered when Miss Parkin was away from her house, albeit with the maximum of £10 0s 0d for cash, and personal valuables up to a value of £125 unless special provision had been made. That meant objects of higher value could be specifically covered but that would attract a higher premium. But no amendments or additions had been made to her policy document and, of course, it was paid up to date. It all looked very clear to me. Then she returned with the teapot.

'So tell me how you lost your handbag, Miss Parkin. And I need to know whether this is a theft or a loss. While I'm taking the details, I'll complete the claim form then you can sign it.'

Miss Parkin had been to Guisborough that Saturday for her regular lunch with a friend, Jane Holden, who was also a former colleague. To keep in touch, they met once a week at the Clarion Restaurant in the main street. This occasion had been no different from any other – they had met at noon and enjoyed a long, leisurely meal before leaving just after 2 p.m. Miss Parkin had then gone to do a spot of grocery shopping around the market before catching the bus home to Ingledale at 3.30 p.m., and it was then she realized she'd mislaid her handbag. It wasn't in her shopping basket as she'd expected but luckily she'd had a return ticket for the bus.

'So do you think it was a pickpocket? Some

light-fingered thief in the crowd taking it out of your basket?'

'That's what I don't know, Mr Taylor. The police asked me that. I know I had it with me when I went into the restaurant to meet Jane, and I put it in my basket which I placed on the floor beside our table. It's a cane shopping basket with high sides, my bag couldn't have fallen out. Jane paid for the meal, you see, it was her turn this week, so I did not need my bag after the meal and it was only when I looked for it to get some money for my groceries that I realized it had gone.'

'And you never used it after going into the restaurant?'

'Well, yes, I went into the ladies' room near the end of the meal and took it with me, to powder my nose, if you understand, and comb my hair, that sort of thing. But I didn't leave it there, the police checked, and I went back for a look. The police sent a constable down to the restaurant to search as well and he questioned the staff, but there was no trace of it. I'm sure I didn't leave it there.'

'So that suggests it was taken from your basket in the street?'

'Yes, it's the only explanation. Jane remembers me having it in the restaurant, in my basket. The police said thieves do that sort of thing, take purses and bags, remove the money and throw the bag away. They think it might be found somewhere, thrown away and minus my money. If it's found, they'll contact me.'

'Well, they'll have a record of your report, whether they consider it lost or stolen, our office will confirm that. So, Miss Parkin, I need a description of your bag and its contents.'

It was a black leather handbag with a brass snap fastener and a shoulder-length carrying strap. There were three compartments and inside was £125 in mixed one-pound and ten-shilling notes, a small brown leather purse containing some smaller coins in silver and copper totalling about £3, various personal papers and letters bearing her address, her pension book, a chequebook, a fountain pen, items of make-up, such as nail scissors, lipstick, powder and comb, and her late mother's necklace.

'Miss Parkin.' I had to ask. 'Can I ask why you were carrying such a large amount of cash?'

'Force of habit, I suppose.' She smiled ruefully. 'I have no real savings, Mr Taylor, I don't need them and besides, I can't save much on my pension. When I draw my weekly housekeeping, I cash a cheque at the village shop, they're very good like that, and whatever I don't spend, I pop into a special

138

compartment of my handbag, changing it into notes as I go along. I've built up quite a big sum, I do that instead of paying it back into the bank. I've always got cash on hand if I need it.'

'That makes sense.'

'I know I'm an former bank worker and should set an example, but I've always felt my little nest egg was safe with me, even safer than leaving it in the house. Until now.'

'We must never give up hope.' I tried to sound optimistic. 'So I need a value for the other things, the bag itself, the fountain pen, toiletries – and that necklace.'

We decided that, apart from the necklace, the bag and its contents were worth about £6 12s 6d at replacement values, but the necklace was a problem.

'I have a photograph of it,' she suddenly said. 'Granny didn't know a lot about it and Mother was trying to discover something of its history. I thought it was rather ugly and didn't really want it, but I daren't give it away, due to the family connection. Anyway, Mother sent a photograph, taken by a professional photographer, to one of those famous auction houses in London. They said they couldn't value it from a photograph but added it looked like a nineteenth-century gold necklace, and suggested she take it to a jeweller for a valuation. I don't think she ever did. When she died, she left it to me, but as I said, I don't like it. I've often thought of giving it away but Mother might not have wanted me to do that, so I just carry it around with me, all the time. Silly, I suppose, but one day I might suddenly decide to give it to someone who's nice to me, who deserves a special thank-you of some kind.'

'So what did the police say about it?'

'Well, I described it as best I could and they said it would be entered in their records along with the bag but I couldn't give a value. I think I said five pounds.'

'If the Premier is to recompense you for this loss, Miss Parkin, we shall need a fairly accurate valuation. Now, I have some bad news which you might know already, and it is that the Premier, like other insurance companies, will only pay a maximum of ten pounds for loss or theft of cash, irrespective of the total amount that was actually concerned.'

'Yes, I know that, I read it before you came. I must live with that, Mr Taylor, it's one of those things. It was a lot to lose but really, I didn't need it, my pension keeps me quite well.'

'But for other belongings, they will pay the current replacement value. I see no problem with the valuation of your bag and things inside, except for the necklace. Do you think five pounds is a reasonable assessment of its value?'

'I think so, Mr Taylor, no more than that. Neither Granny nor Mother were wealthy and I think it was a present to Granny from an admirer – but just you wait there, I'll go and find that photograph.'

She pottered upstairs and returned a few minutes later with the nine-inch-by-six-inch black-and-white photograph depicting a necklace on a white background. It had been arranged in the form of a heart, with a crucifix, minus the Christ figure, hanging from the centre. When I turned the photograph over, I found a typed note glued to the rear – and that contained a brief description. It was described as a gold filigree and polychrome enamel cross and necklace dating from the nineteenth century. Its total length was one yard, i.e. 36 inches. But no value was given. Nonetheless, the fact that it was made of gold and of considerable age suggested a high value.

'Can I show this to someone?' I asked. 'We have an auctioneer and valuer living in Micklesfield. I'd like to get his opinion before I complete your claim form.'

'Well, I'm not too bothered about the insurance, Mr Taylor, it's just that the police suggested I tell you. I will be happy getting enough to buy a new handbag and fountain pen, and I think I can say goodbye to my money and everything else.'

I asked her to sign the claim form before I obtained a valuation so that I could forward it straight to District Office once it was complete. I explained there would be a slight delay of two months or so before she could expect a cheque; that delay was in case the police traced the thief and recovered her property. I left her and drove straight to the home of Paul Richardson, the auctioneer and valuer who lived in Micklesfield. It took him only a few minutes to declare that the necklace was extremely valuable, in his estimation worth something around £500, and so I completed the claim form with that value and managed to catch the last post with it. Then I rang Miss Parkin and she was shocked and surprised, but nonetheless happy that she could expect to receive the Premier's maximum pay out for the necklace, i.e. £125. That was because the necklace had not been specially declared.

Two months later, the cheque arrived at my house and I drove up to Ingledale to present it to Miss Parkin who, by now, had almost forgotten the incident. She invited me in for a cup of tea and some cake, and said she had no idea what she would do with the money. She'd probably put the cheque into her new handbag and keep it there without cashing it, at least until she could decide how to spend it.

And she confirmed there had been no message from the police to say her bag had been recovered, nor had she received any hint from anyone who might have found it. After all, it did contain letters bearing her name and address. This outcome suggested to me that it had indeed been stolen from her basket in the marketplace at Guisborough, and that the thief had kept the money and perhaps the necklace, then thrown the rest away, probably in a dustbin or even into a river to be lost for ever.

The affair might have ended there had not the management of the Clarion Restaurant in Guisborough decided to redecorate. About eight months after Miss Parkin's loss, the restaurant closed for three weeks while the entire interior was cleaned, given a new coat of paint, fresh wallpaper and even a carpet over the wooden floor. And while the huge mahogany sideboard was being man-handled away from the wall, one of the decorators shouted, 'Hey, there's a handbag down here,' and he picked it up. Blowing off the thick dust, he opened it to find Miss Parkin's belongings, including all her cash, the necklace, the fountain pen and her other odds and ends. The manageress was called and she could remember the visit by the police when a lady guest, whose name she did not recall, had reported the loss of her bag and contents. Besides, there were envelopes inside bearing the name and address of a Miss F. Parkin, 5 Moorland Terrace, Ingledale. But how on earth had it got down behind this sideboard? There was sufficient space for it to get down behind it – its back was a few inches off the wall – but it must have been pushed off the sideboard, perhaps accidentally.

And once down there, of course, it was out of sight and out of mind, well away from cleaners' brooms and dusters. The chequebook provided a clue as to the time the bag had found its way to the secure hiding place, and when the manageress rang the police, they searched their records and confirmed it had been reported lost or stolen by Miss Parkin. And everything was still there, including all her money and the necklace. The police rang Miss Parkin with the good news and asked her to call at the police station next time she was in Guisborough, when it would be returned to her against her signature, after she had checked the contents. Then she rang me.

'I'm so delighted, Mr Taylor, really I am, especially after all this time, but what do I do about the insurance money? I mean, I can't accept it, can I? I have my belongings back now so it's perhaps a good job I didn't cash that cheque. It is still in my new handbag, I've never felt happy about cashing it. Shall I return it to you?'

'I think that is the procedure,' I had to say. 'Yes, I'll collect it next time I call on you.'

I called a few days later, when she had her bag once again in her possession, and she handed me the uncashed cheque. She was quite overcome that everything had been returned intact and asked my advice for a means of thanking the staff of the Clarion. I suggested she buy something for the newly decorated restaurant – a nice oil painting perhaps, or a mirror, or she might even consider holding a party for the workmen and staff who had been honest enough to hand it in.

She said she would do something after talking about it with the management – and she liked parties.

'Miss Parkin,' I added before I left her to her happy thoughts, 'can I ask one more thing? How on earth did your handbag get down behind that sideboard?'

'I've been thinking about that, Mr Taylor, and it's funny how things come back to mind eventually. I remember going to the ladies' and I took my handbag, as you do, and when I came out, I decided to collect the coffee cups for Jane and me, you'll remember I was with Jane. The coffee was self-service, from that big sideboard.'

'I'm with you so far.'

'Well, you need two hands to pour coffee and carry the cups and so I put my bag down on the sideboard while I carried the cups over to our table. I intended coming back for it but when I returned, there was an old friend of ours who'd noticed Jane and she came across for a chat. Well, Mr Taylor, I quite forgot about my handbag and wandered out of the restaurant with my basket – and no handbag. I didn't realize until I wanted some money for groceries, and had totally forgotten about going to the ladies', and about collecting the coffee.'

'I can understand that,' I nodded. 'But I still can't understand how it got knocked down behind the sideboard.'

She shook her head. 'And neither can I, Mr Taylor. It is a bit of a mystery, isn't it? I must have knocked it as I was turning away with my hands full of coffee cups, that's the only explanation.'

'That seems very possible, especially if it was close to the edge.'

'Yes, I'm sure that's what happened. But there is another problem. I don't know what to do with that necklace. It seems I can't get rid of it. I don't know why Mother gave it to me.'

'You could always wear it,' I said. 'After all, it has come down the generations into your hands.'

'Do you really think I could wear it? I used to hate it ... but, well, it might look all right with some of my clothes...'

'If you do,' I said, 'I think you should have it insured for its full value, just in case you lose it again. It wouldn't cost a great deal.'

'That sounds a very good idea, but where did I put it, Mr Taylor? When I got my handbag back ... I took it out and thought I wouldn't carry it around in my everyday bag. So I wonder where I put it? I do hope I haven't lost it again.'

Five

'The Bishop walked among the congregation in the cathedral grounds, eating their lunches, and during the afternoon's programme "O praise ye the Lard" was sung by a large crow.'

From a parish magazine

The business generated by my 'surgery' at the Bottle and Jug continued to delight me. One of the benefits was that I did not need to spend so much time canvassing around my widespread agency because most of the people I would normally call upon to seek new business were regular visitors to Micklesfield market. I could meet them there to discuss their requirements. Many were wives whose husbands were out at work during the day; they came to market for their weekly fruit, vegetables and other food, as did pensioners and some men whose work allowed them that kind of freedom. Many of the men spent their time in the Unicorn, no doubt telling their wives they were struggling to produce some kind of deal with a potential customer!

Because I no longer needed to spend so much time canvassing, it meant I had more leisure time at home with Evelyn and baby Paul, particularly in the evenings and at weekends. I found this was very necessary if I was to cultivate my new and rather large garden; certainly, it was capable of providing us with fruit and vegetables, and space for hens and pigs, that being the main purpose of gardens during and just after the war. Most definitely, they were not regarded as places for fun and relaxation!

Another of my tasks was to maintain the house in good decorative condition, although I was aware of the saying that 'All work and no play makes Jack a dull boy'. In the beginning, therefore, work in the garden and on the house was a means of escaping from my day job and I must admit I enjoyed those days pottering about my patch of England and doing jobs around the house.

Thanks to Evelyn's occasional work as a supply teacher, we were able to meet the monthly mortgage repayments whilst affording the necessities of life, even if we were by no means wealthy. There was no spare cash for luxuries but in spite of dreaming of having more to spend, I enjoyed the reduced time necessary to run my insurance business. Less time spent canvassing or collecting meant I could make extra cash at home

– so long as I kept up with the garden and house maintenance!

I earned a few pounds by continuing to sell goods which I obtained by bartering with clients who could not afford their premiums, and I also continued to act as an unofficial agent for Eric Newton of Baysthorpe by selling his beautiful hand-made wooden toys. There was not much income from either of those sidelines, and it was by no means regular, but every extra penny was useful. And then I got a curious request. The telephone rang shortly after seven one Sunday evening.

'It's Nancy Barnes from Crossrigg, sorry to ring so late especially on a Sunday, Matthew, but I need a favour. Urgently. I couldn't think of anybody else who might be able to help.'

Arthur Barnes was a butcher who lived in Crossrigg, and his excellent shop was well patronized over a wide area; his wife, Nancy, looked after the shop while he arranged the necessary purchases from a local slaughterhouse and also toured the neighbourhood in his van, selling meat door-to-door. His territory did not encroach upon Micklesfield, so he was not a competitor of George Wade for whom I used to work. Indeed, the men were good friends and would often help one another if the occasion arose. In Crossrigg itself, Arthur had a reputation for being the cheapest butcher for miles around – I knew this from regular visits to my clients in the village, all of whom said the quality of his merchandise was good whilst his prices were far lower than anyone else.

Whatever he sold in Crossrigg, whether it was a leg of lamb, a joint of beef, pork pies or merely half a dozen eggs, his prices could never be matched. When I had worked for George Wade, he had often commented on Arthur's prices, saying he must be able to keep them so low because he did not employ anyone, other than his wife. Even so, George felt that Arthur was not charging a fair price for his products; he was almost giving them away. In a village like Crossrigg, where the brickworks paid low wages and men were often out of work, this kind of cheap local food was welcomed by the less well-off and there is little wonder Arthur had such a lot of contented customers. From my own visits to the village, I knew the women relied on his low prices to meet their family commitments; quite literally, they could not afford to buy their meat elsewhere. The only problem was getting cash out of them in payment.

It was a surprise to receive that call from Nancy, and I guessed it must concern one of their policies. Nancy and Arthur were both clients of mine, with the Premier insuring their business, their private house and their two vehicles, a private car and the butcher's van. They also had life insurances with the Premier, which meant I was a regular visitor, usually finding Nancy in her shop near the Co-Op.

'So how can I help, Nancy?'

'It's Arthur.' From the tone of her voice, I could sense she was very upset. 'He's been rushed into hospital, Matthew, at Whitby. He'll have to spend a few days there, having tests. They think it might be a heart attack, he was very ill this afternoon in the garden, pains in his chest. It's possible he might be off work for some time.'

My immediate thought was that she was querying the provisions of his life insurance, to check whether he would receive any income from his policy if he was going to be off work for a considerable period. Lots of self-employed people in my Delverdale agency wisely held such a policy.

'I can check the provisions of his policy and pop in to see you tomorrow. Monday is my collecting day in Crossrigg. I do know that Arthur has made provision for an income if he's going to be off work, but I'm not sure of the amount, or when it starts. Some policies require a period of three weeks or even longer off work before the

152

money starts being paid, and of course, the Premier needs the necessary doctor's certificate...'

'Oh, it's not that, Matthew. I know he's well insured, he was always very insistent that we were catered for if anything like this happened. No, it's just that tomorrow is his big day in and around Crossrigg.'

'Of course.' On my own trips to Crossrigg on Mondays, I tried to visit my clients ahead of all other tradesmen. With only a small amount of housekeeping, often due to their husbands visiting the pub or putting money on horses, many wives found it difficult to pay their way. Following payday on Friday, the men would have spent their pocket money in the pub on the Friday and Saturday nights, then more on Sunday lunchtime, and by Monday they would be trying to wheedle further cash from their long-suffering wives' meagre housekeeping allowances – if, indeed, they actually gave their wives any money. Many seemed to keep almost everything for themselves. By Monday, the unfortunate wives had very little to spare, even for essentials – and there was the rest of the week to consider.

Arthur was very aware of this and spent his Mondays delivering meat and collecting his orders for the following week. And he also tried hard to collect any money owed to him.

I knew that lots of local tradespeople were trying to squeeze money from the same limited pot – myself included. It was a genuine case of the early bird catching the worm!

Nancy was saying, 'It's his main day of the week in Crossrigg, Matthew, all his customers will be expecting him, they rely on him but he won't let them have this week's meat until they've paid for last week's. That's his system – they need his meat, it's so cheap and it's the only way he can get his money from some families.'

I had to admit that work in the brickyard was tough, hot, dirty and dusty, with the entire brickworks complex making Crossrigg resemble a small industrial town rather than a moorland village. The attitudes and behaviour of the workforce were also more akin to an industrial area than a village; the men worked hard and lived hard, with some of their families suffering as a result.

'I'm the same,' I replied. 'I always make sure I get into Crossrigg very early if I'm to collect any of my premiums.'

'That's why I'm ringing you. And you used to work for George Wade, he always speaks very highly of you, he was sorry you left.'

At this point, I was still unsure why she was ringing me. She continued to sound upset on the telephone, clearly worried about her husband but perhaps she thought I knew what she was asking? And then, almost as she began to explain, it dawned on me.

'So if it's not concerning your insurance, how can I help?'

'I was wondering if I dare ask you, Matthew, but I know it's your day in Crossrigg on Mondays, and you know the butchering business inside out, so I was wondering if you would do his round for him? You know, take his van and deliver the orders, make a note of next week's in that little book Arthur keeps in the van and collect outstanding debts. It's all written down in his book, Arthur is very methodical ... and, you see, I thought you could do Arthur's round at the same you do your own work. You probably call at the same houses, I'm sure, and it wouldn't add much to your own day...'

For a few moments I was flummoxed and didn't know how to respond. On the one hand, I thought this was a downright cheek, but on the other I knew the Barneses well enough to realize Nancy would not have asked this if it had not been very important.

'I'll pay you, of course, I wouldn't expect you to do this for nothing,' she added, almost as an afterthought. 'And you can always choose a nice joint, something for Sunday dinner.'

'Oh, no, I wouldn't want that, not if I could

do my own work at the same time...'

'Then you'll do it? I don't know how to thank you, Matthew, really I don't. The van will need loading, he goes to the slaughter-house at six to get everything, it'll be ready and waiting in the big fridge but don't forget the liver, kidneys and sausages. Or the chickens and a few ducks. Next he goes to Riverside Farm for his eggs, forty dozen, then he comes back here where I'll have the pork pies ready and his cash tin with plenty of small change. I'll have a flask of tea ready for you as well, with a bait tin, he always takes something to eat on his round, then he's ready to make his first call at eight. Mrs Baxter down near the bridge...'

And so I found myself being rather un-willingly volunteered into returning to my former trade as butcher, albeit in an industrial village notorious for its residents trying to avoid paying their bills. With my own dues to collect at the same time, it promised to be quite a daunting experience but it was too late to back out, Nancy was depending upon me. Tomorrow at six, I would be a butcher once again.

Evelyn thought it was a good idea because it would keep me in touch with my former trade whilst making more business contacts and then she pointed out that if I was using Arthur's van to complete my rounds, I

156

wouldn't need the car. So could I take my motorbike to Graindale slaughterhouse and leave it there while I used Arthur's van? If I did that, she would be able to use Betsy, our car, and she needed some new shoes so she was wondering about a trip to Guisborough, perhaps with Maureen? She could treat Maureen to lunch, as a thank-you for looking after Paul on so many occasions.

And so I agreed but I must admit I did not sleep that night, wondering what I had let myself in for. I woke at five, dressed in some older clothes and found my old butcher's blue-and-white coat, had my breakfast, kissed Evelyn and Paul goodbye, and then collected my briefcase before heading down the garden to the garage. My gallant Coventry Eagle reacted to the first kick of the starter and soon, with my insurance papers in my panniers, I was chugging down the dale towards Crossrigg. There I would collect Arthur's van before heading for Graindale, only a further two miles away, while trying to work out in my head some kind of system which would permit me to collect my premiums while selling his meat.

When I walked into the slaughterhouse, with its concrete floor awash with fresh water, I could smell the blood and raw meat; in my days working in such an environment I had never noticed the overpowering smell but now it was unavoidable, a redolent reminder of my recent past. Realizing I had left a very necessary but unpleasant world, I was greeted by Ted Cleghorn, the owner.

He was a red-faced man with bulbous eyes and he always looked as if he needed a shave. He always wore a long blue-and-white butcher's coat, generally bloodstained, and there were usually white rags sticking out of his pockets. As I walked in, I noticed carcasses of newly killed pigs hanging from the ceiling with freshly ploated chickens on a side table and the entire place felt distinctly chilly and damp.

'By gum, Matthew, you've given up t'insurance job already?'

'No, Ted,' and I explained my present role, realizing that news of Arthur's illness would soon flash about the local villages.

'Aye, well, he's lucky to have you around to help out. Right, his stuff is in that back room, in the big fridge in the usual place. All his stuff has got his name on it. Help yourself.'

And so, with my insurance papers on the front seat, I loaded up the van, checked the notebook in the cubby hole to ascertain I'd collected everything that had been pre-ordered, plus a few extra items to cater, and I added a bit more for possible new customers then settled down to determine my route, using Arthur's notes. With best wishes from Ted, I began my task, not forgetting to collect the eggs, pork pies, cash box and snack before I ventured into Crossrigg.

According to Arthur's list, my first call was on Mrs Baxter at eight; I had to call early because she went out to work and needed to obtain her meat before leaving home. I knew her fairly well – she was one of my clients and if I called late, she would leave the money on the outside window ledge of the pantry.

She was one of the better payers, being a middle-aged woman whose family had grown up and left home but whose husband still worked in the kilns at the brickworks. He was noted for his heavy consumption of beer. That was not surprising, considering the tough and hot work he endured each day. There was little wonder he – and many others – headed straight for the pub after each shift, there to ease their dehydration – but he treated his wife fairly.

Arthur's note said Mrs Baxter had ordered her usual small joint of beef, preferably from a corner with a good amount of fat. Following my visit to her, I would then follow Arthur's list of customers, each stop having their order shown. Some were clear, such as a pound of sausages, a pound of liver, six slices of bacon and half a dozen eggs, but others were rather more vague, such as Mrs Baxter's small joint of beef, Mrs Sharpe's usual mince and Mrs Ward's pork chops. I felt sure I would cope – the customers would explain the details to me. Ann Baxter, a tall good-looking woman with grey hair, came out the moment I eased the van to a halt outside her terrace home and I could see she was clutching her purse in her fist. But when I stepped out of the van, I could see the puzzlement on her round face.

'Don't say you've gone back to butchering, Matthew!' she smiled as I opened the rear doors for her to inspect the contents. 'What's up, has Arthur retired?'

I knew this conversation was going to be repeated throughout the day and so I would have to literally grin and bear it; I explained the situation and she said she would pay me her premiums, then said Arthur would have put aside a nice small joint for her.

I recalled the piece in question, Ted had selected it and I knew from Arthur's notebook which one it was. I picked it up and weighed it.

'That'll be 4s 3d,' I smiled, wrapping it in a large piece of greaseproof paper.

'Oh, no, Matthew. I never pay more than 3s 11d for my joint.'

'This is a very good piece of beef, Mrs Baxter, a corner piece just as you wanted.'

'That might be so, but I have never paid more than 3s 11d. You're overcharging me by fourpence.'

'This is the regular price, Mrs Baxter, Wade's always charge that...'

'And they're well known for overcharging, Matthew. Arthur's not, that's why we allus support him. Arthur's meat is the best in the dale and the cheapest. So either you cut a bit off or you let me have it at Arthur's price. The joint is already cut for me, you know that, and if you look at that book you'll see what I always pay Arthur. Three and eleven-pence.'

I opened the book and then realized the 3s 11d shown against her name was for last week's order. And that meant she wasn't expected to pay for this particular joint until next week.

'I'll let Arthur sort it out,' I decided. 'If this is the same size he always gets you, then I'm sure you're right.'

I knew he always took the money for the previous week before handing over the cur-rent week's order and so I accepted her 3s 11d, marked it 'paid' in Arthur's book, then entered the fact I had handed to Mrs Baxter her standing order for this week which, by my reckoning, came to 4s 3d.

'It's no good you putting 4s 3d down in that book,' she said. 'I'll pay my usual price,

161

Arthur knows that. 3s 11d it's allus been and 3s 11d it is today.'

'Well, so long as he knows what he's doing, Mrs Baxter. I'm sure he has his own system and because he's the boss, he can charge what he likes. I am sure he has special prices for special customers. Even Wade's offer discounts for some of their regulars.'

I felt I had completed a diplomatic deal, hoping that Arthur's condition was not too serious because I did not want to return next week and fight a financial battle not of my own making with Mrs Baxter; although, of course, I could check the situation with Nancy. I managed to collect Mrs Baxter's 1s 6d insurance money at the same time and so I felt I had done quite well. But it was only eight fifteen and my day was just beginning. There were many more calls to make, some involving me as a butcher combined with an insurance agent, and others limited to just one of those roles. There was very little difficulty in collecting my premiums as well as dealing with Arthur's customers. Arthur's meticulous system worked very well indeed; all his customers knew they could not have any meat this week until they paid for last week's and, fortunately, I was sufficiently experienced to know the tricks that some attempted to avoid payment.

When they realized there was a new lad on

the meat van, some of them, young and old alike, tried all sorts of pleas and trickery to avoid paying last week's monies, but I did not succumb to any of their ploys. Among the stories they told were that Arthur had said it was all right to pay for both orders next week, that Arthur always let them carry their bill forward until month end, that Arthur always understood if they'd had a heavy weekend with unexpected expenses and would let them pay next week ... all the hard-luck stories, and 'friends of Arthur' stories came out in just one single day, and I never fell for one of them. And I was paid most of my outstanding premiums.

One curious factor did emerge, however. As I was touring the village in the butcher's van, it was inevitable that, from time to time, I stopped outside houses whose residents did not require meat. I stopped there because I had premiums to collect but in two instances, I was surprised by the reaction of the householders. The first was Mrs Cynthia Carstairs, whose husband was a solicitor in Guisborough. After responding to my ring on her back-door bell, her first surprise was the sight of her insurance man in a butcher's outfit, and the second shock was the sight of the vanload of raw meat outside her smart house.

'Mr Taylor, what on earth is going on? I do

hope you are not responsible for that van outside my house!' She was a haughty woman in her mid-fifties, with auburn hair showing signs of grey.

'Well, yes,' I began as I prepared to launch into the story. 'I'm here for your insurance money as usual but Arthur Barnes...'

'Then take it and go!' she snapped, rushing indoors to find her purse. She did not allow me to explain but left me on the doorstep as she hunted for the half-crown. When she returned, she left the kitchen and walked to the end of her short drive where she looked to the left and right, up and down the street. I followed and signed her book to record the payment. The way she looked anxiously up and down the street made me think she must be expecting someone but she regarded the van as if it was a pile of dog-dirt or worse.

'Er, while I'm here, I wondered if you wanted any meat. I know you're not on Mr Barnes' list for today but I do carry enough spare...'

'Mr Taylor, I do not know why you are here in that garb but I do not buy meat from that van. I obtain mine from the shop! I expect high standards with my meat and I am prepared to pay good money for good meat.'

'Er, this is good meat, very good in fact. It's exactly the same as Arthur sells in the shop.'

'I do not want cheap meat, Mr Taylor, and

164

I do not want my neighbours thinking I cannot afford the best. Can you imagine what they must think, if they believe I am buying cheap meat? Now if you don't mind, please remove that vehicle and if you come again dressed like this for my premiums, please park along the road and take off that silly coat. I want you to understand that I do not want cut-price butchers coming to my door. Or any form of cut-price salesman, in fact.'

'I'm helping Mr and Mrs Barnes...'

'Goodbye, Mr Taylor,' and she rushed inside and slammed the door.

She was not the only woman to react in that way. Another two, both well-off clients of the Premier, made it quite clear that they did not wish to be associated with cheap meat in the form of Arthur's van. One told me to park out of sight and come to her house without my butcher's coat, and the other simply slammed the door and shouted through the letter box, 'Call next week, Mr Taylor, that's if you are still with the insurance. And don't bring that van with you.'

I now realized that there were distinct social divisions in this minor industrial area, with Arthur doing his best to cater for the less well-off. Now I could understand why he charged lower prices. It was his very personal means of allowing the poorer people to obtain meat! I began to see Arthur as a philanthropist, a man working quietly in his special way to help those less fortunate than himself. But he still insisted they pay! After all, he had his own living to make – but in spite of his efforts, many persisted in trying to avoid paying and in my case, one attempt stands out among the others.

I was about three-quarters of the way around Arthur's route, and a similar distance through my own collecting routine, when I had to call upon someone called Mrs Milton who lived on the outskirts of Crossrigg. She was not one of my clients and was not on Arthur's list either, but a message was waiting for me at the village shop where both Arthur and I called regularly. According to the phone call, Mrs Milton had heard I was in the village today with the butcher's van, and as she had company coming on Tuesday night, she wanted some good meat. Could I please find time to call?

She would be most appreciative and hoped I had some additional meat on board. When I arrived, in the middle of that Monday afternoon, I saw the house was in its own grounds and was called Birch House; clearly it belonged to someone much better off than Arthur's van customers, and so I passed through the open gate and into the drive, where I halted outside the garage. The back door opened on to the garage forecourt, and we tradesmen, by tradition, always went to the back door. There was a bell which I rang and the response was that the door opened to reveal a very pretty fair-haired woman in a tan-coloured pleated skirt, smart matching shoes with high heels and a white blouse, open at the neck. I guessed she would be in her mid-thirties and she was slender with a beautiful figure.

'Oh, hello, you must be Barnes the butcher?' and she flashed a dazzling smile at me standing there in my butcher's coat with the van parked behind.

'Yes, but I am not Mr Barnes, I am just helping out today. Matthew Taylor is my name. You left a message at the shop?'

'Yes, it was so good of them to pass it along, and so good of you to come. I did think of coming down to the village and trying to find the van – Mr Barnes is ill, I believe. But I felt that might not be a good idea, you could be anywhere and I'd be chasing around in circles. I'd heard from a lady in the post office that it was butcher's van day in Crossrigg, so I hope you don't mind my impertinence. I am just new here, you see, we – my husband and I, that is – moved here about a month ago and are just finding our way around and getting to know people.'

'Well,' I said, trying to be as helpful as I could, 'Mr Barnes – Arthur – does have the shop in Crossrigg but he was taken into hospital so his wife will not have opened it today. And yes, this is his van, Monday is his day in this village. I'm helping out, at least for today. We'll have to wait and see how he gets on.'

'So you are not really a butcher?'

'Not now, I used to be. Now I work for Premier Assurance, Monday happens to be my day in Crossrigg as well, so I said I would do Arthur's round as a favour. A lot of people expect him on Mondays.'

'Well, that is very nice of you. Can I see what you have to offer?'

'Yes, of course,' and I turned and led the way to the rear of the van, opened the doors and stood back to let her examine the display. The fact she had recently moved into Crossrigg answered my unspoken query about why she wanted the van to call. From what I had gathered from today's experience was that only the poorer people dealt with Arthur's van; the wealthier went to the shop where the prices were more in keeping with those charged by other butchers. There was some kind of snobbery involved in all this, with Arthur's van being the cheap end of his operation. Posh people didn't patronize the van but evidently Mrs Milton was either unconcerned about it or had not yet adapted to, or discovered, that kind of weird local behaviour. Perhaps she might in the days which followed?

'There's not much left,' I admitted to her as she approached the van. 'I've been going round Arthur's regulars, most of them had advance orders but he does carry a few extra cuts.'

'I'm sure I will find something I like,' she smiled.

I stood aside as she studied the contents for a few moments, then she said, 'I think some fillet steak please, Matthew. I can call you Matthew?'

'Yes, everyone else does.'

'Good, then that makes us friends. Now enough for six, please. The best you've got. I have a very important dinner party this week ... steak will be just right.'

I cut the necessary fillets, weighed them and wrapped them in greaseproof paper, then said, 'That will be 12s 6d, please.'

'Twelve and six, it's more expensive in Leeds where I've just come from, but not so good, I'm sure.'

I decided that, as she was a new customer and not in Arthur's books, I should ask for her money today, and then make an entry in Arthur's book so that he might call again – provided she wanted him to. I felt she might decide to visit the shop once she was more settled in and more familiar with the Cross-rigg way of life.

'My purse is upstairs,' she said. 'Come in while I go and get it.'

I followed her into the kitchen where she put the meat in the fridge, then indicated a chair in the adjoining room, and said, 'Sit down, Matthew, I won't be a minute, perhaps you'd like a cup of tea, or something nicer?'

And before I could reply, she had vanished into the hall and I heard her climbing the stairs. A few minutes later she reappeared, now clad in a dressing gown which was held together by a silk rope around the waist.

As, for the briefest of moments, I wondered what she was doing, she stood directly in front of me and threw open the dressing gown to reveal she was naked beneath.

'I'm sure your meat is very good, Matthew,' she smiled. 'And I am very tender...'

But I was already on my feet and heading for the door.

'Sorry, Mrs Milton, I can't ... I mustn't ... I'm happily married ... ' I heard myself spluttering in my embarrassment and disbelief. 'I must go...'

I roared away in the van, then parked a few hundred yards along the road to gather my wits and get my breath back. I had heard of women like Mrs Milton, and in fact had been warned about them during my initiation course with the Premier, but had never thought I would encounter one in deepest Delverdale. It is fair to say that the rest of my round was uneventful by comparison and when I returned to Nancy Barnes, I could see she was smiling.

'It's good news, Arthur's out of danger,' she said. 'He's being brought home in time for tea. It was a bout of very severe indigestion, nothing more, some crab he ate, so the hospital thinks. His heart is fine, at least we know that. Some good has come out of all this and we'll cope now, thanks to you. We do appreciate what you did for us today, and you must take something for your help, Matthew.'

'No, thanks, it's the least I could do,' and I told her I had had an enjoyable day without any problems. I didn't mention Mrs Milton although I thought I should refer to Arthur's low prices. 'Arthur's prices are very low, aren't they?'

'Just on the van, and just on Mondays in Crossrigg,' she smiled. 'It's his way of helping the poorer people. We make up for it in the shop, there are some dreadful snobs in Crossrigg, you know. They pay a little more for their meat even if they don't realize it, and their unwitting contributions help us to keep prices down for the others. Not that we broadcast that, of course.'

'I like the idea,' I said. 'So Arthur's a kind of Robin Hood?'

'Yes, I suppose he is, not that anyone respects him for it. We always get those who won't pay, or who try to dodge paying, but he thinks he is doing his bit for society.'

'I'm sure he is, which is why I couldn't take anything. I completed my own collecting as well, so I'm not out of pocket.'

In spite of my protests, she insisted on giving me some nice fillet steak as a reward, enough for Evelyn and myself, and the thought of steak reminded me to leave a note in the van for Arthur before I left. I wrote in his little book, 'Mrs Milton at Birch House is a newcomer to the village. She bought some steak and paid today. She might want you to call regularly.'

I have no idea whether Arthur called on her, and if so, what happened. In the days and weeks which followed, I saw him around the dale but he never mentioned Mrs Milton. And neither did I.

Helping with Arthur's round was not the only time I was asked to assist others by making use of my earlier training.

During my wartime military duties, I had been a vehicle mechanic specializing in motorcycles, which meant I now did all my own servicing, both of my Coventry Eagle motorbike and Betsy, our family car. Because I had a spacious garage at the bottom of the garden, I was able to take sections of the bike apart, such as the gearbox, and leave the bits lying on the floor until I could reassemble it even if it sometimes meant Betsy living outside for a week or two. Word of my experience with military vehicles soon spread around the dale and motorbike owners would often bring their machines to me if they were causing problems. More often than not, I could effect the necessary repair.

This was another useful money-making sideline and it did not appear to antagonize local garage owners because, quite often, the problems were electrical rather than mechanical. The mysteries of a modern bike's complex wiring system sometimes defeated a village garage mechanic and they were more than happy for me to try and identify the problem. Fortunately, I had retained my army notebooks and they contained everything I needed to know about 490cc WD Nortons, BSAs, Matchlesses, Ariels, Royal Enfields and Triumphs. I also kept my Royal Artillery notes about the maintenance of machine-gun carriers and motor vehicles in general, with Ford V8 and

173

two-stroke engines in particular, including the care of batteries and all the electrically operated components of motor vehicles. I had copious notes on starter motors, magnetos, dynamos, suppressors, lead-acid batteries, fuel-injection pumps, carburettors, tappets, cylinder-head gaskets, timing, sparking plugs, bearings, pistons, lubrication and, of course, a list of the faults which might affect them.

I was also familiar with the usual faults which affected other parts of a motor vehicle, and the means of repairing or remedying most defects.

But a problem with a young man's BSA 250cc motorbike baffled Len Oakley. Len owned and ran Oakley's Garage at Gaitingsby, and he had supplied the bike when new to Brian Roe, a local seed and grain merchant; but there was a problem. When the bike reached 45 m.p.h., it developed a worrying noise which grew louder as the speed increased. It did not produce the noise at speeds below 45 m.p.h., but Brian had never exceeded 60 m.p.h. and so he did not know whether the noise stopped at any particular point. So far as he was concerned, the dreadful and unnatural noise was present at all speeds above 45 m.p.h., growing louder as the speed increased.

Not surprisingly, he had taken the bike

back to Oakley's Garage, where Len had examined it in detail to pronounce there was nothing wrong. When Brian had returned to collect it, Len had said, 'There's nowt wrong with it, Brian. I've checked everything, had the engine running flat out, revved it until the garage roof rattled, jacked the back end up to test the chain while the engine's running in gear, checked the bearings on both wheels, checked all nuts and bolts for tightness, checked the exhaust pipe, the crank case, the steering head and all dampers for slackness and any weakness, done the lot, in fact, and found nothing loose. Nothing rattling. I can't find a thing wrong with it.'

'Did you take it up the road?' asked Brian, not to be deterred by this result.

'No, no need to. Everything's as it should be.'

'Then I think you should take it out. Now. This minute. I'll wait here while you're gone and see to anybody who comes for petrol. Take it up to 45 m.p.h. and beyond, then you'll see what I mean. If you can't sort it out, it'll have to go back to the factory.'

Len, a small wiry individual who wore overalls both at home and at work, had no option and so he took the bike up to the high moor road where he was able to find a long straight stretch away from the restrictive hills and corners of the dale lanes. And the result was just as Brian had said. At 45 m.p.h. the weird noise developed, and as he accelerated up to 50 m.p.h. and then 60 m.p.h., the noise intensified. As the manual specified, he must not take it over 60 m.p.h. during its first five hundred miles. Somewhat alarmed, Len reduced speed and rode back to his garage well below the noise limit.

'So?' demanded Brian when Len had dismounted.

'Aye,' said Len. 'You're right. I see what you mean now. Damned if I know what it is! There's no shaking on the bike, no wheel wobbles, no shuddering when you brake or decelerate, steering's tight, gearbox is smooth, exhaust's not loose, chain's properly adjusted, mudguards tight and not flapping, nowt's loose ... it runs just as a new bike should.'

'Except it makes that weird noise,' grunted Brian. 'It'll have to go back, Len, under guarantee.'

'That all takes time, Brian, and a lot of paperwork. Look, have you thought about Matthew Taylor? He was a motorbike mechanic in the war, he's pretty good. Take it to him, and if he can't fix it, then we'll send it back to BSA.'

'Well, if you can't fettle it, and I can't, how can we expect a young insurance man to know what's wrong?'

'It's worth a try,' said Len. 'Deal direct with him, I don't want a cut.'

And so one Saturday morning Brian Roe, who was not a client of mine, arrived at our house on the BSA. He was in his early forties, a large and friendly man who ran a very successful business. In his overalls, he had ridden the few miles from his home well below the speed at which the noise appeared and when he arrived at our house I was down in the garage, working on my Coventry Eagle. I was not doing anything serious and demanding, merely a spot of lubrication and general cleaning to keep the bike in good condition. Evelyn told him where to find me and so I heard the arrival of the BSA, which sounded perfect, as a new bike should. He dismounted, put the bike on its stand and tapped on the garage door which was standing open.

'Hello, Matthew.'

'Oh, Brian. What can I do for you?' He wasn't one of my clients but I hoped he didn't want to talk about insurance at this very moment as my hands were covered with oil and dirt and I was dressed in my oiliest overalls.

'I've a problem with my bike, Matthew. Len Oakley reckons you might know what it is.'

'Electrical fault, is it? Not firing properly?

Timing, maybe? Missing now and again?'

I strode over to the machine and admired it; it was a new BSA 250cc which looked splendid in its green and cream livery, still bearing the stick-on label on the right-hand side of the petrol tank which warned the owner not to exceed 60 m.p.h. for the first five hundred miles. To run-in the engine meant the bike had to be treated gently during its early months.

'No, it goes very well, no problem starting it, bags of acceleration, comfortable to ride, easy to handle. It's nearly new so you'd expect all that, but there's a problem,' and he explained about the curious noise. After hearing his account, I must admit I had no idea what was causing the problem or what effect it might have on the machine, but I said I would take it for a run up the dale in the hope I could identify the cause and do something about it. (My own insurance covered me for riding motorcycles belonging to other people.) I said I would be about ten minutes so he said he was happy to wait in my garage.

Micklesfield Dale runs from the edge of the village, which is known as Dale End, and extends about four miles into the depths of the moors. The top of the dale is called Dale Head and the dale road is fairly level with a few bends, but virtually devoid of traffic apart from the occasional farm vehicle. I reckoned I could comfortably take the bike to Dale Head and back within ten minutes, and the nature of the road would allow me to experiment at various speeds. Climbing the steep hills which were a feature of Micklesfield meant I could not take the bike up to its problem speed until I reached the open road, but once I reached the church, with the dale extending some four miles beyond, I could give the bike its head.

Accelerating and flicking it through the gears with my toe until I was roaring away in top with the wind whistling through my hair, I watched the speedometer needle heading for the magic 45. And at 45 m.p.h. the noise began. With the wind whistling about my head, it was not easy to listen intently but when I closed the throttle just a fraction, the speed dropped below 45 and the noise stopped. I opened it up again and the noise reappeared, so I accelerated up to 50, then 55 and 60, with the level of noise rising from somewhere on the bike. It was a curious sound but very difficult to pinpoint due to the noise of the wind. And, of course, I couldn't take my eyes off the road at speed to search for the cause! The faster I went, however, the louder the hissing from the wind and even though the puzzling noise was sometimes scarcely audible above the hiss of the wind, I could always hear it.

One description might be that it sounded like a horse blowing noisily through its nostrils, or to some it might sound like hand-clapping which became faster and faster as the bike's speed increased. Others might have said it resembled one of those hand-operated rattles that spectators took to football matches except that the sound was not quite so hard as that made by wood upon wood. A similar noise might be made by running a piece of wood along the ridges of a wash board. I thought there was a definite hint of a metallic sound, so as I strained my ears and racked my brains, I brought the bike to a halt, dismounted, hoisted it on to its stand and began to examine it, inch by inch. Something was loose and rattling against a part of the bike – I thought that was beyond doubt. But what was loose? I couldn't find anything.

As I searched with the utmost care, it dawned on me that the machine itself had not vibrated or shuddered even when I reached 45 m.p.h. or higher although the noise did appear at that speed; the ride at higher speeds was as smooth as any at a lower speed which suggested that if some-thing was loose and banging on the frame, mudguards, gearbox or elsewhere, it would happen all the time to a lesser or larger degree. It wasn't doing that. The noise only happened at 45 m.p.h. or above. And above that speed, I'd had difficulty hearing the noise due to the wind. And the faster one drove, the louder the wind. I began to wonder if the noise was something to do with wind levels.

I decided to ride to the Dale Head and back again, testing the bike at various speeds. Throughout the short trip, the sound was ever-present in varying degrees of volume at 45 m.p.h. and above. I was prepared to admit I was baffled, particularly as the bike was performing as beautifully as any new one should. I was convinced there was nothing wrong with it, except the inexplicable noise.

I turned around at Dale Head and began my return journey to find things exactly as they had been on the outward run. I would have to tell Brian that Len Oakley had been right – there was nothing wrong with the bike. On that return journey, however, I maintained my investigation and then, as I was speeding down the dale at 60 m.p.h. listening to the strange noise and, probably due to my concentration on the problem, not watching the road ahead as I should have been, I was suddenly aware of a deep pothole directly ahead. Acting instinctively and not wishing to swerve violently in case I threw myself off, I rose to my feet.

With both feet firmly on the footrests, I stood up to ride out the bump ahead; it was a device often used by trials riders when crossing particularly rough ground. And as I stood up with my knees close to the petrol tank, rather as a jockey rides a horse, the strange noise stopped. I rattled across the pothole at 50 m.p.h., my bones not being jarred due to my riding position, then I sat down again. The noise resumed. I stood up again. The noise stopped. When I sat down with my knees further apart and slightly away from the edges of the tank, the noise started again. And then I knew what it was.

It was the sticky label which warned owners not to exceed 60 m.p.h. until the engine was run-in. With my right hand on the accelerator, I moved the bike up to 60 m.p.h. The rattling could be clearly heard; then I moved my left hand across the tank to cover the label. As my hand covered the label, the noise stopped. Then I tried doing the same with my right leg. As the noise was sounding, I eased my thigh tight against the tank to smother the label. And the noise stopped.

I could now return to Brian with a clear conscience! Before doing so, however, I eased the bike to a halt so that I could examine the label more carefully. Its leading edge was firmly stuck to the side of the petrol tank, but about half of it, the portion towards the rear, was loose. As the wind level rose, so that loose portion flapped rapidly against the side of the petrol tank to produce the weird noise. I rode home and found Brian waiting patiently in my garage. I dismounted, hauled the BSA on to its stand, and went across to him.

'I've found the problem,' I said. 'It's mighty serious, Brian, there's no wonder Len didn't want to tell you!'

His face fell a mile as he thought about having to return the bike to its makers for what might be a lengthy period, and then the smile on my face told him I was joking.

'I'm joking,' I said. 'I have found the problem, it's one you can cure yourself.'

And so I explained about the flapping sticky label, saying I had left it in position so that he could test it for himself. All he had to do, I told him, was either remove it completely, or make sure every bit of it was firmly stuck to the petrol tank.

'Can I go and try it?' he asked. 'I'll come back in a few minutes.'

'Of course,' and within seconds, he was riding up through Micklesfield, the sound of his bike echoing among the houses as he made for the church and then the dale. I continued to clean my Coventry Eagle until he returned with a big smile on his face.

'You wouldn't believe it, would you?' He looked so happy. 'I bet if I'd sent it back to BSA, they wouldn't have found it.'

'You've got a pothole up the dale to thank for it,' I laughed. 'But that's all, Brian, problem solved.'

'So what do I owe you?'

'Nothing,' I said. 'It was a bit of fun.'

'No, I must pay you, you've saved me hours of agonizing...'

'Is the bike insured?' I asked.

'Yes – ah, funny you should mention that. It is, but I'm thinking of changing my insurance company, not just for the bike. For my business as well.'

'Then come and see me after you've told Len about the bike,' I suggested.

'Rest assured I'll do that,' he promised.

Six

'Question: Could the other driver have done anything to avoid the accident?' 'Answer: 'He could have used the bus.'

From a claim form

One of my larger customers was a construction company known as Kidsons' Builders. I was fortunate in that Kidsons' were fully insured with the Premier, the business being very comprehensively covered for all risks when working on almost any site, but I also had Mr and Mrs Kidson's private insurance. That covered the private car, house and life insurance for both. In other words, Kidsons' was a very good account to have on my books.

With a busy office in Lexingthorpe, Kidsons' workmen and its vehicles in their distinctive green livery with yellow lettering could be seen on sites in most areas of Delverdale and even beyond in places like Guisborough and Whitby. The owner of the business, Albert Kidson, was a hard-working

185

man of vision, always finding locations for new houses, and always managing to keep his workforce busy. If they were not building new houses, they would be repairing old ones, or they might be constructing barns, swimming pools, stables or even something decorative like a garden folly or a flight of ornate front steps. They would repair roofs and cellars, walls and floors and would tackle anything from a castle to a cowshed. They'd even been known to repair a light-house roof and a storm-damaged pier. No job was too big or too small for Kidsons', and the firm had built several post-war council estates in the vicinity, hiring extra craftsmen and labourers for the task.

Kidsons' built private houses too, some on small estates, some in terraces and others detached and individually designed by architects. If anyone in the district wanted a reliable, good-quality builder, they first approached Albert Kidson and he never let anyone down.

Except his wife. She hated the family house he had so lovingly built.

I was aware of that because Lucy Kidson was the company secretary and ran Albert's office in Lexingthorpe. It was she with whom I dealt whenever a policy was due for re-newal or amendment, or whenever I had to collect the premiums. She paid the business premium each quarter by cheque, but preferred me to call in for it rather than post it because it meant she could ask me about any changes in the insurance world, and I could keep in touch with her business. It was a good workable arrangement because there were frequent amendments to Kidsons' parent policy due to the changing variety of work undertaken. Even though Albert had negotiated a very comprehensive umbrella policy for his company, its work and its staff, there were times when special provisions had to be considered, such as when his men repaired the lighthouse roof or fixed the storm damage to one of the piers at Whitby, or repointed some brickwork on a lofty viaduct. In most cases, the Premier waived any increase in premiums because such variable tasks were usually of a transitional nature, the Premier's only stipulation being that they were made aware of the nature of such work, and that the necessary safeguards were implemented.

Kidsons' spacious and airy office was in the grounds of Albert and Lucy's family home, albeit with a separate entrance so visitors did not invade their privacy. Albert had built the house in local stone especially for his wife, and had later added the office block, which included a beautiful suite for her. Without doubt, it was a splendid building, more like a large house than an office. There was a huge suite for Albert, even if most of his time was spent out on site, but it included a massive partners' desk and a large table to accommodate site plans. Adjoining his office was a small conference room in which he could entertain customers, planners, architects and others. Also in the block was a very light and airy foyer where a receptionist/shorthand-typist worked, a waiting room for visitors, a pleasant and surprisingly large and well-equipped kitchen facing south and washroom/toilet nearby. By the standards of other business offices in the locality, this was considered very imposing and most luxurious, and I must admit I enjoyed my visits because the receptionist, a bright blue-eyed blonde in her mid-twenties called Shirley, would always ensure I had a cup of tea or coffee and a plateful of chocolate biscuits as I waited.

Over the months, I grew to know Lucy much better; my first impression had been that she was very businesslike and humourless, a stern-looking woman in her mid-forties with spectacles and short dark hair drawn away from her face and held back with a ribbon. She was always smartly dressed too, in spite of working literally at the top of her own garden, and there is little doubt she contributed heavily towards the success of the business. As time went by, and as I would sit for a few minutes chatting to her while sipping my tea as she wrote out the cheque, I realized she was a very pleasant woman while being hard-working and efficient.

Nonetheless, I could imagine her not tolerating any slackness from either her own workmen or the business people with whom she was in regular contact.

Then one August she decided the entire office block needed decorating and repainting both inside and out, and so, while that work was under way, she and her receptionist moved temporarily into her private house. It was a secluded and comfortable four-bedroomed house called Wren's Nest. There was plenty of room in the big lounge for a couple of desks because most of the files and records could be retained in the office, being moved around as required by the decorators. It was a very short walk from the house to the office block. It was at the private house that I called to collect the premiums later that month. I was shown into the office-cum-lounge and given a chair while Shirley went into the kitchen to make the tea. There was the usual polite preliminary chatter as Lucy wrote the cheque and then I said, 'I like the house, it's spacious and you must enjoy those views across the dale.'

'I hate it!' she said almost vehemently. 'I can't wait to move.'

'But I thought it had been built especially for you?'

'It was, so Albert said, but I hate it, it's not at all to my liking. You need a woman to design a house, Matthew, you need the feminine knowledge of what's needed in a kitchen, where the equipment, sink, cooker, work surfaces, cupboards and shelves should be placed and which way the window should face, where the electric sockets need to be, the best place to put the broom cupboard, the bathroom design ... everything in fact to make housework easier and more efficient.'

'Well, I can't argue against that!'

'Men know nothing about building family houses, Matthew, nothing at all. If they worked in the house, domestic work I mean, they'd appreciate what was needed.'

'I'd have thought your husband would have employed an architect?'

'Not him! Whenever he's built council houses or small estates, architects have drawn the plans and supervised things during construction, but when Albert builds one of his own houses, either for me or for sale on spec, he designs it himself.'

'He's built others for you?' Somehow, I thought Kidsons' had always occupied the house on this site.

'Dozens,' she said wryly. 'Well, maybe not dozens, but quite a lot. More than a dozen, at least.'

'Good heavens!' I did not know how to respond to this. 'So where are they?'

'All over the place! Everywhere between here and Guisborough and even between here and Whitby. Big houses, little houses, a bungalow ... you name it, he's built it for me. There are Lucy houses all over the place, but none of them was right.'

'But the business is here, right here on this site!'

'That's no problem, Matthew. We could sell this house and keep that bit of land with the office on it. There's no need for the office to move as well as us, we've a separate entrance, and in some ways it would be nice for the office to be further away from our living quarters. I wouldn't mind that in the least. It's the house I don't like, not the office. I've no complaints about the office block, I like it.'

'You've told him? That you don't like the house?'

'I'm sick of telling him, Matthew, but he doesn't take the slightest bit of notice. He just goes off and builds another house for me, and then I say I don't like that one, he puts it on the market and starts another. I've tried asking him to let me have a go at designing one, or at least designing the kitchen, but he says he knows best, and claims he knows what he's doing because he's got years of experience behind him.'

'Now I know why this is called Wren's Nest!'

'That was Albert's idea. I've no idea why he chose that name.'

'The male wren builds lots of beautiful nests in the spring, to impress his mate. They are all over the place, in ivy, hedges, tree trunks, outbuildings and even the nests of other birds, but he doesn't complete them. He doesn't include the lining of soft materials, so it's not ready for occupation. His mate goes around and looks at the first one, then rejects it, and so he builds another. She keeps on rejecting them until she finds one she likes. That could be number eight or nine, and if she likes it, she will show her pleasure by lining it with feathers, hair and sheep's wool. Then they both move in.'

'So that's why he calls it Wren's Nest!' and I did not know whether she was pleased or annoyed. 'So is there any common or garden bird where the female builds her own nest?'

I aired a little of my rustic knowledge. 'In the robin's case, the female builds the nest, and similarly the female blackbird also does most of the work on their nest. I think in the blackbird's case, the male might help but it's only a very little. The female goldfinch is also the nest-builder.'

'I know all those birds when I see them!'

'I'm sure other females build the family nests but I can't bring them to mind at the moment. I think in many cases it's a joint operation, with male and female doing their bit.'

'Thanks, Matthew. You know, our office block is better designed than this house, but I must say he asked my advice before the plans were drawn. And he listened to me! I even helped him draw the plans! He'll do that for an office block but not our own house – men!' And she produced one of her enigmatic smiles which left me rather puzzled about her reaction to this snippet. Then Shirley returned with a tray of tea and biscuits, I was given the necessary cheque and for a few minutes we sat and chatted about nothing in particular, with neither me nor Lucy referring to house-building or nest-building. Then I left to continue my collecting around Lexingthorpe.

In the weeks which followed, I learned that Albert had also built some houses for Lucy before their marriage. They'd been constructed during their four years of courtship, the idea being they would move into their new home after the wedding, but she had rejected them all for various reasons. Then he had built the house they now occupied – this was in fact their wedding present to each other, being built some eight years ago, and because Lucy was expected to leave her parents' home upon being married, she was more or less committed to living at what became known as Wren's Nest. Because she disliked it, Albert had then produced more houses, all built while his men were busy with other properties nearby, but she had turned down every one. He had managed to sell them, so he had recouped his expenses.

It seemed nothing pleased Lucy, she'd rejected every one of his offerings before and after marriage, and so she was still living in Wren's Nest and still disliking it. I wondered whether her dislike of the house had resulted in them not having children but there might have been other reasons. I felt, as both were in their forties, they were still young enough to produce a family – but there was no time to waste.

Of course, this domestic saga was absolutely no concern of mine even if I did find it very intriguing and almost comical, although I must admit it did cross my mind that perhaps Lucy was impossible to please. Perhaps she found something wrong with every house because it was her nature to be ultra-critical? She might be wanting perfection while being unable to find it.

It must have been some consolation to her husband that she seemed pleased with the office block he had built – but of course, she was not living there and, more importantly, she had been involved in its design. I was not sure of the precise extent of her involvement, although, of course, Albert's men had actually done the construction. I must admit it was highly attractive and very functional, a model for others in the area, if they could afford it. Such splendid offices did not come cheap!

I thought little more of Kidsons' until my next visit to collect premiums, and this time Lucy said, 'Albert's in his office, Matthew, we were expecting you today. He'd like a word. I'll take you through. Shirley will bring your tea and biscuits in there.'

I was shown into Albert's impressive south-facing office with the huge desk in the middle and he waved me to a seat. 'You don't often find me in here, Matthew.' He grinned widely. 'I'm not an office man, give me an untouched site to work on any day!'

He was a jovial man with thinning brown hair, brown eyes and a healthy tanned face. I was surprised to find him wearing spectacles today but refrained from commenting – some men did wear them to read. We chatted about non-related matters to begin with, such as the state of Middlesbrough football team and whether the Yorkshire Cricket Club should accept players born outside the county. Then Shirley arrived with the tea, and poured it for us.

I steered the conversation towards business. 'Lucy said you wanted a chat?'

'I do, just a bit of advice really, or reassurance!' and he chuckled at his own joke. Shirley disappeared and closed the door, then he continued, 'Insurance, Matthew. You know, in the past, when we've done a peculiar sort of job, like that lighthouse, the piers and that viaduct? We've always contacted you to make sure our policy covered us for doing that sort of special job.'

'Yes, and the Premier respects that. It likes to be kept informed when things differ from the normal. It's just a precaution, but it means you remain covered no matter what goes wrong wherever you are working.'

'Right, so we're about to embark on another peculiar job and need to be sure we're covered for it. I think we will be fully covered, it's not that different from any other building job, but it's best to be certain.'

'Absolutely,' I said. 'So what is the job?'

'We're going to turn this office block into a private house. Now, that might not be as difficult as we think because I've always been one for having an eye to the future, so when

I built it, I made it strong enough to carry another storey and we designed the rooms so they could be easily converted.'

'Well, I must say this suite of offices is superb. But you'll be sorry to leave it, surely?'

'Well, I can do with less office space, speaking personally. As I said, I'm not an office man and Lucy reckons she'll be happier if this was our house. I mean, if you look at it carefully, it could be easily be turned into a house. I've been thinking about it, and I reckon I can easily convert this into a smashing two-storey dwelling house. It's a good site, the structure's sound, the design is in place, it just needs a bit of modification here and there ... I mean, Matthew, imagine this office as a lounge ... and that conference room as our dining room, then new bedrooms upstairs, and a bathroom, two mebbe, and indoor toilets, with a good big modern kitchen for Lucy ... it'll be a luxury house, Matthew, not a luxury office block!'

'Has Lucy put this idea to you?' I felt I must ask.

'She did, as a matter of fact. It was her birthday and I took her out for a slap-up meal, and she put the idea to me then, going on about robins' nests and wrens and so on. But she has some good ideas, Matthew, she designed this office block, you know. Almost single-handed. She has worked in other offices, mind, before she married me. I knew that, I could see she knew what she was doing.'

'I think it's a brilliant idea, Albert. You'll have the finest and most up-to-date house for miles around.'

'And that might get me some big fat contracts to build others, eh? You can't beat setting the standard, Matthew, if you want to create an impression on folks. So what I'm asking is if I need special insurance during that work?'

'You'll need planning permission, for a start!'

'I know I do, but will I need extra insurance?'

'Before we go into that,' I asked, 'you will still need an office while the work's under way, so where will you go during the alterations? You can't work in here while the builders are in. Obviously, you will need insurance if your work records, files, equipment and so on are used or stored elsewhere, even temporarily, and then moved to new offices.'

'Ah, well, they won't be going far. We're going to turn the house into offices. Lucy reckons it'll make good offices, with an upstairs and downstairs. I was always prepared to build an upstairs here, you see, for when we expanded, but we've measured up the house and it'll double the floor space of this office, so that's just what we need. So I need to transfer the house insurance to office insurance, and vice versa, remembering to cater for the work going on in between.'

'I can't see a problem,' I told him. 'All the Premier will need to know is what your plans are, and we can do that on a standard proposal form. It's not a particularly unusual building operation, it's not especially dangerous either, there are no abnormal risks. Even so, you'll need to have both premises fully covered during the transitional period. Just fill in that form and let me have it when you're ready.'

As we chatted afterwards he seemed very excited by the prospect. I realized Lucy had been very clever indeed. Albert had thought she was using her past knowledge and work experience to design an office block whereas, I felt sure, all the time she had secretly been drawing plans for her fine new house. And now, at last, she was going to get it. It was no surprise to learn it would be called Robin's Bower. Bower, of course, is an old word for an attractive dwelling or retreat, or even a nest-like shelter in a garden made from branches, ivy or vines. In addition, of course, bower also comes from the French *boudoir.*

A few months later when I called on my rounds, this time going into the lounge at Wren's Nest due to the energetic building work going on at the office block, I had my usual cup of tea and biscuits with Lucy.

'I'm impressed with your plans for the office block,' I told her. 'I think you'll love it when it's transformed into your house.'

'I know I will,' and she produced that very enigmatic smile.

Within my agency, Lucy Kidson was not the only wife who disliked her house. Martha Blythe also hated hers. She and her husband Geoff lived in No. 1 Lime Terrace at Baysthorpe, a former iron-ore-miner's cottage. It was stoutly built of local grey stone with a blue-tiled roof and was very like the other fifteen in the terrace.

The terrace was on Lime Mount, a steep hill on the road out to Gaitingsby, and from a distance the houses looked like a series of steps, each roof higher than the one below. The houses were on the roadside with the front doors opening on to the footpath which ran alongside. Each house had an enclosed backyard with an outside toilet and wash-house, plus a gate which led on to a back lane where some of the women dried their washing. Upstairs, all the houses had two rather small bedrooms but no bathroom while the ground floor boasted a small sitting room with a coal fire, an even smaller dining room and a kitchen with an adjoining pantry. The kitchen door opened into the backyard. The fire in the sitting room had a back boiler by which people could heat the domestic water, but if they wanted to bathe in luxury they had to carry the zinc-lined bath indoors from the wash-house where it hung on the wall, close all the curtains and keep family and visitors at bay whilst they went about their ablutions with the water cooling rapidly. Washing one's hair while sitting before the fire in a tin bath was never easy, consequently many families owned a large red rubber mat which had to be placed protectively on the rug or floor before the bath was used. Few had carpets in such cottages.

Martha, approaching thirty, disliked her house for several reasons. First, she was something of a snob, with her heart set upon a fine detached house in its own grounds; second, she enjoyed an active social life and liked to invite her best friends home for a meal, but it was hardly the sort of thing one could do in such a tiny house; third, her house was No. 1 in the terrace and therefore at the bottom of the hill with all the others looking down upon it.

She considered that this was highly symbolic, although another reason for her dislike was that when the new bus route had been put into operation, those heavily loaded vehicles heading for Gaitingsby always changed gear right outside her house, which caused ornaments to shake on the mantelpiece and windows to rattle. The noise of full buses groaning up the hill could drown conversation; Heaven knows what it did to the foundations.

Martha's husband, Geoff, was a completely different character. Thirty years old and a salesman for a lubrication company, selling grease, oil and associated products to small garages, he was completely unfazed by anyone with pretensions. He worked hard and was apparently very good at his job, and very knowledgeable about his products. Known to both his company and his customers as a highly reliable person, he enjoyed his work and was a popular character among the garage owners of Delverdale and beyond, and with the villagers amongst whom he lived. One thing he did not like, however, was gardening; consequently a cottage with no garden, and not even a postage-stamp-sized lawn, was Geoff's idea of bliss. He could usefully sweep the backyard from time to time, but he had no intention of spending his weekends cutting grass, digging holes, tending ever-demanding plants or dealing with weeds.

When I became acquainted with the pair because their house insurance and some life insurances were held with the Premier, there were no children of the marriage.

Martha, however, did not believe that wives should work – in her opinion, their mission was to support their husbands in all they did, and to help further their career with a view to becoming a business and social success long before retirement beckoned. Martha saw her future as being married to a highly successful businessman – just like her father. Her father had started life as a salesman for motor-vehicle tyres, inner tubes and valves before owning a chain of high-class dealerships selling cars at the quality end of the market. If her father could do that, then so could Geoff – which was why she had married him, and how she had met him.

He'd called at her father's early garages and believed she saw something of her father in the confident and intelligent young salesman. Geoff, however, having witnessed the problems that successful businessmen had to cope with, the responsibilities they had to endure and the hours they had to work, had decided, long ago, not to become ambitious. He was quite content living in his little house with enough money for his daily needs, and enough time to spend either going to the pub, going fishing, playing cricket or even hiking across the surrounding moors. No. 1 Lime Terrace suited him perfectly, not only because of its lack of a garden, but also because it was cheap to run and easy to maintain. There was the added factor that he actually spent very little time in the house – if he was not at work, he was out somewhere with his pals or down at the pub. In fact, he would have been quite content with a tiny rented property, with the landlord taking responsibility for things like repairs and maintenance, but at Martha's behest when they got married, he had bought the house.

Martha's father, anxious that she should not miss any chance to further her social aspirations, had helped them buy it and so it was the starting point of her dream of married bliss, social success and personal happiness. She and her family regarded it as a modest investment, the idea being to start married life there and quickly move to something bigger and better, and both she and her father had frequently suggested he should sell it. But with six or seven years without Geoff showing any inclination to better himself in any way, Martha had grown to hate their little terrace house. She hated all that it represented, particularly that it was at the bottom of the hill with all the others looking down on her. There was no room for expansion either, and as the years ticked by there is little doubt she felt trapped in No. 1. She would often drop hints to that effect when I called to collect her premiums. Then, after a particularly vociferous battle with the immovable and contented Geoff, she decided that if he wouldn't try to better himself, then she would do something dramatic which would persuade him to change his attitude.

The first thing was to move into a better house. And so she decided they should sell No. 1. After all, wasn't it her money which had enabled them to buy it in the first place? When they'd married, Geoff had had nothing – just like her father when he had married her mother – but her dad had worked and been adventurous and entrepreneurial until he was now a thriving businessman, owner of one of the biggest new-car dealerships in this part of Yorkshire.

There is little doubt that sales of private cars had soared since the end of the war but her father had had the vision to anticipate that and had seized the opportunity to better himself. She hoped Geoff wouldn't want to remain a lubrication salesman all his life ... surely, there was some spark of ambition deep within his body?

When I called to collect the premiums, Martha told me her news.

'We're putting the house on the market, Matthew. I felt it was time we moved to a bigger place and I've got my eye on a lovely old farmhouse at Freyerthorpe. Hollin Beck. It's on the market, as you might know, and I went for a look around it a couple of days ago. I think it would be ideal for us.'

'It's a very nice place.' I knew the house although its occupiers were not my clients. The house belonged to Freyerthorpe Estate and was currently occupied by an elderly farmer and his wife. 'Plenty of outbuildings and land, nice views.'

'Mr and Mrs Ellis are retiring to a cottage on the estate, so the farmhouse is being sold. The estate are merging the farmland with the adjoining spread so they'll be retaining most of the acreage although the house will keep about two acres and all the outbuildings. I like it, it's my sort of place.'

'So what does Geoff think about it?' was my next question.

'I haven't told him yet. I wanted to find another house before I told him I wanted to have everything ready to go with all his queries answered ... selling this place has been in my mind for a few months now, but we need to dispose of it before we can afford another. Dad will help us find the money, I'm sure, he's always been ambitious for me, but I didn't like to put No. 1 on the market before I'd found somewhere else and, of course, with Geoff's work travelling around Delverdale it doesn't really matter where we live.'

I wasn't sure how to react, nor did I have any idea how Geoff would take this. I felt he would be rather upset at her assumption that he'd blindly go along with her ideas, but he was such a laid-back individual he might possibly let her do as she wished, provided he could continue with his easy approach to life. I didn't envisage him as a landowner, and couldn't see him keeping horses or working the earth.

'Well, I hope it all works out,' was the only response I could muster.

'There'll be the insurance to consider,' she smiled. 'Obviously, with a bigger house and more buildings, and all that land, the premiums will rise and you'll need to be told about our removal date so you can make the changes immediately.'

'That's no problem. Just keep me informed and I'll see to it. If you decide to move your own belongings, or get a friend with a lorry to do it, then you'll need cover for the actual transfer from one property to the other, but if you hire a professional furniture-removal firm, they'll have the necessary insurance against breakages, loss, damage and so forth. Even so, I'd advise you to check that they are properly covered.'

The next time I called, there was a 'For Sale' sign outside No. 1. When I arrived to collect the premiums, Martha told me she had put in a bid for Hollin Beck and the estate were looking favourably upon her application.

If they could sell the property directly to her without the involvement of a commercial estate agent, then it would make things very simple indeed, and the price could be adjusted accordingly. And so Martha explained to me that, with the backing of her father, she had put in a bid and all that was needed now was for No. 1 to find a buyer. From that conversation, I assumed Geoff was in full agreement.

A couple of days later, I called at Danny Randall's garage in Micklesfield to buy some petrol for Betsy. As I eased to a halt beside the pump, I was in time to see Geoff Blythe driving away in his Ford. He gave a cheery wave but did not stop for a chat and then, as Danny filled up my tank, he said, 'That chap could sell sand to an Arab. They tell me his house is up for sale.'

'He and Martha have got their eyes on Hollin Beck Farm in Freyerthorpe,' I told him. 'It's a bigger place with more land. The estate are selling it, Martha told me.'

'He says their present house is haunted,' said Danny. 'That's why they're selling it.'

'Haunted?' I expressed genuine surprise at this news. 'I've not heard that tale!'

'According to Geoff, years ago a stage coach ran away down Lime Mount at Bays-thorpe and the horses couldn't hold it. It careered into the wall of Geoff's house and overturned, killing a passenger. They say it's been haunted ever since.'

I thought I knew most of the legends and folklore of Delverdale and district but had never come across this story.

'Did Geoff tell you that?'

'Aye, just now. He says his missus is terrified of ghosts, that's why they're selling up.'

'I thought it was just because she fancied a bigger place.'

'Mebbe that's what she's telling everybody, some folks don't like admitting they believe in ghosts,' suggested Danny. 'Not that I do, mind!'

'You could be right,' I admitted as I followed Danny into his office to sign for my petrol. 'But I've never heard that tale.'

In the days which followed, I was told this story several times. In a small community, like the villages of Delverdale, rumours are prone to spread very rapidly and the goings-on in one village soon become known to the neighbouring communities. Even though the lines of communication were not very modern and certainly not very rapid, old-fashioned gossip seemed to spread like a moor fire driven by wind through dry heather, and once the story of the haunting of No. 1 Lime Terrace was aired it seemed to take on a life of its own. Long before I had chance to discuss it with either Martha or Geoff, I came across it in several village shops, post offices and pubs, including those at Baysthorpe. What puzzled me was why I had not heard it before; unless, of course, it was the unexpected sale of the house which had resurrected a long-dormant tale?

Not long afterwards, I was collecting in the hamlet of Arnoldtoft, where one of my clients was a retired headmaster, Bill Cass. He held a whole-life policy with the Premier. He had been the head of Gaitingsby Primary School, retiring about five years earlier, and he was regarded as an authority on the history and lore of Delverdale. We always had a long chat when I called, his wife producing a cup of tea and some cakes, and I knew Bill welcomed my visits.

He loved telling me about local history and folklore, so this call therefore presented the ideal opportunity to ask about the reported haunting.

'It's supposed to have started with a stage coach,' I added after mentioning the tale. 'The story is that it ran away down Lime Mount and crashed, killing a passenger. I've no dates or names.'

'It sounds like a load of rubbish to me, Matthew.' He chuckled. 'I think I know all the ghost stories from this part of the world, and I've never come across that one. And I've not read about any reports of a runaway coach on that hill.'

As if to satisfy his own curiosity, he went to his bookshelves and took down one or two local reference books, skimming through the indexes to see if there was any mention of the incident, but there wasn't.

'Sorry,' he said. 'I can't help you on that one. Is it important?'

'No,' and I told him how the story had arisen, saying that the Blythes were hoping to buy Hollin Beck farmhouse. 'I'm just curious about it.'

'Well, if I come across the yarn during my researches, I'll let you know, but in my view, it sounds like someone's overactive imagination.'

When I popped into the Fox and Hounds at Baysthorpe one lunchtime to buy a pickled egg and a pork pie for my lunch, I overheard a young couple chatting at the far end of the bar. They were discussing No. 1 Lime Terrace and had obviously been to examine it, both inside and out. I heard the woman say, 'It's quite nice, just right for us, but I don't like those stories about that ghost. I wouldn't want a house that's haunted.'

'There's no such thing as ghosts!' laughed her companion. 'It'll be just a tale!'

'Even so, there must be something behind the story for that sort of tale to be told. I think I'd rather give this one a miss, Alan, let's go and look at that one in Lexing-thorpe.'

I was well aware that once a rumour began to circulate it could rapidly establish itself as a fact, whereupon it became impossible to deny it, and I recalled Danny Randall's reference to it. He'd told me that Geoff himself had told him the story – so was Geoff making up the entire yarn? And furthermore, he'd told Danny that Martha was frightened of ghosts. So why fabricate that tale about his own house? Unless he wanted to terrify people into not buying it ... so was this his cunning way of making sure no one wanted to buy his cottage? It was widely known he did not want to move, that he was quite content in his small home and that he had no wish to become a slave to a garden or bigger premises. If no one wanted to buy No. 1 Lime Terrace, he and Martha would be unable to purchase Hollin Beck Farm.

There was no doubt the rumour was circulating widely in Delverdale, which was not surprising if it had been instigated by a salesman capable of selling sand to the Arabs, and it appeared to have been effective because no one wanted to buy No. 1 Lime Terrace. And then it was my day for collecting premiums in Baysthorpe, with Martha being on my list of calls. I made a mental pact not to refer either to the sale of the house or to ghosts because, I told myself, it was nothing to do with me.

During that day, with several clients wanting to discuss possible new business, I found myself running slightly behind time. Unlike farms where I was expected to join the meal if I arrived around dinner time, I did not like calling at village houses over the midday meal-break period but on this occasion thought I just had time to call on Martha before heading for the Fox and Hounds for my pickled egg, pork pie and glass of orange squash. Although I loved a pint of bitter, I knew its smell would linger on my breath for some time afterwards, and that was not very considerate towards my clients.

In such cases, I settled for a glass of orange squash with my brief meal. However, I just had time to call on Martha before my break. When I arrived, I was surprised to see

Geoff's car parked outside, although I knew that when he was working in the locality he would sometimes pop home for his midday meal. I knocked and was admitted to the small sitting room.

'Oh,' said Martha. 'It's you, Matthew. I thought it was Mr and Mrs Kelly.'

'Kelly?'

'Yes, they want to see the house, the estate agent rang about an hour ago. It's very handy them coming now, with Geoff being here too.'

'Oh right, I'll get out of your way and won't detain you. I can call back when they've gone, it's just the monthly premiums...'

'No, it's no problem, Matthew, I'd rather pay and get it finished. Wait there, I'll get your money,' she said, leaving me to go into the kitchen to find her purse and premium-receipt book.

And the moment she left, there was a knock on the door and this time I heard Geoff shout from upstairs, 'I'll get it, Martha, you see to Matthew.'

As I waited in the sitting room, I heard voices at the front door and then Geoff escorted his visitors through the passage directly into the kitchen. I could hear loud chatter, most of it from Geoff, but did not discern the words because I was not eavesdropping, but then Martha arrived with the premiums in cash. It was the correct amount and I accepted it, signing her receipt book with the amount and date. As I was about to take my leave, Geoff arrived with a middle-aged man and woman in tow.

'Ah, this is Mr Taylor, Matthew, our man from the Premier. If you buy the house, you might want to discuss insurance with him. Matthew, meet Mr and Mrs Kelly, looking around the house, possibly with a view to purchasing.'

'Well, I mustn't get in your way now.' I smiled at everyone and prepared to leave. 'I hope you like the house.'

'Do you insure haunted houses?' Mr Kelly suddenly asked.

'I must admit I've never had that question posed before but I am sure our Head Office would consider it,' I answered diplomatically. 'But I doubt if a ghost would add anything to the cost of the premiums!'

'Ghosts?' asked Martha. 'Why do you ask that?'

'Well, isn't this house supposed to be haunted? They said so in the pub just up the road, and...'

'Haunted?' cried Martha. 'I've never heard that before! Geoff? Have you heard that?'

'He's just told us all about it,' said Mrs Kelly. 'A very honest man, I must say, not hiding the dark secrets of the house.'

'Geoff, have you been concealing this from me? You know I'm terrified of ghosts...'

'I don't believe in them!' I could see Geoff was now in something of a quandary. 'I don't believe a word of it ... ghosts! We've never seen one in here, have we, darling?'

'So what is the story?' asked Mr Kelly, clearly keen to hear the tale in full.

'Have you heard it, Matthew?' Geoff looked at me as if to excuse himself from having to explain it before his wife.

'Yes, but I don't believe it and think it's just a local rumour,' I began, and then related the tale of the coach accident, alleged to have occurred just outside the front door. The Kellys listened with obvious concentration and I concluded by saying there was no evidence of the coach crash or the death, and I said I thought the whole story was just a local tale. I added that such tales often circulated without any foundation.

'A lack of written evidence does not mean the story should be ignored,' said Mr Kelly in all seriousness. 'Many of the best ghost stories are not in any historic records and have no historic foundation, yet they have persisted down the centuries. Tales told down the years by word of mouth invariably become distorted in such a way that they are unrecognizable from the original, but they

216

shouldn't be dismissed.'

His wife added, 'Research can often reveal the true foundation of a ghost story even if repeated retelling has altered it almost beyond recognition. I find this quite fascinating.'

'Look,' Martha said, 'if this house is haunted, you should have told me, Geoff. I don't want to live here any longer, I'll not sleep at night now...'

'And we would like to buy it,' said Mr Kelly. 'Psychic research is our main interest in life and we've always wanted to buy an affordable house with a reputed ghost, so that we can study it at our leisure ... so many haunted houses are manors or castles, way beyond our modest means. So this is just what we want, quite unbelievable. We are happy to make an offer.'

'You are?' Geoff sounded deflated. 'But I would have thought rumours of a ghost would put you off!'

'We are sure it has put off a lot of potential buyers, Mr Blythe, but not us. So shall we go ahead? Show us around, then I will speak to our solicitors and your estate agent, and take the matter from there.'

'Look, I must leave you.' I managed to make my final farewell. 'I'll be in touch later, whoever is living here...'

And so it was that Geoff Blythe's scheme –

for I was sure it was his cunning plan all along – had backfired; in pretending that No. 1 was haunted, he had found a pair of keen ghost-hunting buyers and they moved in eight weeks later. Martha and Geoff moved into Hollin Beck farmhouse at Freyerthorpe, and I dealt with the transfer of their insurance.

It would have been a few weeks afterwards when I again visited Bill Cass at Arnoldtoft. I told him the outcome of the haunted cottage tale and he smiled. 'When you'd gone, Matthew, I searched my old books but the story of the crashed stage coach does not appear in any of them. I think it is merely a figment of someone's imagination. But did you know there used to be a monastery on that site in Baysthorpe? It was destroyed by the Danes in the seventh century or thereabouts, so nothing remains and in fact those cottages in Lime Terrace were built of stones from the derelict monastery and its church. But I've had no reports of hauntings there!'

'Thanks, Bill. Like you, I think the ghost is the figment of someone's very fertile imagination.'

'Then that settles it. But when you told me that tale last time, you said the couple were going to live at Hollin Beck Farm? In the old farmhouse?'

'That's right, it was sold off by the estate.'

'In the early eighteen hundreds, when they were extending the outbuildings, the excavations turned up a skeleton in one of the outer walls. It dated back centuries, to when living creatures were walled up in the belief it ensured a long life and security for the building. This was the remains of a young girl, aged about eight ... and there is a report that Hollin Beck is haunted by that girl...'

'I don't think I'm going to tell Martha or Geoff!' I said, thinking that if Martha came across that tale, she would face a dreadful dilemma. Her dream house – haunted?

When I called at No. 1 Lime Terrace to collect Mrs Kelly's first premiums, I found her in a very happy mood.

'You remember that story of the ghostly coach passenger? Well, Mr Taylor, there is certainly a presence in this house, in the back bedroom. I can sense it ... we both can. We are making more enquiries and although we can't find anything about the coach story, there used to be a monastery in this site, centuries ago, and my husband swears he saw a monk's outline in the early hours of one morning ... we are so delighted, Mr Taylor, so delighted. Our very own ghost!'

'It is an honest ghost, that let me tell you,' I said, dredging up some of my school knowledge from *Hamlet*.

'Aren't they all?' countered Mrs Kelly.

219

Seven

'I was on my way to see the doctor. I was experiencing rear-end trouble when my universal joint gave way, causing me to have an accident.'

From a claim form

Once every three months or so, Montgomery Wilkins liked to pay an official visit, during which he accompanied me on my rounds. He did come at other times, sometimes for just half a day, and I know he found pleasure in joining me on Wednesdays at the market outside the Unicorn Inn. In his role as District Ordinary Branch Sales Manager – Life, it was his job to ensure I was doing my utmost to generate new business, partially from existing clients but also from new ones. The former entailed some sales patter about our new products whilst collecting premiums from people I knew quite well and whose needs I understood, but the latter was more difficult. It meant knocking on the doors of those who were not my clients, and I must admit I did not enjoy that part of my job. I never considered myself to be a high-pressure salesman, but in any case it would not work with the people of the moors. They might be persuaded that some insurances were right for their particular needs, but any attempt to bulldoze them into something alien to their requirements would simply not work. In any case, I thought it a very intrusive means of obtaining new business, preferring to let people approach me if they were interested, but Mr Wilkins appeared hardened to it. He thought he had a duty to inform such people that he could help them in ways they had never even contemplated.

Whenever he rang to say he was proposing to join me, therefore, he expected me to produce a full day's itinerary during which we would visit one or two selected villages, paying close attention to existing clients but also visiting others in the hope of persuading them to take out a Premier policy of some kind. Even if I did not relish calling on people unannounced, it seemed he loved it and regarded it as an interesting and challenging part of his work.

Mr Wilkins was a small man who wore a neat sports jacket, cavalry twill trousers and brightly polished brown shoes with pointed toes. His trade mark, however, was his black beret which he never seemed to remove, even inside clients' houses, and I had discovered that he wore it in honour of Field Marshal Montgomery, the famous wartime leader whose surname he had, by chance, been given as a forename. From Birmingham, and therefore totally unaccustomed to country ways, he had transferred to Scarborough where the Premier's District Office was located. His transfer had been at his own request due to the ill-health of his wife, and fortunately for both there had been a vacancy. I had since learned that the move to the coast had been of immense benefit to Mrs Wilkins, because her health had improved immeasurably. For Montgomery too; his new role had opened up an entirely different world because he had neither been to the North Riding of Yorkshire nor to any other part of the county. Since his arrival, he had discovered just how beautiful and bracing the coast could be, and how magnificent were the moors and dales.

When he rang one morning in May, therefore, I suggested we ventured to two of the furthest outlying villages within my Delverdale agency.

It meant a long drive across the wilds of the moors in the upper reaches of Delverdale but I knew he would take pleasure in seeing something of the countryside. He might even begin to appreciate the difficulties I could face in the depths of winter when the snow was six feet deep or the rivers were in flood – but for that kind of experience, he'd have to join me in the depths of winter. Many townspeople had no idea of the challenges presented by the north and east Yorkshire terrain, even in good weather.

In May, however, the countryside was at its best with the trees in new leaf and blossom along the hedgerows, in the woodlands and around the gardens. It was a time of great renewal with plants growing at a remarkable pace; it was indeed a wonderful time to be working in the countryside and from Mr Wilkins' earlier remarks I do know he appreciated the splendour of the landscape through which we travelled. He had often commented on the air-filling sound of birdsong and found it difficult to accept that newborn animals such as lambs and rabbits frolicked along the verges of the open roads. In his city life, animals were either confined or kept on leads – in towns, you didn't expect to encounter a ewe and her lambs in the middle of the road or pottering down the street.

Here on the North York moors such a sight was common, for the sheep ran unconfined among the heather, although some were kept in fields in the dales. In bad weather, flocks would descend from the moors to take shelter in the villages, but they were not always welcomed. An open garden gate or low wall was great temptation to a flock of hungry sheep. They could clear a vegetable patch or flower garden in minutes! One piece of local lore was that the sheep were good weather forecasters – they would arrive in the villages en masse ahead of the bad weather.

Those on the open moors at any time of year were always at risk from speeding motor vehicles, something the insurance companies were keeping under close observation. I think that is why Mr Wilkins found it so curious that they should run free in this way, but they had done so for centuries, albeit in times when traffic was moving neither so rapidly nor in such a quantity. The death of these valuable animals, however, and the damage such accidents caused to motor vehicles (even with injuries to humans at times), was costing the insurers a considerable amount of money, and there was even talk of fencing in some moorland roads. That is how his mind worked. He saw most things from the perspective of an insurance executive.

His only world seemed to be one of insurance and his conversation was littered with stories of his exploits in Birmingham. He talked of his attempts to persuade people to take out whole-life or endowment policies, his worries about young owners of motor vehicles not being adequately covered and his belief that so many property owners did not update their policies to take account of large and expensive new purchases. He meant things like three-piece suites or expensive fashionable new items like television sets or even valuable antiques, jewellery and paintings. In addition to that, the post-war trend of modernizing the household was one of his pet themes, and he felt that peacetime would produce a marked effect on the wealth of ordinary people. In turn, that would change the kind of furnishings and equipment they would introduce to their homes, all potential markets for a good insurance man.

On one of his visits, he had ruminated on the future. 'I can foresee the time every house will have a refrigerator, Mr Taylor, and if you have a refrigerator, you will fill it with food which will last a considerable time. Now imagine a power cut, Mr Taylor, with the electricity off for a while. What will be the cost of all the ruined food, I ask you? If we can persuade people to take out one of our updated house-and-contents policies, which now include, at no extra cost, the loss of the load within a refrigerator, then we shall have achieved something worthwhile.'

'Not many people on these moors have refrigerators,' I told him. 'In fact, Mr Wilkins, there are many houses without any kind of electricity supply, particularly isolated farms and cottages on the moors and on the outskirts of villages. There's no way they could operate one of those domestic refrigerators.'

'But in Birmingham lots of ordinary people are already buying them...'

'With all due respect, this is not Birmingham, Mr Wilkins. Refrigerators out here are a rarity. Farms have milk coolers in their dairies but they are operated by cold water and don't need electricity. You will find huge walk-in fridges in butchers' shops if they have electricity installed, and you might even get one in a grocer's, but rarely in private houses. The big country estates still use ice-houses to preserve their game and the smaller places have pantries with cold shelves made of stone. Some even use boxes kept at the bottom of rivers and ponds.'

'But times are changing, Mr Taylor, times are changing.'

'You'll find these people take a long time to adapt to change. Even now, ordinary householders copy their parents and grandparents. They preserve their food by bottling fruit or making jam, curing ham or smoking bacon, baking bread and cakes and buns, putting potatoes in so-called pies out in the fields, pickling onions and making cheese from milk, and you can buy tins of dried milk and dried eggs, and tins of all sorts of other things from beans to peas via corned beef ... keeping food here in the countryside has never been a problem. Most of it is eaten too quickly anyway.'

'I appreciate all that, but household refrigerators are on their way in, Mr Taylor, mark my words. The manufacturers are now capable of making them small enough and cheap enough for even a very modest private house and soon they'll be as common in our houses as meat mincers. Remember that when we are trying to sell a house contents policy. Such cover is being built into our new policies, at no extra charge, so we must make the householders aware of future trends. Having that kind of foresight is a sales bonus, Mr Taylor – we, the Premier that is, are ahead of the trend, Mr Taylor, we are working for the future.'

'But if people don't have refrigerators, there's no point in trying to sell them insurance which specifically includes that kind of cover, is there?'

'It's a case of planning ahead, Mr Taylor. If we can sell policies which include risks likely to occur in the future – the very near future, in my opinion – then surely that is to our credit? And besides, one cannot afford to let food go rotten, it is very wasteful.'

'I think you'll find the farmers and country folk out here will think it cheaper to use old food to feed the pigs and hens. They won't turn their noses up if food goes off and smells a bit! Nothing's wasted, Mr Wilkins, and I'd guess that giving it to the animals is cheaper than insuring it. And if we tell clients that additional cover is built in to the policy, they might not agree. They don't get that kind of cover for nowt! They'll still be paying for it one way or another. That's the logic they'll use.'

'Well, premiums are almost sure to rise with the passage of time, that's perfectly sensible and reasonable, but in this case it's also a question of insuring the equipment itself against damage, Mr Taylor, not just its contents. What I am hoping to do – and hoping to persuade our agents to do – is prepare the way, try to persuade people to think ahead, to be ready for modernization, to accept change, to welcome it into their lives in the smoothest possible way. Our actuaries have been working hard on producing attractive new policies aimed at the modern domestic market. It's going to provide the biggest growth industry – they're even talking of machines that will wash the dinner pots! Can you believe that? All we need now is for our clients to be made aware of the way things are moving, we need to get them thinking ahead and preparing for better times.'

We had conducted that kind of conversation on a previous visit but now that Mr Wilkins was due again, I could almost guarantee that his theme was again going to be refrigerators.

I knew he believed modern household-protection policies should be all-embracing, and that they should automatically include refrigerators if and when they were installed in anyone's homes, but to treat that as a sales point would not convince many of my clients. Hard-headed Yorkshire farmers and country folk would not believe an organization like the Premier would give them summat for nowt. That is why I wanted to take him to the more remote part of my agency! I wanted him to confront some fairly stubborn Yorkshire folk with his ideas. I must admit I wondered how he would coax anyone in these moors, especially those without electricity, to even consider refrigerators when thinking of their household policies. I felt he would not have much success, for I had some real characters in mind. I would persuade him to talk to them – but I knew he would enjoy the challenge.

When he arrived in his little dark grey

Standard 10 car, he declined to come in for a cup of tea, reminding me he never drank stimulants and adding he felt we should not waste any more time before heading out to meet our customers. He didn't even come in to admire my new house and office, and so I joined him in his car. The fact we were using his transport meant Evelyn could make good use of Betsy and I know she had planned to take her sister, Maureen, out to Whitby for the day, as a thank-you for looking after Paul so many times. She would often find an opportunity to do that and Maureen enjoyed the outings.

'So, Mr Taylor, where are we heading today?'

'I thought we could visit Walstone and Ingledale, I'm due to collect at both villages today, and both are on the northern edge of my agency.'

'Close together, are they?'

'A couple of miles apart,' I said. 'Separated by a huge chunk of moorland.'

'All right, then, show me the way.'

I took him along the floor of Delverdale, with the road running alongside the route of the River Delver and passing through Gaitingsby, Freyerthorpe End, Arnoldtoft, Baysthorpe and Lexingthorpe. It was after leaving Baysthorpe and Lexingthorpe that we began to climb out of Delverdale and over the heather-clad hills into Sutherdale. His little car coped admirably with the steep inclines as we moved from a leafy valley up to a bleak moorland with miles of unbroken heather and little else. There were no trees on these heights and no stone walls, no barns and no houses, nothing but the call of the grouse and the sigh of the ever-present wind as it moved among the heather. Those heights provided endless views across the moors and dales which intersected them, and, as he praised the freedom this represented while wondering how on earth people made a living from such desolation, we crossed the heights before descending into Sutherdale.

The River Suther, only five or six miles long, was a small tributary of the River Delver, Sutherdale being both the name of the dale through which it flowed and the village which was tucked into moors at its head. Lower down Sutherdale, however, were Walstone and Ingledale, Ingledale being the larger community with a village hall, shop, post office and two inns, the Moorcock and the Miners' Arms. The latter was a reminder of this village's former role as an ironstone-mining centre; that industry had ceased before the outbreak of the First World War.

'We can park outside the village hall.' I

pointed to the brick building as we descended into Ingledale. 'A lot of my clients are within walking distance of there.'

'Don't forget we need to approach potential new clients,' he reminded me. 'When dealing with existing clients, most of your time is spent collecting premiums or effecting renewals. Such regular clients are not really interested in additional policies. From our point of view that does not generate new business, Mr Taylor, and without new business, no insurance company can flourish. We must keep pressing ahead by cultivating fresh clients, by making the opening moves.'

'Yes, I understand that, but I must do my collecting today, I am expected, the money will be ready and waiting.'

'That shouldn't take long, should it? Am I right in thinking most of your premiums will be ready and waiting on window ledges, in outside toilets, sheds, greenhouses and even on doorsteps?' and there was a twinkle in his eye as he reminded me of the custom of these moors. That was something he had never encountered in Birmingham. Anything left outside and unattended there would be stolen.

'Yes, it's just a case of picking it up and noting it's been paid.'

'So why don't I attempt a little canvassing of new clients while you are picking up that loose change? Then you can join me while I am at work and we'll see what progress I make. You might learn something from my expertise and experience, Mr Taylor.'

'Yes, that seems a good idea. Fine.'

'So, is the shop one of your clients?'

From our position on the village hall car park, Wilkins could see the shop on the corner of the hill we had recently descended; it stood beside a small crossroads and was brick-built with a large window full of assorted goods ranging from pans to potatoes. As the only shop for miles around, it stocked almost anything anyone might require in their daily life, from new shoes to tins of fruit, from medicines to make-up, from spades and shovels to pins and needles, pans and pots, bicycle tyres and gardening tools and even baby clothes and shotguns, along with the necessary cartridges.

'No,' I admitted as I prepared to issue him with his first challenge. I guessed he would find it irresistible. 'She is insured but not with the Premier. It's a family shop, it's been in Beryl Potter's family for generations. She's with Moonstone.'

'I'll bet Moonstone Insurance isn't up to date with the fast-moving developments in domestic-refrigeration industry,' he muttered. 'Right, Mr Taylor, I suggest you go and collect your dues while I will begin to soften up this shopkeeper with a view to weaning her off Moonstone. Then you can come and join me.'

I did not tell him I never set about poaching clients from other companies, although if someone approached me when they were dissatisfied with their current insurer, then of course I would accept their business. But Beryl Potter's mother and grandmother had been with Moonstone for as long as anyone could remember and I knew Beryl would never contemplate a change. I did not warn him that Beryl would never entertain him or his ideas – I was interested to see how his worldly ways would impress her. Others had tried; I knew better than even think about trying.

As I set about visiting my clients and collecting their premiums, he disappeared into the shop armed with a briefcase full of leaflets. It took me only a few minutes to collect those premiums left out for me by people living near the village centre, and when I finished I headed back towards the shop. I wanted to hear him in action but Mr Wilkins was already standing outside with a dazed look on his face.

'Success?' I asked as I approached him.

'Mr Taylor, I have never heard such language in my life, not even from soldiers in the trenches. I daren't tell you where she told me to stuff my domestic-refrigeration policy. Then in no uncertain terms, aided by a good deal of Anglo-Saxon references to our human-reproduction capabilities, she advised me to get back to where I had come from.'

'I take it she wasn't interested?'

'You might have warned me!'

'You'd have still wanted to talk to her, you'd have considered her a genuine challenge, Mr Wilkins.'

He regarded me for a long moment and then his face broke into a smile. 'Yes, you're right. I would have ignored your advice. But I shall return. That woman is definitely a challenge and I do not give up easily. Another time, perhaps. Make sure you bring me back here on one of our future forays. So what's next on our agenda?'

'I have more premiums to collect, but I want to make a call at a farm on the outskirts,' I told him. 'There's the monthly premium to collect there, and policy is due for renewal soon.'

'Ripe for canvassing, you think?'

'You'll get a better reception than Beryl gave you. Their existing policies are for the farm machinery and the couple's private car, both needing renewal, so I'll have to set things in motion. But the couple have no household insurance. They might be another

235

challenge for you, but they won't swear like Beryl!'

'Can you guarantee that?'

'I can't guarantee anything, but I think you'll like meeting them. They're a decent couple, Mr and Mrs Cracknell, Don and Betty, and the farm is called West Gill, it's about a mile along the Walstone road.'

West Gill was not on the heights but nestled in a fold within the lower hills which surrounded the farm. It was close to the road with many of its buildings surrounded by deciduous trees, while the River Suther flowed through its fields, lines of alders marking its winding route. Even though it was not exposed to the fierce weather of the moorland heights, the farm was constructed from large blocks of local stone and looked stout enough to survive any kind of climatic conditions. The age of the farmhouse was uncertain but it was known that a house had occupied this site in the early years of the seventeenth century; parts of West Gill had been dated to that period although some of the outbuildings were modern, being built especially to accommodate the Cracknells' amazing assortment of farm machinery. They did not use it all on their land but hired it to others, much of their business being during harvest time. There was a good market in hiring expensive and specialized machinery to farmers who could not afford the heavy capital outlay to buy their own.

We drove out to West Gill and I directed Mr Wilkins into the farmyard and towards the house where he eased to a halt outside the back door. It was standing open and the yard was full of hens, ducks, dogs, cats and even lambs. Fortunately, the yard had a solid base of large cobblestones so we were not plodding through mud as we made for the door. I led the way, reached the doorway and shouted, 'Hello, Betty. It's Matthew Taylor.' I knew the huge farm kitchen overlooked the yard and she would have probably observed or heard our arrival.

'Come in, Matthew, the door's open,' came the hearty response.

'I've a colleague with me,' I called as I advanced into the house. 'Mr Wilkins, from our District Office.'

'He's very welcome and the kettle's on,' and so I led the way along the passage where we turned left into the kitchen. Its picture-style window overlooked the yard and in the middle was a plain wooden table, large enough to seat a dozen people. Several cured hams and sides of bacon hung from hooks in the beamed ceiling, and a large oil lamp with an onion-shaped frosted glass dominated the centre of the room. Other oil lamps occupied places on the mantelpiece, shelves and window ledge, while other shelves were heavy with bottled fruit and jam.Betty, a jolly rather plump woman in her fifties, was baking on a work surface near the fireplace; a fire was blazing and I knew she would be using the fireside oven.

'Mr Wilkins, this is Betty Cracknell. Betty, Mr Wilkins.'

After smiling her welcome for him, she said, 'Our Don's down the fields, Mr Wilkins, but it's 'lowance time so he'll be in shortly.'

'Lowance was the local name for allowance, which was a snack enjoyed during the morning break. Many of these farmers started work at dawn, albeit after a substantial breakfast, but by mid-morning they were usually ready for something extra to eat and drink. They needed a lot of food to ensure they retained enough energy for their long, hard work, hence the 'lowance. In the case of farm labourers, the 'lowance was given to them by their employer, without any charge. That was probably the source of its name – employers of all kinds usually gave their workers some kind of allowance.

After we had chatted about weather, always an important topic for farmers, she asked Mr Wilkins how far he had come this morning. As he explained about his transfer to the office in Scarborough, she busied herself making a large pot of tea and putting scones, butter and jam on to plates, along with some fruit cake and rock buns. I was familiar enough with her routine to take them from the work surface and place them on the table with a setting for Don ready for when he arrived, then I invited Mr Wilkins to be seated. I knew he would not drink the tea, although he would accept a glass of water.

Then I heard Don. There was a loud clumping of feet in the passage outside the kitchen as he kicked off his Wellingtons and replaced them with bedroom slippers before entering. He was a large man, at least six feet five inches tall, with a mop of black hair and dark eyebrows on a face that was almost the colour of stained oak, a result of working out of doors all his life. He wore a pair of overalls and a thick shirt with the sleeves rolled up.

As he walked into the kitchen, a pair of collies followed and, without a word from anyone, went and lay down in front of the fire.

'Now then, Matthew,' he grinned amiably. 'Come to take my hard-earned money off me, have you?'

'The normal routine,' I said. 'But your policy's nearly due for renewal.'

'Ah hadn't forgotten. So aye, we'll go ahead as usual wi' that. We need yon kind of comprehensive cover, wi' all sorts of folks getting their 'ands on my machinery. They don't take as much care of things as Ah do.'

Then Mr Wilkins decided to join the conversation.

'Have you thought about extending your cover, Mr Cracknell?'

'Extending it? For what?'

'The house and its contents. I am always keen to remind potential clients of the risks to a house and its contents, everything from fire to flood, theft, burglary and damage, malicious or otherwise ... you need to consider all risks, Mr Cracknell.'

'This 'ouse 'as been standing 'ere since Oliver Cromwell was a lad, and it's still 'ere, Mr Wilkins, without any fires and floods and thieves or what-'ave-you. Ah can't see any sudden need to be insured, it's not like my machinery, is it? That's used by all sorts o' folks, friends and strangers alike, so Ah need to insure that if they come over 'eavy-'anded or a bit careless in their driving, but this 'ouse is for t'family, as it allus has been. And our family looks after things, so why would Ah need insurance?'

'Well, it's in case something unexpected happens, something that might damage or destroy something valuable...'

'We've nowt valuable in 'ere, Mr Wilkins. You can't say furniture and clothes are valuable, not like machinery. That's valuable because it makes money for me.'

'But suppose a fire broke out and destroyed your entire wardrobe.'

'No problem, Ah've clothes in every bedroom, all been 'anded down from father to son ... Ah've enough suits and jackets to kit out an army, Mr Wilkins, and make no mistake about it, there'll be no accidental fires in this place.'

'But you can't be sure of that, you do have a coal fire, it's burning now, and I see you have oil lamps about the place so there's always a risk...'

'Aye, we 'ave oil lamps 'cos we have none of that electric stuff 'ere. Now if we 'ad t'electric, we might be worried about fires, but not with lamps and wood. They've been burning for years without a problem.'

'But electricity will make things easier in the house, cooking for example.'

'It might send rays into t'food, Mr Wilkins, and we don't want that. Ah don't want my food contaminating with harmful electric rays.'

'So without electricity, you'll not be interested in the Premier's built-in refrigeration insurance?' I wondered when Mr Wilkins was going to mention his current pet subject and almost on cue he produced his latest theory.

'Refrigeration insurance, what's that?'

'Well, if you buy a refrigerator and fill it with food, it will contain quite a few pounds' worth. Now, if the power fails, or the refrigerator breaks down, and it's out of action long enough for the contents to be destroyed or wasted, a good policy would cover you. You could claim from it and recoup your losses.'

'Ah've never 'eard owt so daft in all my life, Mr Wilkins. Why would Ah want to insure food against going bad? My hens and pigs would fettle that anyroad, bad food is cheaper than buying t'real stuff we give 'em, but round 'ere food generally doesn't last long enough to go bad. And besides, Ah've got a cellar full of food, our cellar's been 'ere since t'house was built and it's as cool as a cucumber even on t'hottest summer day. In fact, Ah'll show you. Right now. No time like the present.'

Without further ado, he rose from his chair and stomped from the room with me and Mr Wilkins in hot pursuit. He went into a large back room with a cement floor. In the middle was a heavy wooden trapdoor with an iron ring at one end. He stooped down and hauled on the ring to lift the door and expose a stone staircase leading into the dark depths. Even as the door was lifted, I could feel the chill air from the cellar below. Hanging on a beam near the top of the stairs was a storm lantern which he removed, produced a box of matches from his pocket and lit the wick.

'Down we go,' he said. 'Follow me and watch where you put your feet.'

And as he descended the flame brightened, then he reached up to hang the lantern from a hook of the cellar ceiling and its light, surprisingly powerful, lit up the entire cellar. He reached the bottom and waited until we joined him.

'Now then, take a look around. This is where we keep stuff that needs to be cool. No electricity, no refrigerator, no ice, no running water, no cool air coming in through holes in the wall, just a deep cellar with earth all around it. Cool and dry, just what we want. And t'temperature never varies, summer or winter.'

In the light of the lantern I could see shelves galore, all stacked with Kilner jars full of fruit, jars of jam, tins of food with everything from beans to soup via tinned rabbit and wild boar's head. I noticed pickled onions, cheeses large and small, lots of bottles which he said were home-made wines – orange wine, parsley wine, parsnip wine, may-blossom wine, rhubarb wine, sloe gin, nettle beer, ginger beer and ale too, in a pair of barrels. There were peaches in brandy, cherries in syrup and strawberries in

wine. And on the floor were sacks of potatoes, turnips and carrots.

'You can preserve owt you want,' Don was
saying. 'You can dry it, pickle it, preserve it
in syrup, sugar, jelly, bottles and tins or just
keep it cool and dry. If it's apples, they're
best under the bed individually wrapped in
newspaper, or better still in the room above
a stable full of hosses where t'temperature's
just right. And you can't beat a good com-
pote for keeping fruit ... so, Mr Wilkins, why
would I need a refrigerator? Or electricity,
for that matter. Besides, I've enough space
down here to keep stuff for years, enough to
provide us for as long as we live. I reckon
we've enough stuff to supply other folks an'
all, so if t'weather really closed in for a long
time, we could mebbe sell some of our stuff.
Or even give it away to t'awd folks. I'll bet
you couldn't do that wi' one of your refrigerators, Mr Wilkins. How big will they be?
Enough to hold a good breakfast, mebbe?'

Mr Wilkins did not say anything as he
peered at the shelves and their bewildering
range of contents and then he nodded.
'You've made your point, Mr Cracknell, I
won't pester you again.'

'Aye, well, you weren't to know how we
deal wi' things in t'countryside but Ah'll
make a bargain wi' you. If ever we do get
t'electric fitted, I'll think again about house

244

insurance. And fire risks mebbe. It'll not be as safe as our lamps and fires.'

'You're on!' grinned Wilkins as Don held out his huge hand, spat on it and offered it to Wilkins to shake. He did so, perhaps grudgingly because of the spittle.

'Right, back upstairs you two before my tea gets cold.'

As we were driving away some minutes later, Mr Wilkins said, 'That was amazing, Mr Taylor, it was like stepping back a century or two. But it seems to work, all those different ways of preserving food.'

'They made it work,' I said. 'They had to, sometimes these remote farms were cut off by the snow for three months at a time, with no electricity. It happened in 1947, that great snow. Some farms were cut off for weeks on end.'

'So they stocked up with everything in advance, just in case?'

'Yes, and they still do! It's part of their general way of living. Food and fuel for the household, food and bedding for the livestock,' I said. 'With a bit of planning, they can live for months on what they've got. They're very skilled in the survival arts!'

'I gathered that from the stuff we saw in that cellar. And another thing occurred to me. I bet they survived the war just as comfortably – food rationing wouldn't affect them in the slightest.'

'Absolutely, so can you imagine the Cracknells coping with a small domestic refrigerator?' I said. 'For them, it would be a cruel form of rationing!'

'Point taken! I'll be careful where I mention the word in future,' he nodded. 'Very careful. So, where are you taking me now?'

'I have a handful of collections to make in Walstone, we can be there in five minutes and get them finished before lunchtime. I'm sure you'll find some potential new clients for us.'

'You know, Mr Taylor, I think my office duties are keeping me away from potential customers, I seem to be losing my sharpness. I must get out more and talk to more people, so show me the way. I haven't won a single round today. I do need to generate a new policy of some kind to justify my presence!'

Walstone was little more than a hamlet of pretty stone-built cottages with several farms scattered around its outskirts. There was a handsome parish church which had been modernized in Victorian times, a reading room which dated from the same period, a seat overlooking the River Suther but little else. It lacked a shop, post office or pub. Much of the business conducted by the inhabitants was done either in nearby

Ingledale or further afield in Guisborough, with several of the village menfolk travelling daily to Guisborough for work. I had a few clients there, chiefly motor insurances along with a few household-protection policies and some ordinary life cover, but it was not a wealthy community and few could afford to pay the higher premiums required for the more specialized schemes, however worthy they might be.

Knowing the general financial state of the population, I did not press anyone to consider an insurance he or she could ill afford, and I wanted Mr Wilkins to understand this. Tough sales patter would never be effective in this community; in fact, it could be counter-productive. If any agent tried to persuade these people to take out more insurance with higher premiums, they would simply tell him where to go in no uncertain terms – as he'd already experienced in Ingledale. I hoped he would soon learn that his city methods of urging people to invest in too much insurance would never succeed in these moors. And with that in mind, I remembered another wonderful potential client upon whom he could practise his skills.

We parked opposite the church and I explained which houses I had to visit to collect, and so he suggested we did as before – to avoid wasting time he would visit a non-client in the hope of persuading him or her to join the Premier while I completed my collecting. I said I should finish comfortably within half an hour, and so, after asking which of the houses did not belong to any of my clients, I suggested the lady at Sycamore House, just across the green from where we were parked.

With lots of rooms, it was a large square house standing behind a high stone wall and was far bigger than any other in Walstone. I explain to Mr Wilkins that she might be amenable to some expert advice on the various policies offered by the Premier and explained she had sometimes spoken to me about this but had not yet made a commitment. I told him I had never been able to persuade her – and so he recognized another challenge. He would show this young lad how it should be done!

The lady's name was Edith Gibson, a woman in her late fifties or early sixties who was unmarried but who clearly had money behind her. She was from a wealthy background, her father's family being formerly associated with the woollen industry of the West Riding of Yorkshire. I added that she was not very active in village matters, preferring her own company – and that of her cats. He said he would pay her a visit and if he was not back in his car by the time I had finished my collecting, he would still be in discussions with Miss Gibson. As before, he said I was welcome to join him so that I might share this challenge in the capable hands of a very competent, long-serving insurance executive; he would tell Miss Gibson to expect my arrival. Clearly, he anticipated being there for some time.

My own collecting was completed without any problems apart from one woman, Laura Young, who asked if I'd seen her cat on my rounds in the village. It was missing, she told me, and had been for three or four days. It was a large fluffy tomcat called Plum but I had to confess I had not come across Plum. We knew, of course, that tomcats were prone to wandering away from their homes, often for days or weeks at a time.

And so, after about thirty-five minutes with no sign of Mr Wilkins in his car, I walked across to Sycamore House, let myself in through the tall iron gate and made my way to the front door. There was a bell which I rang, and I could hear its sound deep inside this splendid building, and then the door opened.

'Ah, Mr Taylor, do come in, I was expecting you,' oozed Miss Gibson, a rather stout lady with auburn hair. 'Your colleague is in the drawing room.'

I was ushered along the thickly carpeted passage until we reached the door of the drawing room. She led me inside where Mr Wilkins rose to his feet; he had been sitting on a chair behind a small coffee table laid with pots; I saw there was a cup and plate set out for me; he had a glass of lemon squash with his papers laid out on the floor at his side. Then I noticed all the cats lying around, most of them asleep. They were on the cushions of the settee, in easy chairs, on window ledges and before the empty fire grate, and they were real. There were probably ten or a dozen in different colours, but I did not count them. They did not stir as I entered.

'Sit down, Mr Taylor, and do make yourself at home. Now, coffee?'

She busied herself with the coffee from freshly ground beans as I savoured the scent they produced. I told Wilkins I'd had no problems with my collecting round, and then he said, 'I was discussing insurance with Miss Gibson but it seems there is a small problem she would first like your advice about, being a local man.'

'Well, yes, of course.'

'It's one of my cats, Mr Taylor. Sam. A tom. He's vanished,' she told me with a hint of sadness in her voice. 'I fear he must be stolen. He's been missing for some days now, and I have asked all around the village, but no one's seen him.'

'Stolen? Why would anyone steal a cat?' asked Wilkins.

'For their fur, Mr Wilkins. It doesn't require many cats like Sam to produce a fur coat of some quality. I know that, my father was in the textile business and you'd be surprised how many cats were stolen in Halifax.'

'Ah, I see. It's odd you mention that, Miss Gibson, because I've come from Mrs Young and her cat is missing too. For about three or four days, she thinks.'

'That's about the time Sam went missing. I find that highly significant and just wondered, with you being a local man, whether you had heard any rumours of cat thieves. Do you think I should inform the police?'

'I've not heard any other reports of this kind, Miss Gibson, but tomcats are prone to wandering, as I'm sure you know. I've come across stories of them being absent for months, and then returning as if nothing had happened. If you are worried, then I think a call to the police would be justified. They'll know if there have been any more reports.'

'That's what I thought. Did Mrs Young inform the police?'

'I don't think so, she just asked if I had

seen her cat during my travels, but I haven't. If he's a tom, he's very likely to turn up, and I'm sure he's capable of looking after himself. He's quite distinctive, he's large, black and fluffy, she said, his name is Plum.'

'I can't say I have noticed him when I've walked past her house, Mr Taylor, but my cat is very similar, quite large with long silky fur, black too. I wonder if they are from the same litter?'

'In a village of this size, that's quite likely. Where did you get him?'

'Oh, he just turned up as they do. Helped himself to the food I'd put out for the others and made himself at home. I've had him about four years now. But when you've gone, I shall ring the police.'

'Good. Now, Miss Gibson.' Clearly Mr Wilkins wanted the conversation to return to the more serious matter in hand. Insurance. 'Tell me, is your house insured?'

'No, of course not. Why should I want to spend money on insurance?'

'Well,' and I could see he was about to launch into one of his well-rehearsed sales routines, 'there are two main aspects to be considered. One – the house itself, and two, its contents. Together, that represents a very high value, a huge investment by you but all that is at risk even in the most caring of hands. Fire, flood, storm damage, burglary, theft, things you can't prevent and things that are always unexpected and highly inconvenient, even disastrous.'

'Could I insure my cats?'

'Insure them? What for?' Clearly he did not like being interrupted in mid-flow.

'Theft. You mentioned theft of the contents of my house, and my cats are surely contents, aren't they? They are mine, they belong to me and they are precious, I assure you. Perhaps not in the general sense of having value like paintings and jewellery but they have huge emotional values, all of them.'

'I'm not sure whether we could include cats on a house-contents insurance, Miss Gibson. It is not generally done, cats being able to walk out whenever they want and the cost of the premium, calculated on the risks involved, could be prohibitive...'

'But I am sure a man of your knowledge and experience could find a way of including my cats on a household-protection policy, Mr Wilkins. In case they got stolen, like Sam, or even run over by a passing car. Perhaps if your company will not insure them, you might know of one who does?'

'My company is the finest in the business,' and he puffed out his small chest. 'If we cannot insure cats, then no one can. One obvious problem is that when a cat decides to leave the house, as yours has done on this occasion, it is difficult to state categorically that it was stolen. If it was thought to have been stolen, the police would have to be notified and they would decide whether or not a crime had been committed. We would depend upon their decision, you see, we'd ask for an abstract of their crime report and I am sure most investigations would conclude with the police saying the cat had merely left home. With no evidence of a crime, the police would simply regard the cat as lost, and I know of no insurance company who will insure anyone for losing a cat. The only exception might be for a very valuable and rare specimen, kept either for breeding or show purposes, but those premiums are very expensive indeed and very specialized. Furthermore, there would be stringent conditions attached to such a policy. That form of insurance is generally effected through a mutual system linked to societies and clubs. Now, have you thought about getting a refrigerator?'

'A refrigerator? Why do you ask me that? Is it to keep my cat food in, you mean? And all that milk I buy for them? Or it is something to do with a policy which protects cats? Something associated with the careful storage of their food?'

'I was thinking more along the lines of a

domestic refrigerator for your own household use.'

'Ah, so I repeat – why do you ask that, Mr Wilkins?'

'It's just that our new household-protection policy covers domestic refrigerators, and it includes any loss incurred through power cuts or malfunctioning of the machinery as well as the normal risks such as fire and flood, and we provide that cover at no extra charge. It brings our household-protection policies right up to date and makes us leaders in the current market, Miss Gibson.'

'So if I buy a refrigerator to contain my cats' food and all that milk, you will insure it?'

'That is the deal, yes.'

'So you will insure the cats' food, but not the cats,' she put to him. 'I find that odd and very hard to understand.'

'Well, it's not quite like that.' He attempted some kind of explanation to cope with her impeccable logic. 'It's not specifically cats' food that we shall be insuring, it will be the general contents of the refrigerator, your own personal food.'

'But cats are part of the contents of this house, and you will insure the other contents, like furniture, jewellery, crockery and so forth? I can't see any distinction between a ceramic cat and a real one.'

'Cats are feral creatures, Miss Wilkins, it would be like insuring a chaffinch which comes for its daily feed.'

'Cats are domestic animals, Mr Wilkins, and because they live in my house they are part of my house contents, not like sheep and cows which live in the fields or out-buildings. If you insure a refrigerator with my food in it, then you can insure one with cats' food in it and in turn, that surely means you can insure the cats which depend upon that food. You wouldn't keep a cow's hay in the refrigerator, would you? There is a dif-ference between cows and cats, you see. And if I put my pearl necklace in the refrigerator to hide it from thieves, it would be insured, surely? Not that I am going to put my cats in the refrigerator just to get them insured, but you know what I mean.'

'Erm, I'm not quite sure of your logic, Miss Gibson. Yes, we can insure your refrig-erator and its contents against loss from any cause, and that includes any cat food it might contain. That does not necessarily mean we can insure ordinary domestic cats who have the freedom to come and go as they please, and with no specific value. I doubt if it is possible to put a financial value on an ordinary domestic cat. It is something I would have to check with Head Office.'

'Would you do that for me? I would be so pleased. My cats are very partial to raw liver, you know, I get it from the butcher when he comes on Saturday mornings, and a refrigerator might be a good idea.'

'Right, so can I assume that you might be interested in our new household-contents protection policy? If so, I can complete a proposal form right now...'

'And if the policy does include cats, does that mean Sam will be insured if he doesn't return?'

'I'm afraid not, we can't back-date policies, Miss Gibson. You said he vanished a few days ago.'

'Well, in that case I'm not interested, Mr Wilkins, unless you can find me a policy which includes all my cats. Now, if you will excuse me I have things to do, and in the meantime I shall ring the police at Guisborough to report Sam's absence. You might return, might you? To let me know what progress you make about stolen-cat policies?'

'Yes, of course. Come along, Mr Taylor, we have more calls to make.'

As we were making our way back to his car, he stopped and said, 'Is she the best you can offer in Walstone, Mr Taylor?'

'You said you liked a challenge!'

'She's obsessed with cats. If I can find a policy which includes cats, I think she will buy it, whatever it was for, but there's no way Head Office would sanction a household-contents policy with special provision for the theft of ordinary cats. But you are right – she is a challenge and when I return to the office, I shall do some research to see whether there is a way of devising a scheme to suit her, with or without a refrigerator, but clearly to take account of her cats. I shall return, Mr Taylor, mark my words. People like her do not deter Montgomery Wilkins!'

'Right, well it's time for our break and you once said you'd like to visit one of our local inns? We don't have snack bars and restaurants on these moors, but some of the pubs do a very nice line in pickled eggs and sandwiches, or even cooked ham, tomatoes and pickled onions.'

'Then lead on, Mr Taylor, and this meal can come out of company expenses.'

'Can I suggest the Laverock Inn on the moor above Sutherdale? It's about a mile from here. Mrs Hodgson produces ham sandwiches the size of doorsteps flavoured with her home-made piccalilli, and the beer is excellent.'

'By all means, and although I do not drink stimulants, I am sure the experience will be beneficial to me.'

'I have three collecting calls on the way,' I said. 'And this afternoon we can make more calls in Sutherdale village. We got round faster than expected this morning.'

The first call was at High Moor Farm on the heights above Sutherdale but the farmer always left his premiums on the gatepost at the side of the road. The farmhouse stood almost a mile along a very rough and narrow lane and the premium money – 7s 6d – was always placed there so that my car did not have to endure the rough journey to the house. I asked Wilkins to halt his car while I collected the cash and when I returned he asked, 'Doesn't that money ever get stolen?'

'Not in living memory,' I said. 'This family has always left insurance money out like this, long before I took the agency. It's a relic of the gatepost-bargain days.'

'Gatepost bargain?'

'In bygone times, a buyer would make a bid for an entire field full of cattle but they had to pay before the animals could be removed. They left the money on the gatepost and once it was there, the buyer could take his purchases out from the field. It was called a gatepost bargain.'

'Rather like paying on the nail,' he said. 'We use that term to indicate payment on the spot, something immediate, but the term originated in the custom at markets and corn exchanges when buyers placed their money in special receptacles called nails.

They were very shallow dishes, and they were called nails because they were fastened to the top of a post, and looked very like large nails. There are some outside the Corn Exchange in Bristol even now.'

Having learned a little more about the country's financial practices, my next call en route to the Laverock produced two shillings which had been left on a doorstep, so I recorded that as 'paid', but the third, Mrs Baxter, a young mum in her thirties, did not have the cash waiting outside so I knocked on the kitchen door. She had seen our arrival, recognized me in the passenger seat and opened the door with the 1s 9d in her hand.

'Just before you go, Mr Taylor, I don't suppose you've seen my cat, Tibbles, have you? He's vanished, he's not been home for his meals for three or four days and the children are worried about him. He's a tom and he does wander off, sometimes he's missing all night but never for as long as this.'

'He's not the only one, Mrs Baxter, he's the third missing cat I've heard about this morning, and all in this locality. I just hope we don't have some unpleasant people at work in the dale, like cat-rustlers. So what's he look like, just in case I do see him?'

'He's very friendly, he's a big black fluffy

cat with a bushy tail.'

'Just like all the others. Maybe they're all from the same litter?' I suggested.

'Maybe wandering is in their family?' She smiled. 'Well, I mustn't keep you, I can see you have someone with you.'

'If I do see Tibbles or discover anything about him, I'll get in touch,' I promised.

When we arrived at the stone-built inn high on the moors, we could see it was very dark inside. If the inn had electricity, clearly the owners didn't believe in using it during the daylight hours. The old inn, dating back centuries, was constructed with walls more than a yard thick, a low sloping roof and tiny windows, all designed to keep out the weather whilst retaining the heat.

'I promise I won't mention refrigerators,' said Mr Wilkins as he drew his little car to a halt outside. 'This is my leisure time! Although an inn like this might be just the place to cultivate from the insurance point of view ... but I think they have their own scheme drawn up through their licensees' association!'

I was pleased he was going to relax over the meal; I could find out more about his personal life and interests. I loved this old inn; it was so homely. The interior had stone floors and in the bar when we entered there was a wonderful log fire with several old characters

261

sitting around it. Iris Hodgson, the landlady, was one of them.

'Oh, hello, Matthew. Nice to see you.'

I introduced Mr Wilkins and we ordered one of her famous ham sandwiches each, with a pint of bitter for me and a glass of orange for him. But as we moved across to sit at a table near one of the windows, from where we would have a long view down the dale, I noticed a large black cat snoozing before the fire.

It was very fluffy with a big bushy tail. It was lying at the feet of the men, two of whom were smoking clay pipes and chatting about their gardens.

'Your cat, is it?' I asked Iris.

'No, I don't know where he's come from, he just turned up a few days ago. Made himself at home, he's a friendly old tom but I don't mind him coming here. We need one to keep the mice down, not that he's very active. He prefers to sleep all day but I've no idea where he gets to at night.'

'He's from the village,' said one of the men. 'He's got dozens of calling places, stays for a week or two and then moves on. He'll go back there soon, folks down there who've had him stay all think he's been out courting but in fact he just likes a change of routine, a new taste in food and different company now and again.'

And so we had solved the mystery of the missing cat, all those cats probably being the same one unless, of course, one of them had sired all the others. Was it one cat, or a family? I didn't know and didn't think it necessary to tell those ladies today that their cat was probably enjoying life in the pub. I'd mention it next time I called on them – by then, he might have returned to one or other of his haunts. However, I thought Mr Wilkins might like to impress Miss Gibson with his knowledge of her 'missing' cat because I had no intention of trying to sell her some insurance.

She would talk about nothing else but cats, so I would let her remain one of Mr Wilkins' major unresolved challenges.

The next time I called for a meal at the Laverock Inn, the big black cat had gone. A large ginger one was lying in its place before the fire and I must admit I wondered if Iris Hodgson had a refrigerator at the inn.

Eight

*'A cow wandered into my car. I was later
informed that the cow was half-witted.'*
From a claim form

In 1851, the average life expectancy for a
man in England and Wales was a mere 40.19
years. For a woman at that time it was 42.18
years, hardly long enough for her to experience the menopause. Clearly, a lot of people
lived far longer but equally, many died very
young indeed, hence this low average. By
1937, the man's average life in England and
Wales had risen to 60.18 years, a huge
increase in a comparatively short time, with
the female average rising to 64.40 years.
During the 1950s, a baby boy could expect
to live until the age of 67 and for a girl, the
age was 71. During the century beginning in
1851, therefore, our life expectancy had
risen dramatically, doubtless due to much-
improved living conditions and medical
advances, but from an insurance point of
view it meant that life-assurance premiums

were reduced considerably. Increasingly longer life expectancy meant progressively reduced premiums with longer and better investments for everyone.

It follows that when a person made a proposal that his or her life should be insured for a considerable sum, the insurance company had to be convinced that that person's life expectancy could be regarded as normal or better than normal. Clearly, someone who was suffering from a life-threatening illness or who took part in dangerous sports should expect to pay a higher premium; provided, of course, the insurers would accept him or her as a risk.

This meant a considerable amount of very personal information had to be entered on a proposal form for any type of life insurance, always with the proviso that a certificate from the proposer's doctor or even an independent medical examination might be required. In considering a proposer as a risk, the insurers wanted to ensure that their side of the bargain was not too much of a risk!

Among the personal details required were the proposer's height, weight and age. From those three facts alone, insurance actuaries could make remarkably accurate forecasts about an average person's lifespan – for example, a man of only five feet two inches tall who weighed twenty stone might not be considered a good risk, even if he was only twenty-two years old, and I am not sure what they would make of a fellow who was six feet six inches tall and weighing only ten stone while just reaching his thirty-ninth birthday. And, of course, for every rule there are exceptions. Some eighteen-stone men reaching almost seven feet in height make very good and fit rugby football players and little chaps less than five feet tall and weighing around eight stone can exercise wonderful control over something as large and demanding as a racehorse. Despite all the rules about average people, however, the Premier had an overriding stratagem that each proposal should be dealt with on its individual merits.

Throughout history, Britain has produced some massive people, such as William Campbell, a pub licensee at Newcastle-on-Tyne who was 6ft 3in tall and weighed 53 stone 8lb and who died aged only twenty-two. Another was Daniel Lambert of Stamford, who died at the age of thirty-nine, after weighing 52 stone 11lb shortly before his death. There are others around the world, the heaviest probably being Jon Brower Minnoch of Washington, USA, whose greatest weight was recorded as 975lb before he died at the age of forty-one.

Bearing in mind such statistics, and of

course the associated early deaths, I received a proposal form from a man called Godfrey Harding, who lived with his parents at Lexingthorpe. When visiting my 'surgery' at the Unicorn in Micklesfield one Wednesday, it seemed his mother had picked up a leaflet about endowment insurance. Clearly, she thought Godfrey, aged twenty-eight, should have his life insured for £1,000 through such a policy and so she had persuaded him to complete the form.

He had done so and then sent it to me through the post. I had not met Godfrey nor indeed had I met his mother and knew little about them or their family, my only knowledge being that Mr Harding, senior, was a joiner and cabinetmaker, now retired. However, because this form looked like providing me with at least one new client and some welcome new business in the shape of a high-value endowment policy, I read his proposal with very great interest. Three things stood out on his form – the first was that he was not married, the second was that he did not have a regular job and the third was that his weight was recorded as 'not known' even if his height was listed as 5ft 11in. In my mind, those factors immediately created a mystery, one which I must solve before signing and forwarding this form to District Office. If my bosses received such a form, I would be asked to clarify those same queries, so the answer was to solve them before despatching the form. That suggested a visit to Godfrey and his family at their home.

I rang to make an appointment, giving my reasons, and as a result found myself driving out to Lexingthorpe one Tuesday afternoon for a meeting at three o'clock. Meanwhile, I had made a few discreet enquiries around Micklesfield but no one knew Godfrey, which was not surprising as he lived almost ten miles away, although his father was well known throughout the dale for his wood-working skills. Riverside House was an old water mill; although it retained the millwheel it was no longer functioning and had been secured so that it could not rotate, and the mill was now serving as a private house incorporating a cabinet-maker's workshop.

I drove along the unmade track for about three-quarters of a mile beside the riverbank and eventually reached the old house, which was almost hidden among deciduous trees. From my approach, the house looked almost derelict, its roof and walls smothered with ivy and moss as it rested in the woodland shadows, probably without ever seeing sunshine. I did notice smoke rising from one of the chimneys, however, and the room nearest the millwheel appeared to have lights inside, although I was viewing it from the rear. That, I reasoned, was the woodworker's end of the building, the former mill section. As I approached, I saw an old, almost derelict sign advertising 'Kenneth Harding, Joiner and Cabinet Maker' with his address and telephone number, even though he was officially retired.

When I arrived, I saw a ladies' pedal cycle leaning against the low wall which bordered a small garden at the back door – Mrs Harding's mode of transport, perhaps? It had a basket on the front handlebars and looked in good condition. I parked and walked into the back garden with its stock of growing vegetables all looking very tempting. From there, I could see the nearby yard full of timber and various wooden structures, some complete and others awaiting attention. There was an old van too bearing Harding's name and business details. Really, it was a hideaway but clearly still active as a business. One thing I noticed was that beside each flight of steps, however short, there was a ramp, the kind that might suggest the presence of an invalid carriage or even a child's pram. I knocked on the door; it was the back door of the living quarters. It was standing partially open and a woman's voice called, 'Come in, we're in the parlour.'

I entered bearing my briefcase and was

greeted in the hallway by a tall and very slender woman who would be in her early sixties, I guessed, with well-groomed iron-grey hair tied back in a bun, ruddy cheeks, blue eyes and a nice smile which displayed good teeth. My immediate impression was of a very pleasant person but a quick mental calculation told me she looked rather too old to be the mother of a son of twenty-eight. Or was she? Women did give birth in their thirties or even early forties.

'Eunice Harding,' she introduced herself, extending her hand very formally for me to shake. 'You must be Matthew Taylor, I've missed you at the Unicorn market, I tend to get there very early. But I have seen your leaflets, and it's good of you to come and see us.'

'I'm pleased my so-called office is proving useful!'

'I found those leaflets very useful. Now, my husband will be along in a moment or two, he's in his workshop but I have the kettle on and he'll come and join us for his afternoon tea break. You'd better come in and meet Godfrey. When you rang, you said you wanted to talk to him.'

'Yes, it's about his proposal for an endowment policy, I need to clarify a few points.'

I was led into the parlour, a heavily furnished room with thick dark green velvet curtains, a large settee with two easy chairs, also in dark green, and a fire burning in the grate. But sitting in the middle of the settee, which seemed to be much larger and stronger than most, was a colossus of a man. As I entered, he struggled to get up but his mother said, 'No, Godfrey, don't. Mr Taylor can shake your hand while you are seated, can't you, Mr Taylor?'

'Yes, of course,' and so I shook his hand and introduced myself, thinking he was perhaps suffering from some kind of ailment or disability. I have never seen such a large human being. He seemed to occupy most of the seating space on the settee, which had evidently been specially strengthened; but his hands were small and amazingly delicate for man of such size. However, his general shape and height was difficult to ascertain due to his very loose clothing. He seemed to be swamped in a flannel shirt or smock of some kind which came over his waist and covered his arms, but my immediate impression was one of grossness, with lots of loose and flabby flesh which looked a pale shade of grey.

His face was rounded with floppy cheeks and jowls, but his hair was neatly cut and well-groomed, and a nice shade of dark brown. He had a nice smile too, and welcoming eyes and as I took in my surroundings, I realized that, in the corner of the room not far from the settee, there was a wooden trolley with three shelves, littered with what appeared to be cog wheels, springs and other parts from either clocks or watches. I also noticed in one dark corner a large wooden chair-like structure on wheels – the reason for the ramps outside. As my eyes became accustomed to the darkness, I noticed full bookshelves near the fireside, many dealing with clocks and watches, a magazine rack also full of clock-and-watch periodicals, and a smaller trolley with drawers, one of which was partially open and clearly containing tiny parts of watches and clocks. It was then that I realized I was in the presence of the Clockmaker of Lexingthorpe. I had heard about him, but not having any clocks or watches that needed repair, and not wishing to buy a handmade clock, I had never met him, neither had I associated him with this place or the Hardings. People tended not to refer to him by name – I'd always heard him described as the Clockmaker of Lexingthorpe.

'Nice to meet you, Godfrey,' I said, sitting on the chair near his settee at the invitation of his mother, my briefcase at my side. 'You must be the famous clockmaker?'

'I don't know about being famous.' He laughed easily with a well-modulated voice.

'But it's a living. I can work here, or in my studio in the old mill, near Dad's workshop. I'm working here today, repairing a watch for a man at Guisborough.'

'So you do have an occupation?' I said. 'When I got your proposal form, you said you didn't have a job.'

'Well, it's not a real job, is it? Not like going out to work. It's more of a hobby really, something to occupy my time even if it does earn me a few pounds.'

'Godfrey likes to earn his own keep, Mr Taylor, and although he can't go out to work, his clock and watch repairing, and a spot of clock-making, do earn him a few pounds, certainly enough for his keep and a few extras. He is not married and so there are no dependants, just the three of us.'

As she was speaking, I opened my briefcase and extracted his completed proposal form, along with a blank. Another query had been answered.

'I think we'll complete a new form, Godfrey, showing the fact you do have an income and you are self-employed. I'll list you as a watch repairer and clockmaker. That's one query answered. The next is not so simple. I am sorry to bring up a very personal matter but it concerns your weight. You didn't provide it but we do need it because it helps the company assess the risks involved with your proposal.'

Mrs Harding had not yet left the room to make the tea but lingered, anxious to provide me with her account of Godfrey's problem.

'He never ails a thing, Mr Taylor, he's never been ill in all his life but with him getting on a bit, he'll be thirty before too long, and with me and Kenneth getting older, we are pensioners you know, we had him late in life, he's our only child, so we thought Godfrey should have a life insurance, one of those endowment things where he can save and invest something for the future.'

'A very commendable action, Mrs Harding, but if the Premier is to accept Godfrey, it needs to know more about him, his weight for example.'

'I don't see how that matters, Mr Taylor.'

'It's all to do with the risks attached to one's life, Mrs Harding, very important from a life-insurance viewpoint. The company has a table which it uses to compare weight with age and height, and from those figures it can make calculations. I'm afraid I must include his weight on the proposal form, his application won't be accepted without it, but that could mean my District Office also demands a medical examination or at least a certificate from his regular doctor.'

'Well, our doctor would say Godfrey has

never been ill, Mr Taylor, so surely that must count for something.'

'Most certainly, it would prove he's not an ill person, but the question of his weight remains. I can't guess it – that might be counterproductive.'

'It's always been a problem, ever since he was tiny. We don't know what causes it, Mr Taylor, he's not a big eater, he's careful with his food, he doesn't lie in bed all day but he can't walk far, because of his weight, so he doesn't get any exercise. Kenneth has made him a trolley, for getting about the premises. Like an invalid carriage, one he can propel himself in, a chair on wheels. A wooden frame with a seat which he can propel with his feet, it's over there, in the corner. He doesn't have to worry about steps, you see, he can get around without our help, down to his studio or into the garden, or even down beside the river. And his bedroom is on the ground floor, this house is ideal for him.'

'So has he ever been weighed?'

I found myself addressing my questions to Mrs Harding rather than Godfrey but he seemed quite tolerant of this, apparently because it was always how things were done. His mother did everything for him.

'Not for a long time, not since he was at school, Mr Taylor. Tell him, Godfrey.'

'When I was at school, they made me use

one of those big platform weighing machines in railway-station waiting rooms, I was too heavy for the normal ones the doctor used. I had to weigh myself and make a note of it, with the date. But since I left, the doctor has never weighed me. He did suggest I took myself off to the railway station at Whitby, in Dad's van – the van's adapted for me, by the way – but I've never got round to it. The snag now, of course, is that those railway-station weighing machines, and those you find in gents' toilets, where you put a penny in, well, they only go up to twenty stone and I'm too heavy for them.'

'We did think about the weighbridge, Mr Taylor, where the lorries go, or we could maybe use one in a corn merchant's or a coal yard, but they're all too big and not at all dignified. Not very clean either. It is a problem – even if we wanted to weigh Godfrey we'd have trouble finding a weighing machine able to cope with him.'

'I see.' I was stuck now. Without his weight, I had serious doubts whether District Office would even pass his proposal for consideration by a higher authority. Head Office would want him weighed. I felt I should do my best for him as I felt his proposal should be given special treatment and dealt with on its merits.

It should be sent to Head Office to seek

their authority to obtain a doctor's certificate without any other formality so that his application could be approved even without a declaration of his exact weight. Special circumstances demanded special treatment. Nonetheless, I wondered whether that would be sufficient for him to obtain his endowment policy, although one solution was to grant it, or a similar policy, with a limitation of some kind. Whatever I did, I felt sure his own doctor would support him, particularly as he had never been ill. And, I recalled, the Premier did stress that every proposal *was* dealt with on its merits. I could remind my bosses of that! My own rather inexperienced view was that excess weight alone should not debar him. I knew, of course, that my rather juvenile opinions would not be strong enough to bypass District Office's scrutineers.

'I must find a means of getting you weighed accurately,' I put to him. 'I'm sorry about this, but if I'm to get this proposal past our scrutineers to secure an endowment policy for you, I can't ignore your weight. It's a vital part of the proposal. Fortunately, you are a tall man which goes some way in your favour, and you are not yet thirty.'

'I suppose Dad could always take me to the weighbridge, to join the lorries...' he began.

Then I had a brainwave. 'I've got an idea,'

I said. 'I used to work for George Wade, the butcher in Micklesfield. He's got a special weighing machine for his heavy stuff, like carcasses of beef, whole sheep and massive pigs. It's called a butcher's steelyard.'

'Steelyard?'

'The name's nothing to do with steelyards, Godfrey, it doesn't weigh girders and so on! I think the name comes from a German origin. It's just a specialized weighing machine for large items like half a bullock. It's suspended from a high metal tripod and uses huge hooks to hold whatever's being weighed, so you'd have to sit in a harness of some kind. But it's big enough and strong enough to cope with you. If I can fix things so that you can use it, probably after the butcher's work is finished one day, would you agree to do that?'

'If it means getting myself insured, then yes, I would. And it would mean I have some idea of exactly how much I weigh! I'd welcome that.'

'Right,' I said. 'I'll have words with George then get back to you.'

'I think we should celebrate with a cup of tea,' said Mrs Harding, looking out of the window. 'I see Kenneth is heading this way, he'll be delighted with the news, and he can run Godfrey over to Wade's, Mr Taylor. Even if his proposal is turned down, at least we will have an accurate weight for Godfrey, and maybe the chance to use the steelyard again? Whenever he needs to be weighed?'

I sat and had a cup of tea and some buns with the family, learning that Godfrey had arrived very late in their marriage but that the cause of his excessive weight had never been determined. He'd had all kinds of medical examinations and tests since he was a child, but no reason for his condition had ever been found. He was fortunate he could earn a modest living but there was no doubt his parents were immensely supportive in helping him to do that.

Kenneth Harding agreed wholeheartedly with my suggestion of the butcher's steelyard and before I left to make those arrangements, he took me down to look at his workshop. Obviously, he was proud of it. It was full of beautiful woodwork, much of it small items like jewellery boxes and presentation cases, although there were chairs, stools, coffee tables, ash trays and even wooden spoons made of surplus materials. The workmanship was superb; Kenneth was a true craftsman.

'I'm supposed to be retired,' he told me. 'I don't do the big stuff now, unless I get a special request for something like a wardrobe or chest of drawers, or even a dining suite, but I do make a lot of small stuff. It's not for me, it's for Godfrey. Me and Eunice are a lot older than him, I reckon we won't outlive him, even with his condition, so I'm making all these things to build up a stock for him. He can sell it bit by bit when I'm gone, and he can make extra cash with his clocks and watches. That little insurance will be a big help as well, when it matures; he'll be able to pay for help at home. He'll need help with things like washing and ironing, getting his meals and keeping the house clean. And getting around, he can't drive, he can't fit in the driver's seat.'

'Let's hope we can persuade the Premier to take him on board!' I said before taking my leave.

George Wade readily agreed to let Godfrey get weighed on his steelyard and although Godfrey required a good deal of manhandling and lifting, with a fair amount of cursing plus a few yards of strong webbing, he weighed in at 24 stone 12lb.

George gave me a ticket to prove it and I later included this with Godfrey's proposal form. I also included a doctor's certificate which showed Godfrey had never suffered a day's illness in his life. Then I posted the documents off to District Office, admittedly with my fingers crossed for luck! In this very special case, I knew District Office would forward the papers to Head Office for their decision.

I was rather concerned about the delay by Head Office in responding and must admit I thought Godfrey's proposal would be rejected. Clearly it was being very carefully considered – but it wasn't rejected. They agreed to an endowment policy based on Godfrey's life, but one which was of shorter duration than normal, maturing at fifty-five instead of sixty years of age. The premiums were slightly higher than the normal too but that was to be expected. Godfrey and his family were delighted because in addition to the wonderful support he received from his parents, it provided him with an additional form of security.

I was pleased for Godfrey too. He was one of the biggest men I had ever encountered – and one of the nicest; but in spite of everything, he did manage to get himself insured, thanks to a butcher's machine for weighing very large pieces of meat.

The Hardings, although a small family by comparison with some in the dale, typified the warmth, love and care that existed between some parents and their children. A large percentage of my business came from that source, with parents wanting the best for their children.

Having survived the Second World War,

often with little money and security, parents were looking ahead to a more settled and prosperous future and encouraging their families to do likewise.

I could never forget Godfrey Harding's problem nor the support he gained from his parents, but there were two similar cases. One concerned a maiden lady called Marjorie Catton, a retired civil servant who lived at Oak Tree Lodge, Graindale. It was a neat red-brick detached house in spacious grounds on the edge of the village. It had belonged to her father and mother, with Marjorie inheriting the property upon their deaths, and so, in retirement, she had moved there from London, having worked in the Home Office.

She had settled into village life surprisingly well, and was popular with the local people because she was always willing to help others less fortunate than herself. She would respond in all manner of ways, such as shopping for the elderly and infirm, helping the less articulate to write letters to officials in either the government or local authorities and using her expertise to good effect around the village, such as church events, flower shows, the parish council, the youth club and so forth. One of her acts of generosity was to allow village children to use the tennis court in her grounds; her garden was often full of happy voices and there is no doubt they respected her kindness. For a single woman of retirement age, she had a wonderful rapport with young people. I knew her fairly well because her house insurance, car insurance and a life policy were with the Premier.

I was not surprised, therefore, when I received a phone call from her one July day, asking me to call and discuss a policy for her distant nephew. In fact, the lad in question, Stephen Catton, was her cousin's son so he was not all that distant but it seemed he was lodging with her for a while because he had found a job with Graindale Estate. He was eighteen years old, she told me on the telephone, and she wanted to take out an endowment policy for him. She felt she must do this because he was under twenty-one; as he was not an adult he was unable to enter into a legal contract. She regarded her action as a present for him – she would pay the premiums until he was twenty-one and thereafter the responsibility would rest with him but she felt it would provide him with some incentive to plan for his future. I arranged to call one evening at seven after Stephen had finished work; she said he'd got a job in the walled garden of the estate, caring for vegetables and fruit of every kind.

On that warm Tuesday evening, therefore,

I arrived at Oak Tree Lodge. I could hear the laughter and chatter of children on the tennis court behind the house, and as I walked to the back door, Miss Catton came out to meet me. She was a small, slender woman with nearly pure-white hair and steel-rimmed spectacles; dressed in smart but casual clothes with a multi-coloured skirt and white blouse, she looked very fit and healthy as always.

'Ah, Matthew, good of you to come. We're in the garden, it's such a nice evening and so I have made some cool drinks. Come and meet Stephen.'

I followed her to the west side of the house, well away from the tennis court, and there was an outdoor table with chairs around it, and a jug of what appeared to be lemonade or something similar. Then a sturdy male child materialized from the group of tennis players and made his way towards us; he had not been playing, merely watching.

'Ah, Stephen, come and meet Mr Taylor. Matthew, our insurance man.'

I then realized that the 'child' had the face of an older youth. But he was tiny, the size of a small child and a little more than three feet six inches tall. I knew I was looking at a man suffering from dwarfism or even ateleiosis, the condition which produces midgets. As he approached, I tried not to stare, hoping that I had managed to disguise my initial surprise, but the oncoming youth did not appear to be at all phased by my reaction. I felt sure he was very accustomed to such a response.

'Hello, Mr Taylor,' he greeted me in a slightly high-pitched voice as we shook hands. 'Good of you to come. My aunt has explained, has she?'

'Yes, she wants to buy you an endowment policy but as it's based on your life, I need your consent.' As I prepared to chat to him, he went to one of the chairs with a stool strategically placed near it. Using it as a step, he scrambled on to the chair and settled down as Miss Catton poured the drinks. It was a cool lemon drink, sweet but not too sweet, and wonderful with ice. I waited until the drinks were poured, tasted mine and expressed my approval, and then Miss Catton sat down at the table and asked, 'Matthew, do you anticipate any problems with Stephen's insurance? You can see what his problem is, he is eighteen so I don't have to explain.'

'Life assurance of any kind is all tied up with life expectancy.' I tried to be diplomatic in my response for I was aware that people with this condition did not often live to a great age. 'All the insurance companies who offer life-associated policies have tables of life expectancy produced by their actuaries. These are based on age, height and weight but the Premier always insists it deals with every application on its merits. I see no reason why we can't submit a life-based proposal for Stephen, if that is what you want. I should add that if it is approved, it might have conditions, and it could be rather shorter than normal.'

'Like me!' chuckled Stephen. 'Shorter than normal!'

'An endowment policy would be ideal, Matthew, to mature when he is, say, sixty or sixty-five,' said Miss Catton.

'I'm not sure how the insurers calculate the life expectancy of someone with Stephen's condition.' I felt I had to warn them that his proposal could be rejected. 'But I do know his application will be very carefully and fairly considered.'

'I know I'm a problem,' smiled Stephen. 'I'm not suffering from ateleiosis, Mr Taylor, but I am suffering from dwarfism. Those with ateleiosis tend to die very young, but dwarfs can and do live longer. My three brothers have it too, it comes from my mother's side but I expect to lead a full and normal life for some years yet.'

I explained the various endowment schemes, life policies and term schemes open to him and found him extremely intelligent for one so young, but I had to stress the possibility of acquiring a doctor's certificate or perhaps submitting to an independent examination.

Stephen told me he was always healthy, never suffering from any disease or ailment apart from colds and coughs on occasions and said he would welcome any medical examination the Premier cared to suggest.

'I've nothing to hide, you can see my problem! Everyone can,' he joked.

'All I can do at this juncture, Stephen, is to complete the proposal form which your aunt will countersign, and I suggest you opt for an endowment policy for £1,000 with profits, which will mature when you are sixty or sixty-five.'

'Not younger? I am not stupid, Mr Taylor, and I know dwarfs like me don't often live to a ripe old age, but we do get very mature! I hope I'm one of the latter!'

'Quite, but if we ask for a policy which matures at sixty or sixty-five, it gives room for the Premier to manoeuvre. Whilst they might not accept you as a risk up to that age, they might accept you until you are, say, forty or forty-five.'

'Oh, right. I see.'

'I should add that even in that shorter term, the returns will be very good. It remains a very sound investment because you are starting at such a young age.'

'Ah! I understand. Thank you, and thank you, Aunt Marjorie, for doing this.'

I completed his proposal form, recording that his height was 3ft 5in, that he weighed 5 stone 3lb and that he was eighteen years old. I had no idea what the statistically calculated life expectancy would be for an applicant with those measurements, but added that Mr Catton would be willing to submit himself to an independent medical examination if required.

When the proposal form arrived at District Office, one of the lady clerks telephoned to suggest I had made an error, thinking the height of Mr Catton should really be five feet three inches, not three feet five inches, but I had to correct her, adding that this was not a child. Later, Head Office suggested an alternative to my proposal; they said they would approve a fixed-term endowment policy for Stephen which would cover him until the age of forty for £500 and which would also contain a surrender value after ten years. They made a proviso, however, that if he survived to age forty, they would review the policy with an option of extending it for a further five years with no increase in the premium, and they would do the same if he reached age forty-five. Their mortality tables suggested that statistically few dwarfs lived longer than age fifty.

When I told Miss Catton she was delighted.

'I will tell Stephen's father, I know he has
tried to get insurance for Stephen's brothers,
all without success. Would you mind if they
all approached you?'

'Every application will be dealt with on its
merits,' I replied. 'That's the long and short
of it.'

Another memorable family-orientated insurance policy was slightly different because the
young man in question was already well
insured, and had been for some years. The
family was called Coleman, the parents
being Robert and Marie, and they lived at
Baldby Hall, Baldby. I knew of their family;
a son, Damien, and a daughter, Olive, both
now grown up and living away from home.

Both offspring were in their early thirties,
married with families of their own. I was
never quite sure what Robert did by way of
his business, and if anyone asked, he would
say, 'Manufacturing. I'm in manufacturing.'
I think his business was something to do
with the manufacture of components for the
engines of motor vehicles, boats and aircraft,
but clearly it was a successful enterprise because he owned and lived in a very splendid
mansion. His wife was keen on horsey

country pursuits such as hunting, riding, eventing and point-to-point racing and she kept a string of fine horses in stables at the Hall. For all their wealth and success, they were a very nice couple who would often open the grounds of their home to village fetes, fairs and garden parties.

I knew them because they had their house and contents insured with the Premier, along with their two private cars (his and hers), and life policies for their children. These had been taken out when the children were very small, in much the same way as Miss Catton planned a secure future for her nephew. The policies had continued during the wartime years, the Premier not increasing the premiums because of war risks. Even if someone whose life was assured with the Premier was on active military service, his or her premiums were not increased because of the extra risks which prevailed. Mrs Coleman also had her stables insured with me for she was always conscious of the fire risk, although her animals, including their vets' fees, were covered by a specialist equine-insurance company. As for Mr Coleman's factory on Teesside, it was covered by a specialist industrial-insurance company, a branch of the Premier. Clearly, he was a very important client for the Premier.

I did not often visit Baldby Manor to

collect premiums because Robert had a part-time secretary who worked at the house, and she ensured the monies due were paid quarterly by post. She was very efficient, and the cheques always arrived on time. Nonetheless, I liked to visit the household once in a while, mainly to ensure that the policies were up to date so far as valuation of the house contents was concerned, and that the policies took into account any additional factors or changed circumstances which might have arisen since my previous visit. Mr Coleman would sometimes buy an original oil painting, for example, both for enjoyment and as an investment, and Mrs Coleman would do likewise with French ceramics; consequently such things should be added to the house-contents policy if they were especially valuable. On the occasions when I called at the Hall, I usually dealt with Mrs Coleman, who had a very good understanding of all their insurances. Invariably she produced a cup of tea or coffee, and a biscuit or two. Those visits were always enjoyable.

It was one morning in June when I called at the Hall, having previously made an appointment. The Premier had decided to ask all its agents to visit households likely to contain high-value goods such as paintings, jewellery and antiques to warn them of the increasing number of burglaries and house-breakings in which jewellery had been stolen. In a lot of cases, the value of the stolen jewellery had not been specifically declared upon acquisition and so the relevant policy could not be amended or backdated to provide the necessary cover. It had meant that some of the victims were not insured for their considerable losses.

As a consequence, the Premier wanted all items worth more than £100 to be specifically declared, even if it meant a rise in premiums. Any subsequent loss could be far greater than the increased premiums, they pointed out. In the case of high-value items, jewellery and original paintings in particular, it was also suggested that photographs be taken of the property in question and that vulnerable points of the house be made more secure, such as rear doors, downstairs toilet windows and upstairs windows which were easily accessible. The company suggested that householders, and indeed shop owners and those running small businesses, ask for expert advice from the crime-prevention department of their local police force. And so it was that I embarked on a tour of such properties situated within my agency so that I could preach that message; it was a good means of updating everyone's policies.

One of the houses was Baldby Hall. I had explained my purpose when I rang to make the appointment, and when I arrived, shortly before ten thirty, the Colemans' secretary, Mrs Fairfax, had laid out all the policies on the dining-room table, and had also made lists of the objects which Mrs Coleman thought should be added. I was asked to sit at the table to go through the documents and give my observations on whatever might arise from our meeting. Mrs Fairfax brought in a tray of coffee and biscuits and I settled down for yet another pleasurable meeting with Mrs Coleman.

She produced a list of several items which she felt ought to be listed, such as several brooches, a diamond necklace, a canteen of antique silver cutlery, three new oil paintings of hunting scenes by different artists and a splendid watercolour of Whitby Abbey by John Sell Cotman. She found difficulty placing precise values on the items, but did assure me each was worth more than £100 except for the Cotman watercolour, which she said would one day be worth a fortune. As I made notes and expressed my pleasure at the way she had done all this work, she scanned the life policies. They were not affected by this visit, but she told me, 'The children are grown up now and away from home, but I'm still paying premiums for the policies I took out for them as children. Does your company need to know where they are living now, and what they are doing?'

'It's a good idea to keep the policies right up to date with current addresses, and of course, anything which might materially affect the validity of a policy, such as someone becoming ill or incapacitated, and even getting married and having a family. You've got to think about what might happen if you and Mr Coleman die, your executors need to find everything that's relevant to your estate. We usually recommend you lodge your policies with either a solicitor or your bank.'

'I'll get Mrs Fairfax to bring you their current addresses and an update on their activities. But of course this won't affect Victor, will it?'

'Victor?' I puzzled at the name.

'My son,' she said and I noticed a frown of sorrow fleetingly cross her face.

'Oh, I'm sorry. I had no idea you had another son. I thought there was just Damien and his sister.'

I had to admit I had not studied those life policies in detail, simply accepting the premiums and completing renewal forms when due.

I had never noticed Victor's name but that would have meant scrutinizing the fine detail of the policy document, something I would not do for a conventional renewal. The policies had been taken out many years before my arrival and so I was not familiar with their precise provisions, but it seemed I had missed something. 'Who is Victor?'

'My eldest son,' she said. 'I've been paying his life policy since he was a child, more than twenty-five years now. It is a whole-life policy which will mature upon his death, we bought it for him in anticipation of him marrying and raising a family of his own. A form of security for them rather than him, I suppose.'

'I've never heard of Victor,' I told her gently. 'Where is he?'

'No one knows,' she said softly. 'He was in the RAF during the war, a flight lieutenant with Fighter Command, and he went missing in 1943, somewhere over Europe. Shot down in his Spitfire, so they thought. Missing in action is how they phrased it.'

'I'm sorry, I had no idea.'

'You weren't to know. But I have continued with his premiums ever since, just in case he comes back.'

'But surely he's now officially regarded as dead, isn't he? More than seven years have elapsed since he was reported missing.'

'Legally, perhaps, but not in my mind, Matthew. I believe he is still alive, he'll be well into his thirties now, he was born in 1920. So I keep his policy open, and his bedroom all ready for when he comes home. I can't believe he's dead, you see, I just cannot. Missing is what they said. His body has never been found, neither has his aircraft. So no one can say he is dead, can they? Not with any certainty.'

'That happened in the war,' was all I could think of saying. 'Lots of military personnel went missing, unaccounted for, with no known grave.'

'But I don't think he's dead, I don't accept he's in some anonymous grave. He could have bailed out and be suffering from loss of memory, he might have forged a new life, got married and raised a family, not knowing who he really is ... there are all sorts of things that could have happened to him, so there's always a possibility he might come home.'

'I think you should have declared this,' I said. 'Once the seven years was over, he would be presumed dead, I'm sure that's how the RAF would regard things. That means the policy would cease at death and the sum assured would be paid to his estate. The fact is you cannot insure a dead person in this way, Mrs Coleman. After all, it is a whole-life insurance with the premiums paid throughout the insured person's life, and ceasing on the death of that insured person.

If death cannot be proved, then it must be assumed, in accordance with prevailing law.'

'But he is not dead, Matthew. I know he's not. That's the point I'm making. I want to continue his policy.'

'I think this is one for my boss to resolve! But personally, I would not want you to end this policy if you sincerely believe he is still alive, although I cannot speak for the Premier's official stance on this kind of thing. All they can do is act from a legal point of view.'

'But they can't object, surely? If they believe he is legally dead, I am saving them money! I am paying a premium for a policy which will never be surrendered or never reach maturity. It will continue so long as I keep up the payments.'

'I'll talk to Mr Wilkins about this, the moment I get home,' I promised.

'They won't make me stop, will they?' she asked and I could see the beginnings of distress in her eyes. 'It's just that this is one of those small things which help me believe Victor is still alive. I've nothing else, have I? To show he's alive. But in spite of that, Matthew, seven years' absence isn't long, especially when a war is involved. You hear of people, even now, turning up alive in the jungles of Asia, not knowing the war has ended. Victor could be out there somewhere, not wanting to show himself in case the Germans capture him, or he might have started a new life ... or anything...' and her voice faded away.

I began to think that perhaps she did not entirely believe her son was still alive ... if he was, surely he would have made some effort to contact his family? I began to think Mrs Coleman was struggling to maintain her strong maternal stance in spite of dwindling evidence of Victor's survival. Probably her only consolation lay in the fact his room was always ready and she was still paying his life insurance. In her mind, those two factors convinced her he was alive somewhere in the world. And I must not shatter that belief.

'Mr Wilkins is very experienced,' I assured her. 'He served in the war, he knows what's involved in these matters.'

'I don't want to get any money from this insurance, it's not for me, it's for Victor, well, for his family if he has one, wherever they are. You won't let them stop my payments, will you?'

'No, I won't.'

'I really do want to keep it running until Victor comes home. I want you to understand that.'

'I know.' And I left her.

During the drive home, my mind was in something of a quandary, albeit one I had brought upon myself, for I did not want the Premier's rules to force Mrs Coleman into abandoning something which was clearly very dear and important to her. In its own odd way, that policy was helping her to cope with Victor's fate, whatever it was, and I had no wish to interfere with that. At one point on the homeward run, I almost convinced myself not to mention this to Mr Wilkins, and to allow Mrs Coleman's payment to continue as if I knew nothing about the background; but my conscience told me that such behaviour would be dishonest and could even, in the fullness of time, be detrimental to her and her family. Honesty is always the best policy in such cases and so I made up my mind to ring Mr Wilkins for advice. I would be home before his office closed.

He listened as I carefully explained the situation and when I had given him the facts as I knew them, he said, 'Let the payments continue, Mr Taylor. Mrs Coleman is not alone, Head Office has a long list of families who are paying premiums for their sons who were either missing in action or missing presumed dead. Their motives are exactly the same as Mrs Coleman's but Head Office likes to maintain that list. I shall now add Victor Coleman's name – his full details and his policy number will be in our records and so there is nothing further you need do. Just keep collecting the premiums.'

'But isn't the Premier collecting life premiums for people who are dead?'

'Think of their fate as a kind of limbo, Mr Taylor. No one knows for sure whether they are dead or not, and so long as that doubt persists, the monies are being invested in their names, seven-year rule or not.'

'So they remain fully insured until someone comes along with absolute proof of death?'

'Or alternatively the next-of-kin take steps to make good use of the seven years' absence ruling – the law will presume that a person not heard of for seven years by those who would normally have heard from him is dead. That presumption is not often used for insurance matters, being generally introduced in divorces or even bigamy cases. What will usually happen at the Premier is that the policy will remain active until payments cease, and that will be almost certainly on death of the person who is paying – Mrs Coleman in your case. Because the Premier is aware of the situation, our experts will then encourage the surviving family members to have the insured person formally declared dead, under the seven-year rule. They must seek that declaration, it is not automatic. For example, the solicitor handing Mrs Coleman's estate will be the person to do that. The money will then be released back into the estate of the payer – Mrs Coleman in your case – and she will never know. She will die in the belief that Victor is alive but the money accrued from his whole-life policy will go into her estate, as next of kin, and will therefore benefit the rest of the family. And that keeps everyone happy.'

'So if the missing person does turn up alive many years later, there could be money for him?'

'If the family doesn't spend it, yes, but the Premier does have expert advisers to help in such cases and they will suggest that the surviving family members establish a trust fund for the benefit of the missing person, just in case he or she does turn up alive and kicking.'

'And it could happen!'

'Indeed it could. People missing for years and assumed to be dead can turn up in the most unexpected places. But in the mean-time, we can do something positive once we know the true situation – so well done for bringing this to our attention. I will do what-ever is now required.'

'Shall I tell Mrs Coleman?'

'Just tell her that the Premier is happy for her to continue with her payments and that we are administering other cases like hers.

301

Tell her she is not alone in this – it might help her to know that one of our senior actuaries also lost his son in very similar circumstances and his wife does not believe he is dead. He was missing in action too, like Victor Coleman, and his body has never been found.'

'So he came up with this very thoughtful scheme?'

'Yes. I don't know if other insurance companies operate a similar policy. I think we are unique but we can only introduce it when we know the true family circumstances. So thank you for telling me this, Mr Taylor. It shows you are doing your job with wisdom and sensitivity. You should feel very assured that, according to our records, Victor Coleman is alive and his policy will be kept active.'

'I'll reassure Mrs Coleman immediately,' I said.

Nine

Question: What guarantees may a mortgage company insist upon?Answer: If you are buying a house, they will insist you are well endowed.
From an insurance seminar paper

There is little doubt that my motorcycle-repair skills helped my insurance work. Owners or potential owners of bikes would frequently visit me with their machines if they were not functioning smoothly, and I would try to correct the problem. Often it required only a minor adjustment of some kind, such as the valve timing, attention to the Bowden cable, primary or secondary chains or the carburettor throttle, the cleaning of the oil filters or even something as simple as a spot of lubrication in the right place. Whilst they were with me, they would often ask about insurance and I would give advice, although I tried not to overtly canvass them on such occasions. I would point out, however, that the Premier's comprehensive motorcycle policies were excellent, with first-rate no-claims bonuses; the policies would also cover damage to personal additions to the machine such as Perspex windscreens, metal leg-shields or panniers and their contents.

It was during one of my Wednesday spells at the market outside the Unicorn that I was approached by a youth called Rex Middleton. He was eighteen, a native of Micklesfield who still lived at home and who worked as an apprentice dairyman on a large farm in the village. The farm was owned and run by a family called Bowsfield. Rex was a serious-minded young man, always polite and respectful to others, and he was well liked by everyone.

Tall and handsome with a mop of wavy blond hair, he was a fine cricket player, a good footballer and light enough on his feet to be popular with the girls at village dances. Whenever he appeared at one of the dances, he was guaranteed to attract a host of female admirers but this did not make him big-headed or boastful. He thought they wanted him to show them things like quicksteps, foxtrots and modern waltzes, at all of which he was very skilled. He could even do the Dashing White Sergeant, the Lancers and an old-fashioned waltz.

On Wednesdays, however, he was a regular at the Unicorn, where he enjoyed a few pints, a snack at the bar and a game of darts with men who were often three or four times his age. Wednesday was his full day off work because he worked all day on Sundays at Bowsfield's dairy farm, with most of his evenings being taken up with cricket or football, depending upon the season. Saturday was dance night in either Micklesfield or one of the nearby villages and he got every other Saturday afternoon off work too. That allowed him to play cricket or football for the village teams. Rex was therefore a very busy young man who appeared to enjoy life to the full – he even enjoyed his work, something which did not happen to many of his age, for he had a tremendous rapport with animals of every kind.

During my visits to the market and the Unicorn, I had often seen Rex at the dartboard. He was a good player but not outstanding, although his extraordinary skill was to perform mental gymnastics with the scoring. In a match of, say, 301 or 501 up, he could calculate in his head, within a split second, the combination of singles, doubles and triple scores required to finish precisely at zero.

For those unfamiliar with darts, the standard board is rounded like a clock face and consists of twenty segments, each bearing a score. The top centre is the highest and carries a score of 20 with other scores from 1 to 19 spread around the board, but not in chronological order. On the face of a standard dartboard there is a narrow outer rim in which darts can score double points, and a smaller rim closer to the centre in which the darts score triple points. The centre is the bullseye, which carries a score of 50, although some boards have a small outer bullseye carrying 25.

There are a variety of dartboards too, some of which differ considerably from the standard; for example, the Yorkshire board does not carry triple scores and does not have an outer bullseye while the Lancashire board, sometimes known as a log-end, is much smaller, with its numbers not in the same place as either the standard or the Yorkshire.

There are many of methods of playing darts too, with a lot of variations being used in local inns, but the finest challenge is often considered to be the game known as 501 up. In this, the player must start on a double and finish the game as quickly as possible by scoring a total of 501, but ending on either a double or the bull. In some competitions, where a speedy start is required, it is permissible to start on a straight score rather than a double but the object of the game is to start with a score of 501 and work down to nil. Much of the skill, apart from the ability to throw a straight arrow (a dart), is calculating how many points one needs in order to finish the game on nil, each 'throw' comprising three darts.

And this is where Rex shone, even to the extent of beating older players in this impressive display of mental arithmetic while always finishing on a double. On one occasion, I heard him call to his opponent, 'You need 103 to win, Jack. That's triple seventeen, straight twenty and double sixteen or you could go for straight seventeen, triple eighteen and double sixteen.'

Another time I heard him say, 'Right, I just need 89. I can do it in two darts, triple nineteen and double sixteen, or three darts with a straight nineteen, double fifteen and double top.'

Rex's impressive calculations, always done instantly, were one of the features of those lunchtimes in the Unicorn and I often wondered how or where he had learned to work at such speed and with such accuracy. If anyone asked how he did it, he would merely shrug his shoulders and say, 'Dunno, it just comes into my head.'

It was after one of those lunchtime sessions, when I heard him shout to his pal, 'Twenty, triple twenty and double sixteen, Joe. That's 112 to finish,' that he came for a word with me. I was in the bar enjoying a lunchtime pint when he came to my side and said, 'Matthew, I'm thinking of buying a motorbike. I earn enough to run one now. My dad said I should get you to look it over, check it for faults and things, wear and tear on bearings and so on. And then there's the insurance.'

'It's a second-hand one, is it?' I asked. 'Where are you getting it from?'

'It's advertised in the *Gazette*. A chap at Graindale. A BSA 250cc, five years old. The seller says I can fetch it out on a trial, and he's happy for me to get somebody to give it the once-over.'

'Sure,' I said. 'I'll be happy to do that.'

'How about tonight?'

'Yes, I'll be at home.'

'Great! I can go for it later this afternoon and let you see it whenever you can fit me in. I've got my provisional licence and L plates, and it's taxed so I'll be legal. And I can ride a motorbike, I've ridden my dad's on the farm sometimes – and the chap's insurance covers me to ride it while it's still his.'

'You've obviously gone into this seriously. So how about half past five? Fetch it to my garage, you know where it is? Bottom of my garden.'

'Yes, I know it. Right, I'll be there.'

After tea, I went down to my garage, clad in overalls, and bang on time I heard the arrival of a motorbike. The doors were standing wide open and so I waved Rex inside and asked him to switch off the engine and place the bike on its stand. I then checked all its components, kick-started it to listen for unwelcome noises from the gear-box, engine and bearings, then took it for a short run around the village, testing it on hills, corners and at speed. The brakes and tyres were good too, the lights worked and the steering was firm. This machine sounded very sweet indeed and it handled well. I could see it had been well maintained and had no hesitation in telling Rex it was in very good condition. I thought it was a very sound purchase.

He was clearly delighted with my appraisal and said he would go ahead with the purchase – he'd already negotiated a fair price – but then he mentioned insurance.

'Yes, you need to have your insurance sorted out before you become its owner, or to be precise, before you take it on a public road,' I said. 'The road tax is transferred with the bike, but the insurance doesn't work like that. If you let me know when you intend buying it, I can issue you with a cover note so you can ride it immediately. The certificate of insurance will be issued later.'

'I said I'd take it for a test run and return it afterwards. I've decided to buy it, I've got the money here.' He patted his rear pocket. 'The seller will hand over the registration book when I pay for the bike – I'll do that next.'

'Right, let's get this side of things sorted out now. I'll date and time the cover note for this evening, now in fact, so you're covered as from this moment. But I'll have to ask you to fill in a proposal form, and when it's accepted you'll be issued with the insurance certificate, lasting a year. You'll need to keep it in a safe place in case you are asked to show it to anyone, like the police. I'd recommend fully comprehensive, Rex, it costs a bit extra but it's a very wise thing to do. There'll be the usual no-claims bonus after three years if you have no claims, and you'll get a reduction in premiums when you pass your driving test, and again when you are twenty-five.'

'My dad said I should go for that, so right. Will you fill the form in for me?'

'Yes, we'll have to go up to the house for that, so follow me. You can leave the bike here for now.'

In my office, I found the necessary proposal form while he sat beside me at my desk, and I handed it to him.

'Er, can you fill it in, if I give you the details?'

'Yes, no problem.' There were times this

was far speedier than asking a client to fill in the form, especially if the client was not accustomed to writing or clerical work. It was a feature of my profession, especially whilst among those who worked on the land, that few were confident enough to fill in forms or write letters. 'Ah's nut varry good at book wark' was an oft-repeated phrase, and 'Larning was nivver my strong point' was another. I sensed that Rex was such a person. After all, he had probably left school at fifteen with the sole intention of working on the land.

I asked all the normal questions from Rex such as his full name, date of birth, address, occupation and whether he suffered from any disease, illness or defects of vision which would impair his driving, followed by the make, model and registration number of the BSA, along with its date of manufacture. The fact he had already obtained a provisional driving licence was a factor, although his experience was chiefly driving farm vehicles such as tractors, on land. He provided all the information I needed and I was satisfied he was honest in all his answers, so I asked him to check the form and if he was satisfied with its accuracy, to sign it. I handed him my fountain pen for the task. I could see he was nervous at this point and wondered what was wrong. I saw him licking his lips as he took my pen, placed the form immediately in front of him on my desk and then bent down until his nose was almost touching the paper. He wrapped his left hand around the form with his hand anchoring it, almost like a schoolchild preventing a neighbour from copying his work, and then laboriously began to sign his name.

I've never seen anyone so slow in producing a signature but poor Rex moved the pen in large loops as he created a huge wobbly signature of R. Middleton in what could only be described as a childish scrawl.

'You've read it?' I asked when he'd finished.

'No, but I know it's all correct.'

'You're supposed to read it, to make sure I've got things right.'

'I can't read, Matthew. I can hardly write either. I'm not a scholar, never was.'

'But when I saw you playing darts...'

'Oh, I can do things like that in my head. I can do all sorts in my head, Matthew, but I was no good at school, no good at sums. Not on paper. I got the teacher to ask me the sums instead, and I knew the answers – multiplications, long divisions, percentages. I can do all that sort of stuff in my head, without making mistakes, but I'm no good at paperwork. Never was and never will be. The letters always seem jumbled up and I can't make sense of them. Figures as well, figures on paper that is. Luckily, I don't have to fill forms in at work, that's all done in the office by Mrs Bowsfield, but I can work out milk yields and do costings in my head.'

I talked to him for a few moments about his gift but I knew he desperately wanted to learn to read and write. I knew so little about his condition and although I didn't mention it to Rex, I would have a chat with Evelyn about it, just to see whether the education authorities had any solutions to his problem. If there was hope for him, even as an adult, I would then be in a position to inform him. Evening classes for adults were now becoming very popular.

I walked back down to the garage with him and wished him well, then he drove away on the bike which would soon become his property. As he rode away, I wondered how he would cope with learning the Highway Code and reading road signs, all so necessary if he was to pass his driving test.

Another of my motorcycle customers was Reg Parsons, otherwise known as Parsons the Plumber. A resident of Micklesfield, he was in his early fifties, a jolly man with a permanent smile on his round red face. He always had a joke and a chuckle for everyone he encountered, and seemed to enjoy making people laugh, even if they were polite enough to laugh at stories they'd heard countless times. Married to Alice and with three fine teenage daughters, he lived in a pretty stone cottage near the church; in his garden there was a large greenhouse, his hobby being growing and showing prize chrysanthemums. There was also a range of stone outbuildings in which he stored the requirements of his trade. He kept everything from baths to toilet seats by way of pipes, taps, washers, plungers and sink plugs and in that sense he ran a type of shop. He also acted as a local glazier, repairing broken windows in houses, greenhouses and other buildings, but also installing windows in new buildings. One of his sheds was full of panes of glass, some ready cut to size. He had a collection of about two dozen panes which would fit Miss Pinkerton's greenhouse because branches kept dropping from the trees in her garden and smashing them. Replacing her glass was one of his regular tasks but people could go and buy things from him so that they could fix their own problem.

Although he did some work at home, his main occupation was touring the villages and attending the needs of his many customers, some urgent and some not so urgent. His transport, however, was not a van but a motorbike and sidecar. In large letters, the sidecar bore his name – Parsons the Plumber – along the side, underneath which was the legend 'Glazing work undertaken', plus his address and telephone number.

Reg's sidecar was not the conventional type which could carry one or two people; it was more like a box on wheels. Reg had obtained an old sidecar from a scrapyard and had then removed the body, throwing its remains back on the scrapheap. He had kept the frame with its single wheel, welded it to the frame of his Ariel motorbike and then constructed a large, oblong, wooden box-like container with a flat lid hinged at the edge nearest the motorbike. The box was almost the length of the bike and about two feet six inches wide by a similar depth. Inside was a series of trays resting within a stout shelving framework also constructed by Reg and it was in those trays that he carried his daily essentials. There were trays for all his tools and for his more frequently used spare parts and fitments; he could even carry short lengths of pipe and, if necessary, strap larger items on to the flat lid. He had fitted brackets for that purpose and it was not uncommon to see Reg's combination sailing through the dale with a toilet bowl, a wash basin or even an enamel bath strapped firmly to the sidecar.

Reg was one of my clients. Both his business and his private insurances were conducted through the Premier, and it was natural, therefore, that it included his motorbike and sidecar as well as the stock he carried in his outbuildings. He was comprehensively covered for any unfortunate thing which might happen to his equipment and stock, from fire to flood by way of theft and damage, and his private house was similarly protected. Through a sickness insurance, he was also covered for injuries and illness which might prevent him working for a long period. In short, Reg was a very professional workman who believed in being fully insured.

But the lovely Reg developed two curious problems.

I became aware of the first when his wife, Alice, called to see me one evening. I had no idea why she had paid this visit on his behalf and was not expecting her, but I led her through to my office, offered her a cup of tea and settled her on the chair near my desk. She was a neat bespectacled little person in her late forties with blonde hair always tied with colourful ribbons, and she worked as his secretary. She looked after the invoices, banking and general correspondence and in that capacity was very familiar with all aspects of Reg's business.

'So how can I help you?' I asked after the usual pleasantries.

'It's about Reg's business insurance. Am I right in thinking he is covered if there's an accident, say when he's fixing new pipes in a house? His blowlamp might set fire to something, say some curtains ... he'd be covered? For the cost of repair or replacement? Or if, say, water leaked out of somewhere while he was working and damaged a carpet?'

'The simple answer is yes, but there is a proviso. The sort of damage you mention must be the result of a genuine accident, something unforeseen and not due to carelessness or negligence. I think you'll not find any insurance company that will offer protection against carelessness or negligence by the policyholder. If a worker is careless, then the insurance of the customer might be activated to recover the costs from the workman, because in such cases there's always the question of liability and compensation for loss or injury caused by third persons. Or, of course, the householder might just send a bill for the damage. I think most would do that rather than go to law.'

'So Reg would not be covered if he was careless, or even incompetent, that's the message? But of course he's not careless or incompetent. Everyone knows that.'

'Right,' I said. 'But we don't insure against

317

a policyholder's own incompetence or care-lessness. They can't make capital out of their own failings, that's the logic behind it. So is this a problem?'

'Yes, in a way,' she said. 'He's been getting careless lately, nothing too serious but probably more due to forgetfulness than outright carelessness.'

'Such as?'

'Well, he went to install a new water closet at a house in Ingledale and was just finishing off in the afternoon when he got an emergency call to a burst pipe a mile away. He left the WC job in a rush and said he'd return as soon as he could. But he forgot. The first thing I knew about it was when the house-holder sent us a bill for cleaning up the mess. Reg had forgotten to go back and clear up after himself.'

'I'm sorry, Alice, but he'd never be covered for that kind of thing.'

'It's not the first time it's happened. Just lately, over the last few weeks, he's been called back several times to clean up after jobs he's supposed to have finished. It's un-like him, he's usually so careful and pays great attention to leaving a job in a clean state, often cleaner than when he started. It's costing us money, Matthew, because he has to return to clear up the mess which means he can't do the next job he promised so he gets behind with his work and folks start pressing him to get on with things.'

'You've spoken to him about it?'

'Just to ask why he's suddenly being so careless, it's costing him his reputation, Matthew. I can see people are going to stop employing him if he's not careful.'

'So what's his reaction?'

'He just shrugs his shoulders and says he forgot, he said he's very busy but he always is, that's a good thing in his profession. He promises to be more careful in the future, but then a few days later the same thing happens again.'

'Have you thought about a work sheet for each job? With compartments he can tick off when he's finished? You could check whether or not he's cleaned up after himself, or he could check for himself if he took the form out on jobs with him.'

'That's an idea! But there is another thing.'

'Another insurance job?'

'It might be, I'm not sure. He keeps losing his tools.'

'Having them stolen, you mean?'

'I don't think so. He's losing them, leaving them behind or something. Recently he's lost a blowlamp, a hand drill, three claw hammers, umpteen spanners and even two twelve-foot lengths of piping.'

'So where on earth would he lose things

like that?'

'I wish I knew. He's searched high and low for them, went back to where he'd been working but they weren't there. Losing a valuable tool can often mean he can't finish a job and it means a special trip into Guisborough or Whitby to get a replacement. I'm wondering if he can claim off his insurance for those?'

'If they were stolen he could certainly claim, but he'd have to notify the police and make a formal complaint of a crime. But losses, through carelessness, will not generally be covered, unless the objects are specially mentioned in the policy. That's usually the case if something has a rather high value, not necessarily a financial value. It could be something with a sentimental value.'

'But if I go away on holiday and lose my wedding ring, I am covered by my household policy, aren't I?

'Yes, that's because the ring, and other jewellery, has to be specially mentioned in the policy document and the premiums take account of those risks. Loss of tools used for business can't be covered by your domestic house-protection policy, Alice.'

'So even though Reg is not doing these things deliberately, we can't recover the costs through his insurance? Is that what you are saying?'

'As I said, clients cannot benefit from insurance, Alice, they can only be compensated but they must not contribute to the loss. If you think Reg needs to have his business tools insured against accidental loss, then I can see about having the policy amended but it will almost certainly mean listing all his tools with individual values, and it might also mean a substantial increase in premiums.'

'Even that might be cheaper than replacing the things he loses, taking into account the time needed to go and buy them. I don't know why he's suddenly started to do this but it must stop somehow.'

'We're talking of loss rather than theft, Alice. He's already covered against theft. But loss of tools is hardly the same and I don't think we can insure him against neglecting to return and complete his jobs either. It could be argued he is personally contributing to those conditions, and that could suggest he is negligent.'

'I hope you didn't mind me asking.'

'Not at all. In my view, Alice, he's got something on his mind which is making him careless. I think that needs to be sorted out first, find out what's causing him to behave like this. Have you thought about having the doctor talk to him? Or is it money? Once we find out what's the cause of this, we can worry some more about whether or not his work tools can be insured against loss. I can talk to my District Office about it. But I repeat, we can't insure clients against their own carelessness or negligence whilst at work. His customers' own third-party insurance should cover that kind of thing if he upsets any of them in a big way – that's if they are insured for such things! Most householders aren't!'

'I'd better leave things as they are just now. Thank you, Matthew, thanks for giving me time to talk to you, I had to mention it to somebody. I'll talk to him before I decide what to do next.'

She left and I could see she was somewhat despondent and I sensed there was some kind of problem affecting Reg, something he did not want to discuss even with his wife. What was happening to him was so out of character and I wondered who else she had spoken to about it. Those of us who knew Reg realized that something was not quite right – so who was going to approach him if his own wife couldn't? But it was not my problem – I must not get involved in the personal dilemmas of one of my clients; it was up to Reg and Alice to sort out things for themselves.

It would two or three weeks later, as I was driving Betsy, my little car, on the return trip after collecting in Baldby, that I saw Reg's familiar motorbike and sidecar parked on the roadside. He was with it but was slumped over the handlebars of his machine, the engine being switched off. I halted immediately and ran across to him; he was fully conscious but groaning loudly and clutching at his chest. I didn't know what to do. It was a very isolated place and for a moment I was undecided. Then I knew what I could and should do. He needed treatment in hospital – that was blindingly obvious, and Guisborough was about twenty minutes away, closer than Whitby and also closer than Dr Bailey's surgery in Micklesfield. I had no idea whether Dr Bailey would be there or not but reasoned I couldn't take that risk – it was now 4.30 p.m. and surgery didn't open until six so the doctor might be away from home, visiting a patient somewhere.

Hospital was the answer. My mind made up, and knowing I must act swiftly, I ran to help Reg off his bike.

'No, Matthew, leave me, I'll be all right in a minute or two.'

'Leave you like this? Here? No way, Reg! I can't ignore this! You need a doctor, urgently.'

'No, no I don't, it'll go off...'

'No it won't ... I'm not going to be responsible for you if you won't let me help. Come on. Into my car.'

He took a lot of persuading, both manual and verbal, before I got him into the rear seat of my car where he could lie down; I had to leave the bike but felt it – and its load – would be safe until I could make arrangements to collect it.

And so, with Reg alternately groaning loudly and then lapsing into long silences as his face turned grey while he clutched at his chest, I hurtled across the barren moors to the quiet market town of Guisborough. The hospital, a former workhouse, was in Northgate. I had no trouble parking outside the main door.

'Matthew, there's no need, I'll be as right as rain, just you see ... it's happened before, it's not my heart, I know it's not.' He was still protesting as I left him to run inside for help. Once the urgency of the situation dawned on the receptionist, the staff reacted with bewildering speed, with Reg protesting that he was much better now and he could even walk without any help.

Nonetheless, the still-protesting Reg was hoisted on to a wheeled stretcher and whisked down one of the corridors for an immediate examination.

I decided to wait until I had some kind of news – I would have the task of notifying Alice. A nurse brought me a cup of tea and a newspaper as I waited on a chair near the entrance. The time seemed to pass so dreadfully slowly with no sign of activity and then, after about three-quarters of an hour, a doctor came towards me – with Reg walking behind, looking somewhat sheepish and embarrassed but surprisingly fit and well. He looked as if nothing ailed him.

'Sorry about all this, Matthew, really I am. I feel such an idiot...'

'So what was it? I thought you were dying!'

'It's happened before, like I said ... I knew I'd get over it soon...'

The doctor then said, 'It was good of you to react so quickly, Mr Taylor, if this had been a heart attack, you would have saved his life. I'll leave you to get Mr Parsons back home safe and sound, and he can tell you all about it. Goodbye, Mr Parsons and I'll be in touch with your own doctor,' and he left us.

'So it's not a heart condition?' I put to Reg as we walked out to my car.

'No, they've given me a thorough examination and my heart is like that of a twenty-year-old. I'm as fit as I could be. I'll tell you what, that was the best thing that could have happened to me, getting that examination done. I knew it wasn't my heart, I always get over it like now but it's bad while it lasts.'

'So what's the problem?'

'You'll not believe it. Indigestion. Chronic

indigestion ... more of an allergy really, it seems I've started to react violently to some foods, it's called an intolerance.'

At this point, I remembered Arthur Barnes, the butcher from Crossrigg. I'd done his round because they thought he'd had a heart attack, but it seemed he'd reacted violently to something he'd eaten. Crab in his case. 'I've heard of this,' was all I could think of saying.

'It's likely to be pork or perhaps milk, with the poison building up over the years until it reacts like this. In the past, I might have had a bit of wind or a spot of burping, but now it's got to the poison stage. I have to see Dr Bailey and he'll book me in to Whitby Hospital for a check, they'll do tests but in the meantime I have to lay off pork and anything coming from a dairy – cheese, milk, ice cream...'

We were now standing near Betsy and so I asked, 'How many times has this happened, Reg?'

'Dunno, exactly. Quite a lot. I've usually sat it out on my bike, somewhere quiet, but I've never told anyone because it always goes off after a while. To be honest, I wondered if I was having warning signs about heart attacks but didn't like to make a fuss in case I got laid off work. I can't afford to be ill, Matthew, in spite of my insurances! Lately,

I've made a mess of a few jobs of work, forgot where I'd left things or what job I was supposed to be doing, lost things, forgot where I put them, worrying I suppose, suffering like today and then getting over it. I didn't really think it was my heart, it seemed more linked to my belly, but you can't be too sure, can you?'

'So in spite of your worries, you didn't go to the doctor?'

'No, you don't, do you? Not when you're a feller, not when you're self-employed with all those jobs waiting ... you can't afford to be ill and put off work. I was never ill for long, just an hour or so. I suppose I thought it might go away altogether one day ... daft, eh? Not going to a doctor. But it has gone away, I feel fine now. And it was my stomach, not my heart. That's the good news.'

'Come on, let's get you home. At least you've had the all-clear from a doctor so far as your heart is concerned, so now it's down to your diet. And I think you should tell Alice what's been going on.'

'I'll have to, won't I? I have to tell her not to give me pork sandwiches or custard with my apple pie or milk in my tea and I do love Wensleydale cheese with pickled onions ... I had a ploughman's today, it was good!'

'A ploughman's? With all that cheese ... no wonder you're suffering!'

'I think it was ploughman's which caused it before. Looking back and listening to that doctor, I seemed to get mighty ill after eating them. He said it was all that cheese, too much for my battered innards!'

'It's been gradually poisoning you, Reg, so listen to what the experts say.'

'Aye, I will.'

And so we drove home.

I did not tell Reg that Alice had spoken to me but it did occur to me that his earlier lapses had all occurred during the afternoons shortly before he was due to finish a job of some kind, and probably after he'd enjoyed his hefty ploughman's lunch of cheese and onions or whatever Alice had given him.

She might now work out that his expensive lapses had been caused by whatever he'd eaten for lunch. Severe indigestion of this kind, more than just wind or momentary excess and probably the result of an allergic type of reaction, had often been mistaken for a heart attack, I learned later.

As for insuring his workman's tools against loss, I never proceeded with that idea. If the insurance companies decided to produce that kind of policy for workmen, they'd make a loss in no time at all! Workmen are notorious for leaving tools and equipment behind.

I saw Alice later and she smiled knowingly,

telling me that Reg had now reformed and was on a strict dairy-free diet with stern reductions in his consumption of pork products, including ham and bacon but especially cheese. It seemed dairy products were causing the real problem. But I don't think he lost any more of his tools and was never again criticized for not cleaning up after finishing a job.

So far as my own Coventry Eagle motorcycle was concerned, I made sure it received regular runs and was well maintained, even if I did not use it a great deal. Whenever Evelyn wanted the car I would use the motorbike, but tried to restrict those rides to the summer months. I liked to meet my clients in a clean condition, and not swamped in a mass of protective weatherproof clothing.

It was an early but very hot June day when I decided to take the motorbike out for a collecting trip to Lexingthorpe.

I did not need to dress up in my heavy weatherproofs so I sallied forth in my sports jacket and flannels, albeit with a pair of gauntlets on my hands and stout boots on my feet. My collecting book and other stationery were in my panniers and I was feeling very content. The sunny day gave me a feeling of euphoria; I was enjoying my work, I seemed to be doing very well with lots of new business while Evelyn was thriving on her occasional supply-teaching duties. I was meeting my mortgage repayments and other domestic outgoings, albeit with little cash to spare, but my work meant my income was sustained, much of it depending upon the commission I earned. That was very valuable – a substantial period off work through illness would make things very difficult, I realized, even if I was well insured. I could appreciate Reg worrying what would happen if he'd been made to stop work through sickness.

With those thoughts ranging through my mind, I was travelling down a winding hill near Great Freyerthorpe End and have to admit that my mind was not completely on my driving. I was thinking about our domestic world, about paying for the large house and keeping pace with its maintenance and I did not see the problem ahead. There had been a fierce shower of rain the previous night and although the road was dry, there was a deep patch of gravel which had been swept across the road on one of the sharp corners. I did not see it until too late.

The front wheel hit it and skidded on the loose gravel and the next thing I knew was that I was hurtling through the air towards the high drystone wall at the other side. The bike was sliding noisily along the gravel behind me and then my head hit the wall as the bike followed and landed heavily on my right leg.

Then everything went black. I woke up in Whitby Cottage Hospital with Evelyn at my bedside and it took a long time for me to find my voice.

'What happened?' I croaked.

'You had an accident, Matthew, you've got concussion and a broken leg. You'll just have to rest, you'll be allowed home soon but you'll be off work for about six weeks.'

'But who'll do my work?' I groaned, thinking of all that lost commission.

'I will,' said Evelyn.